DEADLY MEANS

CAROLYN RIDDER ASPENSON

SEVERN RIVER PUBLISHING

DEADLY MEANS

Severn River Publishing
www.SevernRiverBooks.com

ISBN: 978-1-64875-440-1 (Paperback)

ALSO BY CAROLYN RIDDER ASPENSON

The Rachel Ryder Thriller Series

Damaging Secrets

Hunted Girl

Overkill

Countdown

Body Count

Fatal Silence

Deadly Means

Final Fix

To find out more about Carolyn Ridder Aspenson and her books, visit
severnriverbooks.com

For Jack
Love you always.

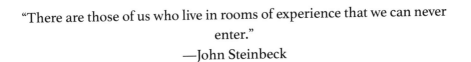

"There are those of us who live in rooms of experience that we can never enter."
—John Steinbeck

1

Two hundred files. We'd been sitting in the investigation room for hours going through two hundred cold case files searching for something that, as my partner Bishop had said, tickled our fancy. I cringed at the thought of Bishop's fancy—whatever that was—being tickled. "We've got one stack of files left. If we don't find something reasonably interesting, we're going to have to investigate Bobby Joe Pyott's missing tractor." I shoved a few files around the large investigation room table until I found that file and jabbed my finger on it. "From 1992." I dipped my head back. "Shoot me now."

Bishop laughed, and an overgrown clump of salt and pepper hair slicked to the side of his head jiggled. "Remember when our biggest investigation was busting kids for stealing drinks and candy from the park and recreation field concessions stands? We could still be doing that."

My eyes darted from a particularly uninteresting cold case file to his face. I narrowed them purposefully. "Do not put that out in the universe."

He wiggled his eyebrows. "Just watch what you wish for."

"Thanks for the life lesson, Dad." I winked at him. The father in Bishop couldn't help sneaking lessons into his conversations. On the back end of fifty, he believed his vast life experience benefited others. I trailed behind him in years, though not in experiences, but I knew everyone had to learn their lessons in their own way and time.

I tossed another boring file onto the growing stack on the floor and rummaged through the bottom stack of case files we'd yet to review. We hadn't investigated anything exciting in over two months, and my constant griping and whining annoyed everyone, including myself. I grabbed a file and opened it. "Five dollars stolen from the counter of a fruit stand in Alpharetta back in 1981?" I shut the folder and dropped it onto the top of the no files, shaking my head in disbelief. "Probably fifty murders reported in Chicago that same year and yet no one cared enough to report a five-dollar theft." I felt my eyes roll. "What is wrong with the people of my hometown? Does justice not matter?"

Bishop's upper lip twitched. "I sense sarcasm in your tone."

"Ya think?"

"Chicago is a big city. In 1981, Hamby was still part of Alpharetta, and mostly farmland. I think there were maybe three thousand people on the census?"

I dropped another case file on the uninteresting stack. "Of course, you would know that. You're a cesspool of useless information."

"Not really. A former city councilman wrote a history of Hamby book. It's in my bathroom."

"Thanks for sharing." I tossed another ridiculous case file onto the no pile. "We need something to do. I can't sit around watching Michels pick his nails much longer."

He sipped his coffee. "You're really champing at the bit, aren't you?"

I pressed my lips together. "I'm bored." Mostly, I needed something to keep my mind off my significant other and his undercover assignment with the DEA, but work had hit a new level of boring.

"When you first started here, you said you wanted to get away from the pressures of big-city crimes. Welcome to your dream coming true."

"I didn't think it would be this slow. And you know that was only part of why I came here." I'd come to Hamby after my husband was murdered, to honor what he and I had planned for our retirement. "I knew it would be slower here, but missing tractors and petty cash crimes? I just can't."

Bishop's eyes softened. He wouldn't get snarky over anything having to do with Tommy because he knew watching someone you love be murdered is nothing to joke about, and he respected that.

I drummed my fingers on a stack of files.

"Is this need to be busy really about boredom or is it about Kyle?"

And in came the thing I didn't want to discuss. I crossed my arms over my chest and tried to make light of it. "Are you trying to psychoanalyze me, because I'm not paying you to be my therapist."

"Consider it a perk of the job."

"Thanks, but I think I'll pass." I'd had more than enough psycho-analysis when Tommy was murdered.

Bishop's expression turned serious. "I didn't mean to—"

"You didn't. Don't worry about it." I'd done my best at keeping the guilt over my husband's murder at bay. Sometimes it worked, sometimes it didn't. Grief is eternal, and it mutates like a virus, fighting to keep me locked inside the bowels of guilt and despair. There was no changing the past, and when I accepted that, I focused on the good memories and moved forward as he would have wanted.

Bishop reviewed a file and chuckled just as dispatch came over the landline's intercom. "Detectives, we had a report of a 10-17 with one injured. Patrol is requesting assistance for a 10-62 at 342 Mayfield Drive. Repeat 342 Mayfield Drive."

"This is Detective Ryder. I'm with Detective Bishop. Copy that. ETA—"

Bishop held up his hands and wiggled his fingers.

"Approximately ten minutes."

"Fire is en route. ETA seven."

"Copy that," Bishop said. He smiled at me. "Well. Looks like you got your wish. Let's go dig our teeth into this one."

We both stood and adjusted our equipment belts as we headed to Bishop's vehicle.

"What's up with you and the strange phrases? Dig our teeth into? champing at the bit?"

"What's wrong with using common phrases in conversation?" he asked.

"That's the thing. They're not common. They make you sound old."

"Which I am." He climbed into the driver's seat. "And don't knock being over fifty. You're practically knocking on its door."

Ouch.

~

FALL HAD ARRIVED EARLIER than usual, and a light breeze carrying a hint of burning leaves skimmed across my cheeks as I stepped out of the vehicle. The chill surprised me and annoyed Bishop.

"It's colder than I expected," he said.

"It's too early for this, but at least it's not winter," I said.

I'd worn a black Hamby Police Department windbreaker over my white department polo and a pair of fitted Silver brand jeans. Bishop wore his usual, a pair of pleated chino pants with a casual blazer over his white department polo.

I snapped photos of the home and Bishop jotted down details as we reviewed the area.

"But winter's there, staring us down, waiting patiently to stab us in the back with another snowmageddon or worse."

I pivoted left and photographed the street, then did the same from behind on my right.

I grew up in a duplex in the Irving Park area of Chicago with neighboring homes stacked like dominos squeezed into postage stamp–sized lots. The Hamby mini-mansions were so big, they could fit three duplexes on just their first floors. It had taken a while to adjust to the rolling expanse of lots and large homes in town. Hamby residents liked showing off their money in big ways. Big homes, big cars, big egos.

Mayfield was the top of the top. The elite community where money and status determined your likability rank. It was so uppity the residents voted to allow potential buyers to purchase homes, and if someone didn't get in, the wealthy in Georgia added them to an undocumented blacklist.

The sheer size of the home dominated the main drive into the Mayfield golf community.

"Aside from the front doors, everything looks fine out here," Bishop said. "The landscaping is fantastic but draws attention to the house."

Outdoor lights dotted the landscape and framed the sidewalk to the wooden double front doors. They'd stuck a sign announcing their security system in the flower bed near the front steps.

"The size of the house draws attention," I said.

Officer Gregory met us at the door. I checked for a security system camera or doorbell camera but couldn't find any.

"What's the situation?" Bishop asked.

Gregory, a young and newer officer, stood about six feet. His shoulders spanned about that in width as well, his perfectly V-shaped torso proving he spent a lot of time in the gym. He didn't tower over Bishop, but he'd intimidate suspects just from his looks. Muscle didn't always amount to strength and skill, but he'd have to learn that on his own.

"Home invasion. Family is Kelley. Husband, Jared, wife, Kelsey. Three men dressed in black forcibly entered the home, all carrying. Told the husband to get the cash and jewelry or they'd kill the family. They zip-tied the wife and children to dining room chairs, then forced the husband to open the safe. According to him, they took approximately $150,000 in cash, and maybe $50,000 in jewelry, including the wife's wedding ring on her finger. Then they zip-tied the husband to another chair, smacked him around a bit, then left."

"Injuries?" Bishop asked.

"Black eye, but that's about it."

"The sign says they've got a security system." I pointed to the corners of the porch ceiling above the door. "Where's the cameras?"

"Husband said the sign is only for show."

That didn't surprise me.

"How'd they call 911?" Bishop asked.

"The wife moved her chair across the floor and removed her husband's cell phone from his pocket. She held it with one hand, and he dialed 911."

Impressive. "Who cut the zip ties?" I asked.

"I did, but not before making sure to photograph everything. I've bagged them and placed them on the dining room table."

"Thanks," Bishop and I said in unison.

We slipped into our booties and gloves and headed inside to two screaming children, a crying woman, and one pissed off husband holding a bag of frozen peas against his left eye.

"I want the police chief here now," he said to a uniformed officer.

Bishop side-eyed me. I groaned under my breath.

"Mr. Kelley," Bishop said.

The man whipped around and glared at us. "Are you the chief?"

"I'm Detective Rob Bishop, and this is my partner, Detective Rachel Ryder."

The man gave me a once-over. What a slimeball. His family had just gone through a traumatic situation, and he was checking me out.

"I demand to see Chief Abernathy!"

"Sir," I said. "The chief isn't here. You've got us."

"How about you let the paramedics tend to you?" Bishop asked.

The man waved his hands. "I'm fine. It's nothing."

Bishop pointed to the bag of peas. "That's going to defrost in a minute. They'll give you something that'll last longer."

The man's tone softened. "I don't want you talking to my wife and kids. They're upset. They don't need to relive this."

"We'll have a look around first. The paramedics will help your family. We'll come back when we're finished," Bishop said

The paramedics escorted them all outside. The children's high-pitched screams faded as they walked out the door.

Bishop checked his watch. "We've got five minutes until the husband comes back in." He called Chief Jimmy Abernathy at home and put him on speaker. "Just a heads up. We've got a home invasion in Mayfield. Male vic is demanding to see you."

"Mayfield? Great. Anyone hurt?" Jimmy asked.

"Male got punched in the face. He'll probably have a black eye, but that's about it."

"Anyone else home?"

"The wife and two children, both young," Bishop said. "Perps zip-tied them to chairs, and they watched the husband get punched."

"Son of a bitch. Text me the address. I'm on my way." He disconnected the call.

We walked the perimeter of the area where the sitting area and dining room connected. Large columns separated the different rooms in the open floor plan. Open floor plans weren't my thing. Everything lumped together without walls in my line of sight triggered my type A personality into overdrive.

I pointed to a few of the expensive-looking knickknacks scattered around the space. "Looks like they've got some expensive things here. Why weren't any of them taken?"

"Maybe they wanted to get in and out quickly, so they just went for what was in the safe?" he asked.

"Maybe. But seems odd to me. Get what you can and get out, right? If they'd zip-tied the family to the chairs, wouldn't they have enough time to at least grab a few other things?"

"You'd think."

Officer Gregory walked up. "Nikki's here. Is it okay for her to get started?"

Nikki Parks, our crime scene technician walked in. She smiled at Gregory. "Did they give the approval?"

"They didn't even get a chance to answer," he said.

Nikki blushed. Bishop and I shared a side-eye glance. Was there something going on between them? A while back we'd learned Detective Justin Michels and our former tech, Ashley Middleton, were an item, but since Ashley didn't work for the department, it wasn't a problem. Gregory and Nikki dating went against city policy, though that hadn't stopped anyone. Tommy and I weren't supposed to date either, and we ended up married.

"It's fine," I said. "Chief is on his way. The husband is volatile. Let's get this done as quick as possible."

"Will do," she said. She walked away with Gregory watching.

Bishop cleared his throat. Gregory scurried away like he'd just been busted for sneaking a piece of candy before dinner.

"Interesting," Bishop said.

I shrugged. "Not my business."

The husband walked back in. Bishop checked his watch. "Four and a half minutes."

"Is the chief on his way?"

"Yes," I said.

"I don't want to deal with anyone other than him. Did you know that officer took photos of us before he cut the zip ties? What the hell is that? My children could be permanently damaged from this, and he's taking photos?"

"Sir," Bishop said. "I know it seemed inappropriate, but the officer took the photos as evidence. Normally, responding officers don't touch anything at a crime scene, but since your family was zip-tied to chairs, he didn't want your children further traumatized, and cut the ties."

Jared Kelley blinked. "Oh, I didn't think of it that way."

"That's why we wear the badge," I mumbled under my breath.

"We've been assigned the investigation, sir," Bishop said. "So, the sooner we get started, the sooner you can have your home back."

Kelley laughed, then dragged his hand down his chin. His eye had swollen closed. "You think we're going to stay here? You've got to be kidding. The damn house can go on the market tomorrow for all I care."

"That's your decision, sir," Bishop said. "But we still need to know what happened."

Jimmy Abernathy entered, strode over and introduced himself to Jared Kelley.

"About time you got here," Kelley said.

Jimmy's expression didn't change, but I knew what he was thinking. "I only come to crime scenes at the request of detectives, Mr. Kelley. I'm sincerely sorry for what your family has gone through. Trust that Detectives Ryder and Bishop will find the intruders."

"Can you assure me this won't happen again? Maybe put a patrol outside the home? Provide security of some sort?" Kelley asked.

What happened to putting the house on the market?

"Unfortunately, I can't designate an officer to watch over your home, however, you can contact a private security company for assistance."

"You want me to pay to protect my family?" Jared Kelley's nostrils flared. "Isn't that your job?"

"Mr. Kelley, the police department maintains law and order. It is your responsibility to ensure your family is protected."

Kelsey Kelley stumbled inside. She'd gripped an officer's arm and giggled. "Whoops. I almost tripped." She giggled as she headed toward us.

Jared Kelley rolled his eyes. "My wife needs me."

"Mr. Kelley," I asked. "Where are your children?"

"We asked the neighbor to get them. They don't need to be here during this." He rushed to his wife.

"He sent his kids to the neighbor's?" I asked. "What the?"

"I don't have a response to that," Bishop said.

"Ditto," Jimmy said.

THE SCENE OFFERED little evidence for Nikki to gather. She bagged and tracked what she could, including the zip ties, and headed back to the department. She wouldn't catalog them until the next morning, which Bishop and I agreed was fine.

The Kelleys sat on a large leather sectional. Mr. Kelley sat on one side while his wife sat with her two children glued to her side on the other.

"Why must my children be here for this?" Mr. Kelley asked. "They were sleeping just fine at the neighbor's."

"They may have noticed something you two didn't," Bishop said.

"You're going to question them? I'm not comfortable with that."

"Understood."

"Mr. Kelley," I said. "Why don't you have a security system or video cameras?"

He pressed his lips together. "We live in a gated community with private security. We don't need them."

I kept my mouth shut. Telling a victim he's an idiot wouldn't get me high marks on my next review.

"Did the intruders ask for anything other than cash and jewelry?" Bishop asked.

"No. I already told the officer this. Can't you get it from him?"

"Sometimes people remember additional details after the initial questioning," I said.

"Whatever. Like I told the other guy, they just wanted what was in the safe. Told me to unlock it and give them the cash and jewelry."

"Was there anything else in the safe?" I asked. "Important papers like your will, maybe?"

Kelsey Kelley was all smiles still, though a little less stoned than before. "My diamond bracelet was in there. Six carats. And they took my wedding ring off my hand. Four carats."

"Just the money and expensive jewelry," he said. "I keep documents locked in my desk." He lightly touched his eye and winced. "It was like they knew I had a safe filled with money and jewelry. Like they had been assigned to get it and only it."

He had a point. Criminals were usually opportunists. Why hadn't they taken anything else?

Bishop rubbed his eyes. "Did the intruders touch anything in the safe?"

"They had me get it all and put it in their bags, and they were wearing latex gloves anyway."

"Where's the key for the safe?" I asked.

He removed his keys from his keychain. "Here."

"You carry it on your keychain?"

"Yeah, why wouldn't I?"

If he didn't know the reasons, that was on him. "Does your wife have a key?"

"Yes. She keeps hers in her jewelry hutch in our bedroom closet."

I motioned for an officer to come over. "Please check for a key in the jewelry hutch in the parents' bedroom closet." I added, "With gloves on," as he rushed away.

"Have you told anyone how much cash you keep at home?" Bishop asked.

"My buddies and I joke about it occasionally, but it's not them. They have a shit ton more than me. What would they need mine for? Besides, the guys that broke in were bigger, and I think Hispanic."

"What makes you say that?" Bishop asked.

"Because the one doing the talking had an accent."

I pursed my lips. "They wore face masks, correct?"

"Ski masks."

"We're going to need you and your wife to come to the department tomorrow and look through some mug shots. First thing would be appreciated."

Jared Kelley blinked. "I have a nine o'clock tee time."

"Looks like you don't anymore," I said and strode away. I'd had enough of his entitled attitude.

2

It was after two a.m. by the time we got back to the department.

"If that woman's drugged up again . . ." Bishop yawned.

"I feel bad for the kids." I bent my elbows next to my ears and stretched them back as far as I could. The extension felt like a mini-massage.

"We can file the report in the morning." He leaned against his desk and tipped the screen of his laptop closed. "Or later this morning, that is. Let's go home."

"Works for me," I said. "I'm exhausted."

Bishop looked at me with soft eyes and a worried brow. "He's okay, Rachel."

I shifted my weight from one foot to the other and stared at the pencil holder on his desk. Bishop and I have been partners for several years. We finished each other's sentences, laughed at our own inside jokes, and knew what the other was thinking before they said it. "You don't know that."

"I know that if he wasn't, we'd know."

"That's not a guarantee." Sometimes when drug enforcement agents' covers were blown, they disappeared for years until someone finally bragged about the kill or used it for a lighter sentence. "Nothing's guaranteed."

"Stop thinking the worst."

"In my experience, the worst usually happens."

"Because you expect it. You will that stuff to happen when you focus on it."

"Are you studying Buddhism or something? All this strange talk is making me nervous."

He chuckled. "I'm just being positive. It makes a difference."

"I have to talk to Cathy about this. She's making you all squishy and soft."

He pushed his chair away from the desk. "Let's get out of here."

We walked to our vehicles without another word.

I wiped the growing spray of fallen leaves from my Jeep window. In the next month the trees would all pop with a rainbow of fall colors, adding more traffic accidents to our records. Leaves made roads slippery, and, inevitably, some distracted driver would take a curve too fast or hit their brakes, hit a patch of leaves, and cause a collision.

I took the long way home hoping the drive would relax me. It was only an extra five minutes, but they were better than an extra five lying in bed fretting over things I couldn't control. Over the past few months, I'd averaged no more than four hours of sleep on the nights I'd slept, and my racoon eyes proved it. I'd spent a lot of time distracting myself from my worry over Kyle, but in the dark of night, it crept in and sprouted tentacles, smothering my brain with fear and sadness. Every possible outcome played on my internal movie screen. Making assumptions took an emotional toll, but it was hard to stop. Knowing nothing about Kyle's mission sent my mind wandering into dark places. I'd lived in those dark places after Tommy's murder, and it took years to climb out of the pit. A pit I'd promised myself I'd never fall into again, but there I was, hanging onto the ledge with one hand.

My beta fish Louie swam up to the edge of his water condo as I dropped his dinner pellets into his home. "Hey, Louie. What'd you do today?" He swallowed up all the pellets, so I tossed in a few more. "We had a home invasion. No clues, no motive, a jerk victim, and his stoned wife. I feel for the kids." He chomped down the additional pellets and swam into his big shell to snooze. He'd never been much of a talker. "Goodnight, little guy. See you in a few hours."

I showered and tossed on something comfy to sleep in, then I lay in bed begging my mind to shut down. Finally giving up, I texted Ashley Middleton for an update on Kyle. It was late, and she was probably sleeping, unless the DEA had her on scene.

Her response came quickly. *Nothing yet.*

I SLEPT FOR ABOUT AN HOUR, then got dressed and headed to the range to shoot some before work. Detective Lauren Levy stood in aisle three firing off a magazine. Each shot landed on the target's head. I put on my ear and eye protection and muffled the sound of her shots. Their tangy firecracker-like smell penetrated my nose as I emptied my bag in the aisle next to her.

After recovering from our near death experience during the serial killer investigation, Levy was promoted to detective and partnered with Michels.

She slid fresh bullets into the magazine, racked the gun, and positioned her feet hip width apart facing the target. She aimed her weapon and pulled the trigger in rapid-fire succession, each bullet zinging through the air with a loud and smelly blast. They all hit in the appropriate range but weren't as impressive as the others. She rubbed her shoulder and grimaced.

I removed my ear covers. "You okay? You're wincing with each pull."

"I've got some shoulder pain, but I'm working through it. Heard you landed a home invasion last night in Mayfield. Bet that was fun."

"I'm not sure I'd use that word."

She laughed. "Beats working a cold case. Any idea who did it?"

"Yes. Three men, all dressed in black with black ski masks. The one who spoke had a Hispanic accent."

"Dead giveaway every time."

"Right? You'd think criminals from other countries would learn to fake a U.S. accent so it would be harder to catch them." I removed my department-issued Glock and prepared to shoot.

Levy watched. I set the target back as far as it would go, then shot. After moving the target closer, shooting more, then moving it closer, and shooting it again, I finally finished.

"Damn," she said. "Look at that!"

I'd hit the same area, the kill shot, each time, creating a golf ball–sized hole. "I practice a lot."

"I knew you were good, but I didn't realize you were that good."

We shot a few more rounds, placing bets on who could draw a circle with their bullets, and playing a shooting version of basketball's horse. I won every time, but Levy didn't care. It wasn't that she couldn't shoot. I'd just had more practice.

"Seriously," she said. "You been spending more time here than usual?"

"Not a whole lot else to do."

"Copy that."

I packed up to leave as we talked. "I've been at this a long time. If I couldn't shoot well, I would have left the field years ago."

Levy and I had become friends over the months since the accident. I'd visited her in the hospital and spent time with her at home while she recovered. Almost dying together bonded people, plus, I genuinely liked her and we had things in common. She was an excellent cop and was becoming a great detective. Most importantly, she'd run Michels through the ringer, and I loved watching that.

"You heading in?" I asked. "I'm getting coffee. The husband and wife are coming in this morning and the husband's an a-hole."

"And you want to rev up to what, kick his ass?"

"Maybe."

She laughed. "Coffee would be great. Maybe Jimmy will let Michels and me assist since we're so bored."

"There's a cold case about a missing tractor circa before electricity."

Her eyes widened. "Seriously?"

I laughed. "It's not from that long ago, but yes."

"That tractor's buried in the landfill in Buford by now."

"Or covered in kudzu somewhere on one of the old horse farm properties." I hitched my bag over my shoulder.

I BOUGHT four coffees at the nearby Dunkin' and handed them to Bishop, Michels, and Levy when I arrived.

"The Kelleys are here," Bishop said. "The husband's in a mood."

"No way?" Sarcasm dripped from my words.

He sipped his coffee then licked his lips like he'd just had a taste of heaven. "Jimmy requested an update before we meet with them."

"What's to update?"

He shrugged. "Maybe that Jared Kelley didn't end up in the hospital?"

"We already knew that," I said.

"Let me rephrase. He's lucky one of us didn't put him in the hospital."

I angled my head to the side. Bishop wasn't cranky often, but his stiff posture and terse tone said he teetered on the border of pissed off. "You okay?"

"I'm fine. I just hate entitled a-holes who think they're better than us."

I tossed back the last of my liquid energy. "I'm with you on that." I dropped my empty cup into the kitchen trash can, and said, "Let's get this party started."

Jimmy leaned against the corner of his desk, one heel crossed over the other with a smile plastered onto his face. "Tell me you caught the guys already."

"Arrested and convicted in night court," Bishop said. He shrugged. "The wife was stoned, so we didn't even bother asking her specific questions. We got the kids back, but they're too young to interview. We have confirmed Jared Kelley is an asshole."

I blinked. Bishop rarely got angry.

"Noted," Jimmy said.

"It yanks my chain that people like him think they can demand things from us."

"I agree, the guy's an asshole," Jimmy said. "But assholes deserve justice, too."

It was hard not to laugh at that.

Jimmy continued. "You know how this works. Home invasions are tough to solve, especially when the perpetrators are masked up. We'll let them look through the mug shots. It probably won't help, but at least it'll show we're trying. This is Mayfield. Half that community golfs with the mayor. We've got to do our due diligence. Nikki took prints from everywhere. Maybe we'll get lucky, and something will get a hit."

"The guys wore gloves," I said.

"Right," he said. "But we don't know if they ever removed them. Listen, we can't make magic happen, so, make sure the Kelleys understand that, all right?" He looked at Bishop.

Bishop nodded.

"I'm giving Michels and Levy the assist on this. It'll be a great place for Levy to get her feet wet."

"She'll appreciate that," I said.

"Good." Jimmy pushed himself off the corner of his desk and walked toward the door. "Now, let's go welcome our guests."

Michels and Levy followed us to the conference room where the Kelleys waited. "Anything we should know?" Levy asked.

I rattled off the key points of the crime.

"Sounds like fun," she said.

Mr. Kelley stood when we walked in. "Have you found who took my money and jewelry?"

"Our money and jewelry, honey," Mrs. Kelley said.

At least Kelsey Kelley wasn't stoned.

"We're working on it," Bishop said. "We've got some more questions, and then we'd like to have you take a look at some photos."

Jared Kelley crossed his arms over his chest. "You mentioned that last night. What's the point of looking at photos if they wore ski masks?"

"It's procedure," I said. "And they may trigger a detail you didn't realize you knew."

My nose twitched. Either the overnight cleaning crew had sprayed something floral smelling in the room or Kelsey Kelley had dumped a bottle of perfume over herself.

"That's unlikely," Jared Kelley said.

"Mr. Kelley," Jimmy said. He pointed at Levy and Michels. "These are Detectives Michels and Levy. They're here to assist Detectives Bishop and Ryder with the investigation. We'll do everything in our power to find the men who invaded your home, but we can't do that if you're not willing to help. Do you understand?"

Mr. Kelley's Adam's apple bobbed up and down. "Understood."

"Great," Jimmy said. "Now, I'll let them get to it." He walked out of the room and closed the door behind him.

His eyes widened. "He's not staying? I said I wanted him handling this."

Had he not just acknowledged what Jimmy had said? "Mr. Kelley, Chief Abernathy runs the entire Hamby Police Department. He doesn't investigate home invasions."

"I'll call the mayor."

I eyed Bishop. He shrugged.

"Feel free," I said. "We'll start with Mrs. Kelley then."

Mr. Kelley glared at me, but I held my ground until he finally sat down. He refused to look at me, and I couldn't have cared less.

Bishop and I sat across from the couple while Michels and Levy sat at the table's ends.

"Mrs. Kelley," I said. "We haven't had the opportunity to ask you any questions, so Detective Levy and I would like to take you to another room."

Jared Kelley's eyes widened. "Why do you need to take her to another room? Why can't we answer questions together?"

Bishop cleared his throat. "Sometimes it's easier for victims to speak privately with officers."

"It's fine, Jared," Mrs. Kelley said. Her demeanor teetered between annoyed and angry. "I am perfectly capable of talking to the detectives without you babysitting me."

Levy and I made eye contact.

"Great," I said. "Follow us."

We escorted Mrs. Kelley into a small interrogation room.

"I'm sorry it's so sterile, but we only have the one conference room available at the moment."

"I understand." As she sat, she said, "I need to apologize for last night. Jared gave me a Xanax to calm my nerves. He knows I hate that stuff. He told me he was giving me ibuprofen for my migraine, and I was so discombobulated, I swallowed it without checking."

What a winner that guy was.

"Has he done that before?" I asked.

"Given me drugs? No."

"It must have been stressful going through what you have," Levy said. "Can you tell us what happened? Start from the beginning."

"Sure." She cleared her throat. I had just tucked the kids into bed. We let them stay up until nine on weekends. I was in our room getting into my pajamas when I heard the front door burst open and men screaming. My husband kept shouting, no, no, no. I ran toward the stairs to see what was going on." She took a breath. "I should have called 911 right then. Honestly, I'm not sure why I didn't."

"Did the men see you on the stairs?" I asked.

"Yes. One was halfway up when I came out of our room. He grabbed me by the arm and made me wake up the kids. I begged him to leave them alone, but he forced me to get them." Her voice was calm and even. "He promised me if we did everything they said, no one would get hurt. I had no other choice but to believe him."

"And you got your children then?" Levy asked.

"Yes. They were scared, of course. The man forced us downstairs and zip-tied us to the dining room chairs. They covered our mouths. It was awful. I was afraid if my kids kept crying, the men would do something to them."

"How old are your children?" Levy asked.

"Lacey is four and Canon is six."

"What happened next?"

She exhaled. "The man told Jared to take him to the safe. He told him if he took him to it nothing would happen, but if he fought him, they would shoot us." Tears filled her eyes.

Levy handed her a tissue box from the small credenza behind her.

"Thank you."

"Did your husband argue with the man?" I asked.

"Oh, God no. Not then at least. He might be a pretentious jerk, but he loves us. He took them to the safe and gave them everything in it."

"Did all three men speak?"

"Two. The one that came upstairs, and the man Jared took to the safe. The other man was responsible for the zip ties."

"Do you have any idea of their race?" I asked. I wanted to see if she thought the same about the one man as her husband had.

"The two who spoke had Mexican accents, and the one who zip-tied us had dark skin, so I'm pretty sure he is, too.

"You saw his skin?"

"I saw his wrists."

That was something. Not much, but something. "What happened next?"

"They came downstairs. The one guy zip-tied Jared to the chair. Jared told him to f-off, and the guy punched him in the eye. They told us if we made any noise, they'd come back and kill us."

Jared Kelley hadn't told us that.

"After they left, Jared tried to get to the scissors in the kitchen, but he fell onto his side. I scooted my chair over to him and got his cell phone from his pocket. I shimmied the chair so I could hold the phone near his hand so he could call 911, but he couldn't. Thankfully, he could activate Siri to make the call with my voice."

"Go on," I said.

"The next thing I knew, the police arrived, and then Jared had rushed the kids to the neighbor's without telling me. He gave me the Xanax right away, so the rest? I really have no idea."

"Mrs. Kelley, do you work?" I asked.

She licked her lips. "I'm home with the children."

"What does your husband do?"

"He's the president of Surface Solvents."

"What do they do?"

"Honestly, I only half listen when he talks about it, but I know it's a chemical company that works with flooring." She twisted her hands into a ball then released them. "I should know that, but . . ."

"No worries," I said.

"How long has he been with the company?"

"Oh, for at least six years. We moved here for the job. From Chicago."

I hadn't noticed the Chicago dialect or accent. "I'm from Irving Park."

"Really? We were just outside the city, actually. Evanston. But I'm not from there originally. I'm from Michigan. We met in college."

"How are things going for your husband and the business?"

"You mean is it successful? Yes, definitely. Jared can be an asshole, and frankly, he is a lot of the time, but he's good at what he does. He knows how to turn on the charm when it's to his benefit. My kids are perfect examples of that."

"Are you aware of anyone at work who might have an issue with him? Maybe a disgruntled or former employee?"

Her eyes widened. "You think someone who works for him did this?"

"We're just covering as many bases as we can," I said.

"Oh, yes, got it. I don't know of anyone, but we don't talk much about his work. You'd have to talk to his assistant for that stuff."

Her expression went from nervous to annoyed when she said that, so I dug deeper. "His assistant?"

"Erica Higgins. I have her number if you'd like it. She can tell you all about his business, and how she's fucking my husband."

Ouch. That had to hurt. I felt for the woman. If Tommy had ever cheated on me, I'd have his balls hanging from my Jeep's rearview mirror. Kyle's too. "Is it possible something happened between them recently?"

"I wouldn't know, but if you think she was involved in this, I'd say no. She's young, and naïve, and I'm not sure she's smart enough."

"You'd be surprised at the things people do." I asked her a few more questions related to her husband's work, but she didn't know much.

"Have you considered getting a divorce?" Levy asked.

Mrs. Kelley blanched. "Why would I do that?"

"Because your husband is cheating on you," Levy said.

"If I left him for an affair, I would have done that six months into our marriage. This is just what he does."

Wow. Just wow.

"How are your relationships with people in Mayfield? Have you or your husband had any run-ins with anyone?" I asked.

"Of course not. We have gatherings all the time and play golf and tennis together. We're one big, happy family."

In my experience, no community was even close to being one big, happy family. "Families fight all the time. Maybe they argued about a golf game or politics?"

She laughed. "Jared is a horrible golfer. He can't even play mini-golf, and practically everyone in Mayfield aligns politically. If anything, they spend their time hating on the government in general." Her voice softened. "Not problems, exactly." Her cheeks reddened. "There is a group here, but we said no, and that's created a little tension lately." She pressed her lips together then added, "But it'll be fine."

"A group?"

"You know, a social group."

I wasn't sure I understood. "I'm sorry. I don't understand."

"Swingers, detective. They're swingers."

3

The mug shots were a failure, though we'd expected that. Jimmy assured Jared Kelley we would do our best to find the men responsible for breaking into their home. Jared demanded it be quick because his wife insisted they stay there, and he didn't want it to happen again.

Bishop, Jimmy, Michels, Levy, and I met in the investigation room to discuss what we'd learned. I struggled to keep the smile off my face but failed.

"What in the devil's hell are you smiling about?" Bishop asked.

I cleared my throat. "Mayfield's a swingers community."

"You didn't already know that?" Bishop asked.

It must have been old news. "I've been a little focused on hunting down serial killers and saving people's lives. I don't have space in my brain to store stuff like that."

Jimmy laughed. "You really didn't know, did you?"

I ignored the chief of police but only because he was the father of my goddaughter. "Even I know that, and I haven't been here as long as you," Levy said.

I glared at Michels. He held his palms up. "Not saying a thing."

"Y'all are funny."

Bishop laughed. "You just said y'all."

"I did not."

"Yes, you did," Jimmy said.

I looked at Levy. She cringed. A quick glance at Michels got me palms up again. "Someone punch me the next time I do that." I placed my hands on the table, palms down. "Okay, now that we've got that out of the way, can we get to the investigation?"

"Swingers aside," Bishop said. "Jared Kelley has two disgruntled employees. One was denied workers' compensation coverage for a broken arm. The other he fired without severance."

"Sounds like a nice guy," Levy said.

"Ask his assistant. He's screwing her," I said.

"Right," she said.

"The wife tell you that?" Bishop asked.

"Though she used a different descriptive for the activity."

"Ick," Levy said. "Guarantee the assistant's under thirty."

"And a double D," I said, smiling.

"All right." Jimmy forced us into focusing. "I have a stack of files on my desk, and I'd like to get home before ten tonight, so can we get moving here?"

"Right," Bishop said. "Jared Kelley can't think of anyone else, and has no clear reason for the break-in."

Michels said, "Levy and I checked through six months back, and other than a golf ball through a window and a few teenagers blaring their car radios at night, no disturbances of any kind have been reported in the community."

"Clean as a whistle," Levy said. She whistled for added effect.

Jimmy stood. "Sounds like you start with the assistant. She can provide more information about the other two." He pointed to Levy and Michels. "You two get started on the second round of door-to-doors. Let me know if anything breaks." He walked out of the room.

"What crawled up his butt?" I asked.

"The mayor called for an update," Bishop said.

"Ah, got it."

∿

JARED KELLEY WORKED off Old Milton Parkway in Alpharetta. Bishop chose State Route 400 instead of Highway 9. Traffic on 400 was perpetually stuck in rush hour, but every intersection on Highway 9 came with a stoplight. Deciding which would be better always ended in a toss-up. Both sucked and picking the lesser of two evils was always just a guess.

"We need to look into Kelsey Kelley," I said.

Bishop flipped on his signal to change lanes. "You think she had her home broken into? I think that's a stretch."

"He's had multiple affairs, the first starting six months after they got married."

"And in our update Levy said she had no intention of divorcing him."

"She's a stay-at-home mom completely reliant on her husband. Paying an attorney might be hard, and she might lose big. She has the place robbed, that covers the attorney fees, and she gets to keep the jewelry."

"We can't rule it out yet, but I don't see her for it. She'd have to find the men to do it. Do you see her doing that?"

"Don't underestimate the power of a pissed off woman."

"You think I don't? I'm divorced, and I have you for a partner. We can talk to her again."

"I wasn't asking for permission," I said.

"When have you ever done that?" He turned off the exit ramp and immediately stopped in back-to-back traffic.

I flipped around and checked the traffic behind me. The congestion appeared to go on forever. "Where are these people going? Don't any of them work?"

"Where were all the people going in Chicago traffic?"

"To hell in a handbasket, as Lenny would say. He's like you with the catchy phrases."

The wrinkles at the corners of Bishop's eyes deepened when he smiled. "How is Lenny these days?"

Lenny Dolatowski and I had worked together at the Chicago PD, but growing up, his family and mine shared a wall living in a duplex in Chicago. His daughter Jenny was my best friend. I barely had relationships with my parents, and Lenny had become my family. He'd been there for me when Tommy died, just as I'd been there for him when a drunk driver plowed into Jenny on Lake Shore Drive. We'd bonded in ways that could never be broken. "He's good. Like you, he's got a lady friend."

He raised an eyebrow. "Really?" He cleared one light. Only five to go before we had to turn for Kelley's office.

"I don't know much about her, but I hope she's not taking advantage of him."

"Why would she be taking advantage of him?"

"Lenny's a softie. I just . . . I don't know. I just don't want him getting hurt."

"He's a big boy, and a former commander for the Chicago PD. He'll be fine."

"We'll see." I detached my bun from its clip and hair band, gathered the fly-aways, then put it back together, only tighter.

Bishop turned toward me, then back to watching traffic. "Why are you nervous?"

"What makes you think I'm nervous?"

"Because you adjust your hair when you're nervous."

Did I? "Just got a lot on my mind." That wasn't a lie.

"Maybe we should talk about it," he said.

I knew what *it* meant. Kyle. "Can we not go there right now? I need to focus on the investigation."

"Yes, ma'am."

Fifteen minutes later, we'd gone a mile and turned into the Kelley business's parking lot. We determined who would handle what on our way inside. The office took up the entire third floor of the building. The elevator opened into a small lobby leading to a closed door. A framed note on it said, *please ring bell*. Bishop did.

A woman's voice came through the speaker. "Surface Solvents. May I help you?"

"Detectives Ryder and Bishop from the Hamby Police Department, ma'am," Bishop said. "We're here to see a Ms. Erica Higgins."

"One moment."

A loud buzz burst from the door a few seconds later. Bishop opened it and let me through first.

The receptionist smiled from her desk. "She'll be right with you."

"Thank you," we said in unison. Bishop side-eyed me. It appeared that Erica Higgins had expected us even though we hadn't informed her. Jared Kelley must have.

I examined the small lobby area. The only ways into the office area were secured doors on each side of the reception desk. One opened, and a young woman walked out.

"Detectives," she said. "I'm Erica Higgins. Come on back."

Bishop and I shared a look. Erica Higgins was exactly as Levy and I had described. Big boobs sitting so high on her chest they almost touched her chin and somewhere under thirty. If I had to guess, I would have said twenty-three. She wore a tight-fitting dress and her long, blond hair pulled into a clip on the left side. A dangling silver earring with an emerald hanging from it swung as she talked.

Most definitely looking for love—or money—in the wrong places.

"Please," she said as we stepped into a conference room behind her. "Have a seat." She fiddled with the earring. It was a nervous reaction. Why was she nervous?

I sat and started, changing my questioning from what we'd discussed earlier. "Miss Higgins, thank you for seeing us. May I ask how you knew we were coming?"

She blinked, then sat at the end of the oblong table. "How I knew—I, uh, Mr. Kelley called last night and said you might be stopping by."

Bingo! "And did he tell you why?"

"He said his home was broken into and money and jewelry were stolen, and that the mayor thought you might be coming by. He also didn't expect to be in the office today."

Of course, he'd already talked to the mayor. Poor Jimmy. "Got it," I said. I removed my small spiral notebook and a pen from my pocket and jotted down notes as we talked. "Did Mr. Kelley give you any details about the incident?"

She watched something behind us. Bishop turned around to see what she'd been looking at. "No, ma'am. Not really. He just said the house was broken into and money was taken from the safe."

"Nothing else?" Bishop asked.

"No, sir."

"How long have you worked for Mr. Kelley?" I asked.

She bounced in her seat. "Oh, for almost a year now. It's a great job. Jar—Mr. Kelley is great to work for."

"And you're an administrative assistant?"

She sneered at me. "No, ma'am. I'm an executive assistant."

"I didn't know there was a difference."

"There's a big difference. An administrative assistant does basic things like type out letters, take phone calls. Nothing too involved. Executive assistants handle everything from the basic tasks to managing schedules, prepping for meetings, and making executive decisions so their boss can handle urgent matters. Though we do so much more than that."

"So," I said. "You make executive decisions for the company?"

"I'm capable, if that's what you're asking, but I've only had to do it a few times. Mr. Kelley and I have a strong relationship and we communicate often. He would be lost without me."

"Does that strong relationship carry over into anything personal?" I asked.

She blinked. "I'm sorry, I'm not sure I understand."

"Do you have a sexual relationship with your boss?"

Her jaw dropped. Her eyes shifted to Bishop and then back to me. She scooted her chair back. "I don't see how any of this is your business." She stood.

"Sit," I said. "We're investigating a crime where your boss's wife and children were tied up and their lives were threatened. Everything related to Mr. Kelley and his family is our business. Are you still involved in a personal relationship with Mr. Kelley?"

She sat and stared at me with her mouth slightly opened. When her eyes moved to Bishop, he said, "If your personal relationship with Mr. Kelley has ended, we need to know."

She licked her lips and looked down at the table. "We're still together. We're in love."

I wouldn't have used the words together or love, but if she'd led herself to believe she was more than an object in his eyes, it wasn't my business to argue.

"Where were you last night?" Bishop asked.

Better him than me.

"Do you think I did this?" She rolled her eyes and sneered at us. "What reason would I have to break into my boyfriend's home?"

"Maybe Mr. Kelley decided to end things, and you wanted revenge?" I said. "Or, maybe you found out he's not ever going to leave his wife, and you wanted to make him suffer?"

"He hasn't broken up with me, and he won't. I told you, we're in love. He's preparing to divorce his wife, by the way. He even talked to an attorney. I know because I made the appointment."

Repeatedly defending something usually meant that it wasn't true. "If all of that is true, then you shouldn't have a problem telling us where you were last night."

"Did that bitch tell you to come here? Did she say I did this?" She crossed her arms over her chest. "What about her? Is she a suspect? She's horrible to him. She threatens to take the kids from him all the time. She hates him."

"Ma'am," Bishop said. "Please answer the question."

She huffed. "I was home. I have a roommate. You can call and ask her if you'd like."

"We'll need her name and number."

"Also," I asked. "May we have your address and cell number?"

She gave us the information.

"Miss Higgins," Bishop said. "Is there anyone that might have a reason to be upset with Mr. Kelley?"

"Finally you're looking for other people to blame."

"Anyone in his personal or business life have problems with him?"

She dropped the agitation in her tone. "We have a group of friends we see occasionally, but most of the time it's just us. As for here, I don't think so. He did have to let someone go recently, but she was like, ancient, so I doubt she'd do it."

"May we have her name and phone number?"

"You'll have to get that from human resources."

Bishop had said Jared Kelley had mentioned two people, so he asked about them.

"I'll have to get you with human resources for that as well."

"Understood," he said.

"Did you know his wife is drunk all the time? And she's a terrible mother. Always playing golf or tennis with her friends and leaving the kids with a sitter for it."

We'd just jumped into a deep lake of young woman drama, and we'd drown if we didn't get out soon. Thank God Bishop rescued us before it was too late. "Noted. Is there anything else you think might be important for us to know?"

She bit her bottom lip, then said, "No."

I removed a card from my pocket. "Here's my information. Please call me if you can think of anything else."

Bishop did the same.

"I'll take you to human resources."

"Thank you," Bishop said.

～

AN HOUR later we had the information surrounding the issues with employees and their contact information, as well as the ancient woman— she was forty-two—Kelley had recently fired, but we didn't believe any of them committed the crime.

I shifted my body in the passenger seat of Bishop's department vehicle and asked, "How old do I look?"

The corner of his mouth twitched. He didn't even bother glancing at me. "An antique is something older than twenty-five. It's safe to say his executive assistant is an antique."

"You didn't answer my question."

A smile stretched across his face. "Remember the power of a pissed off woman thing?" He tapped his fingers on the steering wheel while waiting for the light to turn green. "I feel sorry for that girl. She's so young. She has no idea he's using her."

"What she said validates my thoughts on the wife," I said.

"Only if any of them are true, which is unlikely. Cheating husbands always make the wife the bad guy."

"Still need to have another conversation with her."

"And I think a come-to-Jesus meeting with her husband."

"Agreed," I said. "Did you see the emeralds on her earrings? Those ain't cheap. She might be emotionally damaged from this, but at least she'll end up with some expensive jewelry."

He laughed. "Is that really how you look at it?"

I exhaled. "Yup."

"I don't understand why these young girls go for older married men."

"They're either looking for a sugar daddy, or they think something will come from it. They're attracted to married men because they represent something they want. A stable relationship. A family. Someone who loves them enough to marry them."

"That's pitiful."

"Right." I dialed the roommate's number.

The girl answered on the second ring. "Hello?"

"Is this Brittney Chambers?"

"Who is this?"

"I'm Detective Rachel Ryder with the Hamby Police Department. I'm calling to verify Miss Erica Higgins's whereabouts last night between the hours of six p.m. and one this morning." I gave a large window of time to cover any possible holes in Erica's story.

"What is this regarding? Is she in trouble?"

"We're investigating a break-in at Mr. Jared Kelley's home, and we're verifying the whereabouts of several employees. It's standard procedure."

"She was home, and she would never go near Jared's house. He's told her not to, and she's stupid enough to do what he says. For the record, the guy's a piece of shit, but she would never do anything to hurt him. She actually thinks they're going to get married."

People thought John Wayne Gacy wouldn't hurt anyone as well, and he'd murdered thirty-three boys and men. "Thank you," I said.

"Sure," she said, and disconnected the call.

"Seems like the roomie isn't a fan of the married boyfriend," Bishop said.

"The roomie must be smart."

"When do you want to talk to the Kelleys again?"

"Now is as good a time as any," I said.

~

A MAN CARRIED a new front door up the steps to the Kelleys' porch.

Jared Kelley stood on the bottom of the steps and barked orders at the guy. When he saw us walking up his driveway, he stopped. "Excellent. You have an update already?"

"I'm afraid not," Bishop said. "But we would like to talk to you and your wife again. Individually, please."

He raised an eyebrow. "What? Why? We've told you everything we know."

The door man jogged down the stairs and toward his truck.

Bishop turned and watched the man, then looked back at Kelley and said, "We can do this here or inside. Which would you prefer?"

He narrowed his eyes but climbed up the stairs and into the house.

Kelsey Kelley saw us from the kitchen. "Did something happen?"

"They want to talk to us separately," Jared Kelley said.

"I'll take the kids to the basement to watch TV," she said.

We sat at the breakfast table as she left.

"What questions?" Jared Kelley asked.

"Have you had any work done to your house recently?" I asked.

"Not since last year."

Bishop went for the gold. "Tell us about your relationship with your assistant," Bishop said.

"My assistant? What does she have to do with this?"

I didn't have the patience to skirt the truth. "Let's just cut to the chase, okay? We know you're having an affair with Erica Higgins. Have things been okay?"

He laughed. "Erica and me? You're mistaken."

I exhaled. "She confirmed it. Nice emerald earrings, by the way."

His face reddened. He glanced at the basement door and whispered, "She didn't do this. She couldn't. She doesn't have it in her."

"Every woman has it in her," I said. "Does she know you aren't planning on leaving your wife?"

"What? Uh, yes. Of course. This is just a thing. It doesn't mean anything."

"I think you should have a talk with her about that."

He blinked. "Are you going to discuss this with Kelsey?"

"Mr. Kelley," Bishop said. "Three armed men broke into your home and threatened your family. We have to address every possible angle to find those men."

"Jesus Christ. Kelsey didn't do this. Can't we just drop that?"

No, but he didn't need to know that. "Why did you have that much in cash in your safe?" I asked.

"I'm investing it. Just haven't had a chance to do it yet."

"Why would you not deposit that in an account?" I asked.

"I sold a valuable piece of sports memorabilia, and I haven't had a chance to deposit the money yet."

"You said you and your friends joke about how much cash you have lying around," I said. "Have you done this in groups or around people other than your friends?"

"My golf buddies?" He laughed. "If you're asking if we go around bragging about how much money we have, no. A neighbor works for an investment company. He likes to talk about the market, so we discuss it then."

"Is it possible one of them is having financial problems?" Bishop asked.

"I doubt it, but I can't say for sure. You never know what goes on behind closed doors."

"We're going to need the names of your golf buddies," Bishop said.

"Let me get my cell phone."

"You can write them down while we talk to your wife," I said. "Why don't you switch places with her?"

He rolled his eyes. "Fine."

Kelsey Kelley was less talkative than earlier, and a lot less friendly. "You didn't arrest the whore?"

"We haven't arrested anyone," Bishop said.

"Mrs. Kelley," I said. "You mentioned you had no plans of divorcing, correct?"

"As I said, why would I? I have a perfectly comfortable life."

"Your husband has cheated on you multiple times."

"And I told you that myself. If I wanted to get divorced, I would have done it by now."

"Do you have access to the family money?"

"Why wouldn't I?"

"Is your jewelry insured?"

"Yes." Her eyes widened. "Oh, my God. You think I did this, don't you?"

"I think a woman who's been married to a serial cheater might get frustrated and desperate."

"And have her own money and jewelry stolen? You have got to be kidding." She held her palm up and looked around the large space. "Why would I give up all this? It's more lucrative for me to stay with him."

"Do you normally keep that much cash at home?" Bishop asked.

"*I* don't, but one of the men Jared occasionally plays golf with invests for a living. He wanted to give him a shot, so he sold some stupid sports jersey and hasn't deposited the money yet."

We left the Kelleys' place with nothing more than what we started with and returned to the station.

Bubba, our tech genius, Nikki, Michels, and Levy joined us in the investigation room.

"I've got nothing," Nikki said. "Considering they were dressed for success, finding any DNA was unlikely. Honestly, this looks like a well-planned invasion by experienced criminals."

"Except they only took what was in the safe," Levy said. "If you're tying up a family and threatening their lives, why not go for a big get?"

"There's a reason," I said. "We just have to figure it out."

"Did your door-to-door uncover anything?" Bishop asked.

"We spoke with the gate guards and got access to their videos, but nothing shows anyone even attempting to enter, but they don't have full coverage of the outskirts of the community," Levy said.

Michels gave his input, confirming our feelings about Jared Kelley. "A few neighbors in close proximity to the Kelley home think the husband is shady."

"Did they say why?" I asked.

"He comes and goes at all times of the day and night."

"So, he doesn't keep regular hours," Bishop said. "He runs Surface Solvents. How many flooring emergencies can there be in the middle of the night?"

"My thought, too," Michels said. "Maybe the guy's having financial problems and wants the insurance money, so he cashes out some stocks or something, sticks it in his safe, and hires someone to hit the house?"

"He and the wife said the money came from the sale of a valuable sports jersey," Bishop said. Maybe there wasn't one."

"We'd need something more than a maybe to get a warrant to check his financial records," Levy said.

"Agreed," Bishop said. "Let's verify the sale of the jersey and see where that takes us. We all know the odds of closing a break-in are slim."

"Let's run that by Jimmy first. Kelley's connection to the mayor could pose a problem."

Bubba cleared his throat. "Regarding his business, there are two Surface Solvents in the local area. One is a fireplace repair company. Kelley runs the other. There are no pending lawsuits or grievances filed against the company."

"We don't think it's about his work," I said.

"Am I the only one thinking this is random?" Levy asked. "Like Nikki said. It's not the first invasion the perps have committed, but it wasn't a personal crime. More just a crime of opportunity?"

"I'm moving that direction," I said. "The house is the first thing you see coming up the road, and it's massive, so that might be appealing to thieves."

Michels leaned back in his chair. "I say it's the wife."

"I don't think so." I shrugged. "Some women forgive indiscretions because they're accustomed to a certain lifestyle."

"That's pathetic," he said.

"Didn't say it wasn't."

Levy exhaled. "Does that mean it's back to digging through cold case files for something to do?"

"My small lab could use a remodel," Nikki said. The sides of her mouth twitched. "Nothing a few nails and some shelves won't fix."

"I think I'll pass on that one. I have a phobia of any project that includes tools."

I laughed. "When in need of home repair help, don't call Levy."

"Hey, we all have our issues."

Wasn't that the truth? I needed my hands, feet, and ten other people's hands and feet to count mine. I stood. "Okay then, I'll go ahead and let the chief know where we're at. I'm not looking forward to hitting the cold case files again."

"We need to tell him Kelley called the mayor," Bishop said.

I opened the door. "Five bucks says he already knows."

4

Savannah sat in front of Jimmy's desk bouncing Scarlet on her knee while the toddler chewed on a plastic handgun. She ranted on about a parking ticket she'd received in Alpharetta.

"Well," I said. I jutted my hip out and leaned against the doorframe. "The media would be all over this. Hamby PD's chief gets wife off criminal charges as daughter plays with gun."

She yanked the gun away from Scarlet. "That's not what's going on here."

Scarlet's mouth dropped into a frown as her eyes widened.

Jimmy slid his chair back toward the wall, then held his hands close to his ears. "Get ready for it in one . . . two—" he pointed to his daughter and said, "three," as the scream burst from her tiny mouth.

Savannah glared at me. "Thank you."

I popped from the doorframe and plopped into the chair beside her. "What? All I did was state facts. The media would twist this scene to their benefit. You're the one who upset my goddaughter."

If looks could truly kill, I'd have been dead on the spot. I reached for Scarlet, who gladly climbed into my arms, then stuck her thumb in her mouth, and stopped crying. "Look. I'm magic."

"You're a lot of things," Savannah said. "And thank God one of them is magic with your goddaughter. Most of the time."

"I'll take that. Where in Alpharetta was the ticket?"

"The Avalon. How was I supposed to know the meters weren't free after six p.m.?"

"By reading the sign," her husband said. "It's ten bucks. Just pay the thing." He turned his attention to me. "Any update?"

"That's why I'm here." I updated him on our efforts and what we didn't find.

"You don't see the wife for it?"

"No. If anything, I'd say we should dig deeper into the husband, but with his connection to the mayor . . ."

"I don't give a damn about his connection. Get the name of the person he sold the jersey to. If he balks, we pursue. If the sale checks out, we've done our due diligence, which is our job."

"The mayor called. Kelley called him last night bitching up a storm about how we aren't taking this seriously, so checking him out is a great way to show we are."

"If that doesn't give us anything, we're dead in the water. It could be a random break-in."

"Then you all will get to revisit the cold case files," he said.

Savannah blew a bubble with her gum and it popped. Perfectly timed, too.

I was just going to argue against the cold case files when the school superintendent knocked on Jimmy's doorframe and walked into his office without an invite. "Abernathy, we need to have a come-to-Jesus meeting about your Hamby High School officer."

"Off to work," I said. I carted Scarlet through the door as Savannah grabbed her purse and diaper bag.

Savannah and I became friends during my first big case with the department, and before Jimmy was promoted to chief. As nearly total opposites who shared a *tell it like it is* attitude, our friendship worked, and she was a shining star in my life.

We crossed the pit and sat in my less private cubicle.

She whispered, "I cannot stand that man. He's so cheap, he wouldn't give a nickel to see Jesus ride a bicycle."

I laughed. "That's a new one and said with perfect inflection, as always."

"People like that bring out my southern sass. You know he's in there saying the board doesn't want to pay for police representation because there haven't been any issues."

"There haven't been any issues because the school board is paying for police representation."

"I know that," she said. She unlatched her child from my arms. Scarlet fought hard, but Savannah won. "But that man doesn't have the sense God gave a goose to think like that."

I bit my bottom lip. She was full-throttle southern sass, and I wasn't about to stop her. I enjoyed the show. "You've really got your undies in a bunch over this guy, haven't you?"

She blinked and then grinned. "Have you been googling Southern sayings again?"

"Maybe."

Her eyes widened. "You have! That's my girl. I once googled Chicago sayings but each one included the f word. I had no idea it had so many different meanings."

I pressed my lips together. I wanted to respond with something using the word, but Savannah despised it, so I didn't. "It's universal."

"And awful."

"My favorite Southern saying is *her pants were so tight you could see her religion.*"

Bishop, Levy, and Michels walked in and immediately fought for Scarlet's attention. Five minutes later, she was out like a headlight and sleep-nursing the heck out of a pacifier.

"Y'all have work to do," Savannah said. "I don't want to keep you from those cold cases."

"Fun times," Bishop said.

"I'd rather be changing Scarlet's diapers than reviewing cold cases," Levy said.

Savannah smiled as she headed toward the door. "Don't tempt me with that offer."

~

BISHOP and I called Jared Kelley and asked for the name and number of the person who bought the shirt while Levy and Michels returned the cold case files to storage and grabbed a few others.

He wasn't pleased. "First you accuse my wife of paying someone to steal from us, and now you're accusing me? You should be out looking for the real thieves."

"We're investigating a crime," Bishop said. "It's our job to approach it from every possible angle."

"The mayor's going to hear about this."

"That's fine," Bishop said. "But we still need the information."

He huffed and cussed under his breath. "Give me a minute."

The contact verified the sale of the jersey, and we prepared Jimmy for another call from the mayor.

"I expected it," he said. "But I'm glad the sale checks out."

"Well," Bishop said. "Time for round two of the cold case files."

We met Levy and Michels back in the investigation room and shared the news. They handed us each a box.

I set mine on the floor. "I'll be right back." I walked to a private area and called Ashley.

"Rachel, I'm sorry. Still nothing. You know how these things work. He won't want to risk his cover being blown unless he's got an important update."

"Thanks, Ash. I just thought I'd check."

"No problem. Hey, can you tell Justin to come straight home tonight? I'm cooking."

"Will do."

We never referred to Michels by his first name. He had been Michels for so long, Justin didn't flow easily from my mouth. "Hey," I said to him once I set my box on the table in the investigation room. "Ashley said don't be late because she's cooking."

Bishop looked up from a file with a raised eyebrow. "Is that meant for all of us?"

"No," Michels said.

I laughed. He'd been territorial and protective of Ashley since she'd been abducted by a serial killer. Ashley was strong, and she had recovered both emotionally and physically. Michels, however, couldn't let it go, and I doubted he ever would.

"Hank Pendley's cow was stolen," I said. I skimmed the file. "Forget it. Hank and the suspects have been dead for twenty-plus years."

"That cow's long gone then," Michels said.

"What about this?" Levy asked. "Bobby Pyott, known to others as Baby," she chuckled and held up the man's mug shot. "Doesn't look like a baby to me."

"Not at all," I said.

"Anyway, he's wanted for stealing his girlfriend's purse and beating her alleged lover over the head with it."

"When was this?"

"Nineteen eighty-six."

"And he's still wanted?" I asked.

"Actually," Bishop said. "That was a big one. Bobby disappeared the day his girlfriend reported the incident."

"And they never found him?"

"Nope. Rumor has it the alleged lover, the son of the Alpharetta mayor at the time, killed him."

"That might be fun to look into," Levy said.

"Nothing ever came from it. No investigation, no search. Nothing. Word is the mayor paid the police chief to walk away."

"Oh, the juicy lives of small-town Georgia," Levy said.

"Let's put it aside for now," Bishop said. "Most of the people involved are gone."

We found nothing else. Jimmy vetoed Baby Pyott's disappearance and sent us home. Bishop and I walked to our vehicles together. "You doing anything tonight?"

"Watching *Yellowstone* and eating a bag of carrots," I said.

"A bag of carrots?"

"I haven't been to the store in a while."

"I'm cooking for Cathy. Chicken parmesan. Would you like to come?"

"It's a full bag of carrots. I'll be fine."

"Eating carrots sounds disgusting, and I don't want you to starve."

"I'll be fine, but thank you."

He climbed into his vehicle, saying, "If you change your mind, come on by."

I headed straight home and did as I said, watched *Yellowstone* and ate carrots, but only a few. The last time I saw the clock, it read ten fifteen. When my phone buzzed me awake, it was after midnight. "Ryder," I said with a groggy voice.

It was dispatch with another home invasion in Mayfield. "Chief wants all of you and Detective Bishop on it. I've already called him."

"Shit," I said as I disconnected the call. I rushed to dress, checked my weapons, and called Bishop on the way out the door. "ETA?"

"Ten tops. You?"

"Same."

"Guess the last one wasn't random," he said.

"And probably not about Jared Kelley, either."

"Nope."

Jimmy picked up on the first ring and skipped a greeting. "When we catch these bastards, I'm nailing their asses to the wall." He paused. "I don't get enough time with my family as it is, damn it."

"So, you're en route?"

"Five out."

"See you there."

I parked on the street behind Michels's truck. "Looks like it's going to be another long night," he said.

Jimmy stormed by dropping f-bombs.

"He's pissed this is taking time away from his personal life," I said. "Tread carefully."

Bishop walked up beside me. "We're all pissed it's taking time away from our personal lives."

They headed toward the home.

Levy arrived shortly after while I did what I always did, took photos of the home and the area around the scene. The home shape was a smaller version of the Kelleys' but with a different elevation.

Levy walked with me to the porch. Bishop and Michels stood at brick stairs leading to the double-doored entrance.

"Yikes," Levy said. "Glass doors."

Glass shards covered the marble floor just inside the foyer, leaving just a small frame of glass attached to the actual doorframe. There were no other doors. Why someone would have just glass doors baffled me. Especially in a community with such expensive homes. People often picked appearance over safety. It was too bad.

I checked for security cameras or digital doorbells and pointed out the one installed in the left corner of the door area. "Doesn't look broken, so, maybe they've got our suspects on video."

"I won't bet on that," Bishop said.

Levy stared at the broken glass in the doors and said, "Who has storm doors but no real doors?"

"Is that what those are called?" Michels asked.

"They're a version of them," I said.

Levy leaned in through the broken door. "Damn. If this was the same perps, it looks like they leveled up."

A patrol officer agreed. "I was at the first one. It wasn't this aggressive."

"How's the family?" Bishop asked.

"Husband's beat up, but he's refused medical care. The wife is pretty shook up. Kid seems fine."

"Name?" I asked.

"Blahut. Alan and Lisa. Kid is Dylan."

"Where are they now?" I asked.

"In the kitchen," he said.

"Thanks. Hey, do me a favor. Get people on the edges of the community. We need to look for any fence holes, etcetera. Anything that someone could get through without being seen."

He said, "Yes, ma'am," and jogged down the porch steps.

"We're going to have a look around," Levy said.

"Sounds good," Bishop said. "We'll be with the victims."

A man, woman, and a teenage boy sat at the kitchen table. The boy's neck was locked in a bent position, his eyes glued to an iPad.

"Mr. and Mrs. Blahut," Bishop said. "I'm Detective Rob Bishop, and this is my partner, Detective Rachel Ryder. We'd like to talk to you about what happened tonight."

The man studied Bishop carefully, his eyes traveling up and down Bishop's body. I made eye contact when he looked at me. Instead of scrutinizing me, he looked away. Eye contact always intimidated people, and it was an easy way to gauge their emotions. Mr. Blahut was angry, but he was also nervous.

The man had taken a few more punches to the face than Jared Kelley. One eye had nearly swollen shut, his left ear bled, and he needed stitches on his lip.

"Alan Blahut," he said.

Before he finished, I said, "You need to have that ear looked at. Let me get you a paramedic."

"No, I don't need one. I'm fine."

"Sir, your ear is bleeding from the inside."

"Because some asshole just beat the shit out of me. Tell me what you're doing to find them."

Bishop and I shared a glance. If the man refused treatment, there wasn't much we could do.

I turned toward his wife. "I'm Detective Ryder. This is my partner, Detective Bishop."

She sniffled. "I'm Lisa, and this is my son Dylan. We're okay. They didn't hurt us, just Alan."

Her husband interrupted. "Is this connected to the Kelleys' break-in? Is someone out looking for the men who did this?"

"We've got officers searching the community," Bishop said.

"Mr. Blahut, can we get a copy of the video on the camera outside?" I asked.

His nostrils flared. "The damn battery's dead."

"I told you that last week," his wife complained. "You didn't charge it?"

"I've been busy," he said. "You can charge it just as easily as I can."

"If you'd put the charger back in the drawer, maybe. I keep telling you to put your stuff away, but do you ever listen to me?"

"Damn it, Lisa. Not now!"

Bishop cleared his throat. "Can you tell us what happened?"

The man exhaled. "We were uh, watching TV. Dylan was up in his room doing whatever it is he does. Next thing I know, I hear glass shattering in the foyer. I get up and check, thinking it's a deer or bear or something, but it's three guys dressed in black with ski masks on. They all had guns. One screamed for me to stop. He had his gun pointed at me, so, I stopped. Dylan ran downstairs." He looked at his son. "I guess he heard the glass and screaming because he never uses the front stairs. Matter of fact, he rarely hears anything either."

I glanced at the kid. He hadn't changed positions. "What happened next?"

"One of the men grabbed Dylan. The guy who talked asked if anyone else was home. I said no, but my wife came into the foyer right after that. The third guy grabbed her. They took us into the kitchen, tied them, and told me to give them all my money and my wife's jewelry, or they'd kill them both in front of me, then kill me. I got the stuff, then they tied me up, beat my face because they were too afraid to do it with my arms free, and left."

"What did they take?" I asked.

"All the cash in the safe. Over three hundred thousand dollars. All in hundreds, rubber banded in groups of ten thousand. My wife's wedding ring, a pair of diamond earrings, an emerald bracelet." He shifted toward her. "What else was in the safe?"

"I don't know," she said. "I guess all my expensive jewelry."

I noticed a wedding ring chock-full of diamonds on her hand. "You have two wedding rings?"

"This is my casual one. The other is five carats. I don't like wearing that to play tennis or go shopping."

Casual? I wouldn't have called a ring with four large diamonds casual. I worked a jewelry store robbery two years into my career with the Chicago PD. They'd smashed the glass cases and lifted several expensive pieces including a five-carat solitaire diamond ring. I wasn't a jewelry person but looking at the photos of that thing had made me drool. "And they didn't make you give it to them?"

She glanced at her husband. "I guess they didn't see it."

"Did they look for jewelry anywhere else?" Bishop asked.

"No. She's got a jewelry drawer in the closet, but they didn't even go in there," Alan Blahut said. "It all went so fast. I think they wanted to get in and out."

"Yet they took the time to attack you after tying you to the chair?" I asked.

"They said it was a warning. The guy who pointed the gun at me dragged me over and threw me in the chair. The other guy zip-tied me to it, and then the first guy smacked me with the butt of his gun." He touched his bloodied ear.

"Did you pass out?"

"Yes," his wife said. "He needs to go to the hospital."

"I'll go after we're done here."

Bishop spoke to Mrs. Blahut. "We're told you called 911. How did you do that tied up?"

She pointed to a pocket inside her sweater. "My phone is here. Those assholes were too stupid to look. I just told Siri to call 911."

Kudos to the wife.

Bishop asked Mr. Blahut, "Were you able to see any of the men through their masks?"

"No.""

"But one spoke to you? Did you sense an accent?"

"Definitely Hispanic."

"What about you?" he asked the wife.

"I was focused on my son, but I think Alan's right. At least the one was Hispanic."

I had to ask the son twice if he saw anything.

"No. The one dude took my phone when I came downstairs."

"Did he give it back to you?" Bishop asked.

"No. He threw it on the floor and laughed."

"Mr. Blahut, where are you employed?" Bishop asked.

"Spectrum Group. I'm a wealth manager. Money manager to some, but it's more detailed than just money."

"How are things at work?"

"If you think one of my peers or clients did this, you're wrong. They're not like that."

"Everyone's like that when they need to be," Bishop said. "Have you had any problems with anyone through your business or here in the community?"

He vehemently shook his head. "We are good people. We go to church. We donate to important causes. We volunteer. We don't cause trouble, detective. Are there people that don't like us? Probably, but I wouldn't know who."

"Mrs. Blahut, what about you? Do you work?"

"I run the family."

"Have you had any problems with anyone in the community?"

"Of course not. Alan told you, we're good people."

"No issues with anyone, say, over a tennis match or something between the kids?" I asked.

"When I've had problems, I've worked them out quickly. I don't have time for drama."

Bishop spoke to the son. "Can you tell us what you saw?"

He looked up from the tablet, then automatically back to it. "What I said before. I saw the dudes with my dad, then one of them took my phone and tied my mom and me up."

"Did you see them hit your father?" I asked.

"Oh, yeah."

Dear God. I couldn't deal with the kid. "Did you see them tie him to the chair?"

"Yeah, but like, I wasn't really paying attention."

His father lost it. "Jesus Christ, Dylan! Stop being an idiot and tell the police what you saw." He leaned his head to the side and pressed a bloodied cloth to his wound.

I motioned to one of the officers. "Get a paramedic in here, please."

She said okay and darted off.

To Mr. Blahut, I said, "You need to have that looked at."

"I don't need—"

"Alan, stop yelling," his wife said. "He'll let the paramedic look at him, and my son wasn't paying attention. He does that sometimes."

"How the hell could he not pay attention? It's the first time since he was a toddler he didn't have a damn phone in his hand."

"Sir," I said. "We need you all to stay calm."

He curled his lip at me as his wife said, "He gets pissy when he's sick, so I'm assuming getting beat up would elicit a similar response."

I'd begun to feel sorry for each of them. "Dylan, where is your phone now?"

"You guys took it. When can I get it back? My tablet doesn't let me text."

"Soon. When the man took your phone, did you notice anything about him? Maybe you can recall his eye color or saw some hair?"

His head bobbed back and forth like a turkey did when running. "Oh, yeah. He had yellow eyes."

I raised an eyebrow. "Yellow eyes?"

"The white part was all yellow. It was gross."

"Jaundice," Bishop said. "A sign of liver disease."

"Did you happen to notice the color of the rest of his eyes?" I asked.

"Sorry. I just kind of like, you know, went to another place in my head. I do that sometimes."

The paramedic arrived, and an officer ran inside. "Detective, we found an opening in the fence, and there's hundred-dollar bills lying near it."

5

Nikki held up a baggie containing a small bundle of cash. "Twelve hundred. All in c-notes." She'd already marked off the area appropriately and pointed to the metal chain-link fence with three strands of barbed wire on top. "Someone cut it and pushed through. Unfortunately, there's no way to tell if it was our guys or someone else. But," she held up another small baggie. "I did see red liquid on the broken area. I scraped some off, and if it's blood like I think, I'll move forward with it, but it's a very small amount, and I can't verify without a test."

"That small amount could be the key to finding our intruders, so thank you." I studied the area. "It's not close to either home. Why go deep into the community when there's enough homes here to hit?"

"Maybe they cased the area?" Nikki asked. "Saw their best options?"

"That would mean they were behind the gates before," Bishop said.

"Right," I said. "And to get through that gate they'd be on the list."

"Or work here," Bishop said. "They could have easily cased the homes. We'll need to get an employee list."

"I'll get Michels on that now," I said. I contacted him on the radio.

"I'll check at the security gate," he responded.

"I pointed at the opening and said to Nikki, "Think you can get any prints off it?"

She exhaled. "Maybe a partial or two."

"Understood. It's likely the fence cutters wore gloves, but we should still check."

"I'm on it," she said.

Bishop and I thanked her and headed back to the Blahut home.

Mr. Blahut had been taken to the hospital, and his wife and son were just leaving to meet him there.

I stopped them as they walked into the garage. "Mrs. Blahut," I said. "Are you close to the Kelleys?"

"Close? I'm not sure I'd say that, but we do socialize with them. Dinner, get-togethers, that kind of thing."

"What about golf or tennis?"

"Sure, but that doesn't mean much. Everyone plays together at one time or another." She opened her car door and stepped inside.

"Kelsey Kelley mentioned a particular social group involving some of the community members. Are you and your husband a member of that group?"

Her entire body stiffened. Her eyes shifted from me to her son and back. "No."

"Thank you. We'll need your family to come by the department tomorrow to answer some additional questions and look at some mug shots."

"I'll see how my husband is doing." She closed the door and backed out of the garage, honking at the officers standing in the driveway.

I walked over to Bishop standing outside near the front door.

"You think they're connected," Bishop said.

"Wealthy community. Limited home security. Looks like someone's been casing the community. It'll happen again."

"Yup."

I glanced at the front door. The broken glass hadn't been covered. I radioed for an officer to contact the community's maintenance department and see if they could at least board it up for the time being. "I'll have an officer stick around while the maintenance department cleans up the glass and covers the doors. Let's go home. We can pick up early tomorrow."

"Sounds like a plan," he said.

~

"PRINTS ON THE CASH RAN CLEAN," Nikki said. "And I couldn't get anything from the fencing. Not even a partial. Good news is the red stuff was blood. It's not much, but I'll try to develop the DNA profile and see what happens."

"Thanks," Bishop said. "We need something to break this open."

I sipped my Dunkin' coffee as I listened and read through the newspaper article about the two invasions, then, during a break in conversation, I read the headline out loud. "Hamby police have no suspects in two home invasions in Mayfield Golf Community." I tossed the paper across the table toward Bishop. He'd picked up his coffee just before the paper landed in its spot. "Our community relations liaison did the interview. Did any of you talk to her?"

Everyone shook their heads.

I hated that Jimmy had hired a communications liaison. We'd had no problem dealing with the press, and at least that way we could manage what they knew. "Then how does she know?" I asked as Jimmy walked in.

"How does who know what?"

Bishop held up the paper with the front-page headline about the invasions in full view. "Taylor Cooke said we have no suspects."

"She's correct," Jimmy said.

"But shouldn't she have spoken to me or Bishop?" I asked.

"Not if she spoke to me." He sat at the head of the table. "I gave her the information."

"It shines a bad light on us, chief," Bishop said.

"Be that as it may, we do not have any suspects, and we need help from the community. Listen," he said. "The news is already all over this. Cooke did her job. Gave them little information and they added the rest."

I groaned. "I freaking hate the media."

"They're not fans of us, either," Bishop said.

I crossed my arms over my chest. "Don't get me started on that."

"So, where are we?" Jimmy asked.

Bishop gave the update. "No recorded prints on the money, none off the son's phone or fence. Camera at front door has a dead battery. It's a wealthy community with crappy security and a broken fence. Ryder and I think it'll happen again."

"I'd bet my money on it being an inside job," I said.

"I agree," Jimmy said.

"Maybe an employee," I said. I turned toward Bishop. "And we can't rule out a resident."

Bishop dragged his hand down the stubble on the sides of his face. "We're still determining the relationship between the two families."

"Good. Do what you need to do. I'd like to keep the mayor off my ass, so please give me another update at the end of the day." He stood and left the room.

No one spoke for a minute, until Bubba finally broke the silence. "He's been in a bad mood for a while now."

I wondered why. Was it something other than the mayor and work? Was something going on at home I didn't know about? Would Savannah have told me? She'd always been open about their relationship, or so I'd thought. "I'm sure he's tired. Scarlet's been waking up at night."

"I'm not looking forward to that," Nikki said.

We all stared at her. Her eyes widened. "Not now! When it happens. Geez. I'm not pregnant now!"

~

THERE WASN'T much for Nikki to do, so she went ahead and cleaned up her lab. She was singing along to a country song when I walked in.

"Oh, hey," she said. A flush of red swept up her neck and landed on her cheeks. "I didn't hear you come in."

"Is that Blake Shelton?"

"Good guess."

"I know some of his stuff."

"Cool. What's up?"

"Just wanted to say thanks for your hard work. I appreciate you putting in the late hours and being so loyal to the job."

She shrugged. "It's not like I've got anything else going on. If I ever get into a relationship though, things might change."

"What about Officer Gregory?"

She shoved a tray into a slat under her lab table. "What about him?"

"I think the two of you might have a little something going on."

She blushed again. "Really? What makes you say that?"

"Just a hunch."

As I walked out, she grabbed the door and said, "Tell me what you know!"

I turned and pretended to zip my lips shut.

THE BLAHUTS ARRIVED to look at the mug shots. Like the Kelleys, they didn't recognize anyone.

"Mr. Blahut," I asked. "What's your relationship to Jared Kelley?"

"We're friends."

"Good friends?"

"I'd say we're building up to that."

"Have you ever talked to him about his finances?" Bishop asked.

"You mean about investing through my company? I don't sell our services to my friends. You know the saying, don't shit in your own backyard."

"Have you had any work done on your home lately?" I asked.

"No."

"What about the swingers group? Are you a part of that?" I asked.

"Excuse me? A swingers group? I wasn't aware that kind of thing happened in Mayfield."

Lisa agreed. "That's disgusting."

I didn't believe them. "So, you've never been asked to participate?"

Lisa stared at the ground while her husband barked out an adamant no.

After asking the Blahuts the same questions we asked the Kelleys, and coming up with nothing, we sent them home.

"That was another dead end," he said. "Give me five and meet me at the back exit, and put on your happy face. We're going to talk to the community manager."

I pointed to my face. "Resting bitch face *is* my happy face."

"You know what?" He unlocked his department vehicle's doors but didn't bother opening mine. "You're right."

THE ENTRY GATE REPRESENTATIVE, as she'd called herself, had us pull around and wait in the waiting lot for the community's manager.

It annoyed me. "She couldn't just let us go to the office?"

"Did you see the scowl on her face? She takes her job very seriously."

"Right? I'm pretty sure she's got a sawed-off shotgun on the floor in there."

"In these parts, you never know."

A man tapped on Bishop's window. He didn't see him coming, and jerked in surprise, nearly hitting his head on the roof of his car. He rolled down the window, but before he could say anything, the man said, "Come on over to the office."

He walked us into his office. The floor-to-ceiling windows with a golf course and lake view anchored the space. Large wood built-in bookcases framed the sides of the room and reached the ceiling as well. I suspected his ornate wood desk cost more than my Jeep.

"Please, have a seat. I'm Dan Swift. You're here about the break-ins, I presume?"

"Detectives Ryder," I pointed at Bishop. "And Bishop."

He leaned back in his chair. He wasn't tall, maybe five foot eight, and his head wasn't visible over the chair's back. Probably the reason he wore his hair poufy on top.

"These break-ins are quite alarming. Do you have any suspects?"

"We're not at liberty to share specifics on the investigation, sir," Bishop said.

"Oh, right. My apologies. Tell me then, what can I do to help? We pride ourselves on maintaining a safe community, and I'd like to make sure that continues."

"Then check your fences," I said.

He blinked. "Excuse me?"

"You have a broken fence toward the back of the neighborhood," Bishop said. "We believe that's how the intruders gained access to the community."

He furrowed his brow. "I'll have that fixed today." He opened his side drawer and removed a folded paper. "Can you locate it on the map?"

Bishop easily pointed it out. "We'll need to conduct interviews with employees."

"Of course," he said. "The employees are all vetted before they're hired. None have criminal records."

"That could simply mean they haven't been caught," I said.

"That is true. I can't imagine you'd think someone in the community is involved. Our residents are vetted before they're allowed to purchase homes. None have criminal records either."

I purposefully tilted my head far to the right and opened my eyes wide as if to say, *seriously?*

He leaned back. "Right. They may not have been caught." He ran his hand through his hair. The product slathered through it divided it into thick chunks. "I'll get that list, but only on one condition."

Okay, the guy needed a swift kick in the ass, and I was about to give it to him. "Excuse me? Are you trying to negotiate with law enforcement?"

He waved his hands in front of him. "No, no, that's not what I'm doing. Please, I'm just asking that you don't make your theory public. We work hard to maintain a certain appearance, and we'd like to keep it that way. We have several empty lots for sale, and even more pending sales. We don't want to lose residents."

"We'll do our best," Bishop said. "If possible, we'd like to talk to any previous employees as well."

"Give me a moment." He stood and walked out, closing his office door behind him.

"He's sweating," I said. "And annoying."

Bishop studied the view through the window. "I wonder what it would be like looking at that every day?" He glanced at the file folders on Dan Swift's desk. "You think he's hired someone with a record and doesn't want us to know?"

"If he could get a felon at a lower pay rate, I wouldn't put it past him," I said.

Bishop took a deep breath. "That won't look good for Mr. Swift."

"Nope."

Swift returned with a file folder a few minutes later. "This is everyone. I included past employees for the last year. We purge their information if they're over a year old, but corporate keeps them. If you'd like, I can request an order?"

"We'll let you know," I said.

"Again, I would appreciate you keeping this confidential."

"We'd like to begin interviewing employees. Is there somewhere we can do this privately?"

"I'll set you up in one of our event rooms and contact the department managers. Will you be together, or interviewing separately?"

The list was twenty-five pages long, though not all were currently working. I texted Michels and Levy and asked for help. They gave an ETA of fifteen minutes. "Together," I said. "And we'll have two more detectives arriving soon. Can we get a room for them?"

"Yes, detective. Follow me."

Bishop and I interviewed Chad Wetherson, the golf course manager, first. The man was in his mid-thirties, and wore a white long-sleeve button-down shirt with an open collar under a solid gray sweater vest.

"Mr. Wetherson," Bishop said. "What does a golf course manager do?"

Wetherson straightened in the chair and pushed his shoulders back. He rested his hands on his lap. "How much time do you have?" He chuckled. "The list is long, but in general terms, I manage the maintenance and repairs of everything on the course, including landscaping, the restrooms, you name it."

"Does that include the golf shop?" I asked.

"Just the course. There are other managers for the shop and taverns."

"How many people work under you?" Bishop asked.

"Right now? Six, but during our busier seasons it can get up to fifteen."

"Isn't fall a busier season?"

"All the seasons are busy to some degree, but in order, it's summer, spring, fall, then winter."

Bishop jotted down Wetherson's responses. "Any of the six on staff now new hires?"

"No, sir. In fact, I just dropped five employees because the season is unusually slow."

Great. More people to locate and talk to.

"Do you handle the interviews?" Bishop asked.

"Yes, sir, but they're initially screened through our HR department."

"So, they interview them first?"

"Oh, no. That's not what I meant. They go through the applications and pick the appropriate applicants, and then send them to me."

"And from there?" Bishop asked.

"I interview them. If I like one, HR will run a background check. If it comes back clean, we make a job offer."

"Have you ever hired anyone with a criminal record?" I asked.

"No, ma'am."

"What about undocumented persons?" Bishop asked.

Wetherson blinked. "I, uh . . ."

"We're only here for the home invasions," Bishop said. "We don't care about immigration status."

"Oh, well, yes, we do, but they pay federal taxes, and we run background checks on them as well."

Some undocumented immigrants chose to pay federal taxes in hopes of it helping them gain citizenship in the future. Undocumented individuals who committed crimes and were arrested often left the country if given bail, but they'd come back with new identification and a completely new name. It was nearly impossible to get ahead of that game.

"You don't have anyone you're paying under the table?" Bishop asked.

He glanced at the door then leaned forward. "Just one, but I did just let another guy go."

"Do you have his contact information?" Bishop asked.

"Which one?"

"How about both?"

"I think I have cell numbers. I can't say whether HR has addresses, but I can check. I'm pretty sure we have the one's information."

"We'd appreciate that. What's his name?"

"Carlos Martínez. I know he's from El Salvador, but that's about it."

"Did he apply for the position?" I asked.

"No, ma'am. Another employee asked us to hire him. In fact, it was the other undocumented employee. We interviewed Martínez and he was hired, but it wasn't my decision."

"Whose decision was it?" I asked.

"HR. I didn't want to take that risk. Too many undocumented workers could cause us problems with the feds."

"What about the other one?"

"Diego Perez. He's here today."

"Is he from El Salvador as well?" Bishop asked.

"I think they're related, but I can't say for sure. I can get him for you next if you'd like?"

"We'd like that," I said.

He made a call on his cell. "Benny, can you get Perez up to admin?" A few seconds later, he said, "Really? How long?" And then, "Okay, thanks." He set his phone down. "Diego Perez hasn't shown up for four days. That means he's no longer an employee of Mayfield. I can get you his address from HR, but I can't guarantee it's right. Also, we take photos of all employees for their files. I can get those for Perez and Martínez and anyone else you need."

"We'd appreciate it," I said. "For all of them."

The number he had for Martínez was fake, but we'd expected that.

We decided to interview the employees away from the business office, hoping that would make them more comfortable. Wetherson set us up with an older man first. Juan Gonzales. He'd been with the community for five years.

We waited in front of the maintenance shed for Gonzales. A Latino man in jeans and a red cap walked over.

"Juan Gonzales?" I stepped forward and held out my badge.

"Yes," he said.

"Good morning. I'm Detective Rachel Ryder and this is my partner, Rob Bishop. We'd like to ask you a few questions."

Gonzales didn't seem pleased by our presence. He wiped his hands on a rag and stood with his arms at his side. He was a sturdy, middle-aged man, with a mustache and a kind face. I doubted he knew anything about the break-ins, and probably didn't care to associate with any of the other employees.

"Do you have any suspects?" he asked.

"How about we ask the questions," Bishop said. We asked him where he was on the night of the break-ins.

"With my wife at home. I am not like the others. I have been at this job for many years. I am a good employee, and I would not risk my job."

"Have you noticed anything out of the ordinary recently?" Bishop asked.

"How do you mean?"

"With your coworkers, or just around the course in general?"

Gonzales thought for a moment. Finally, he said, "Well, there was one thing. It was about a week ago, maybe two. I was working late, and I saw some people sneaking around the golf course. They were careful to stay out of sight, so I couldn't get a good look at them. But they were definitely up to something."

"Can you tell us any details about them? Maybe what they were wearing? Did they have on hats? Were their faces covered?"

The man thought for a moment. "They were wearing dark clothes and masks," he said. "That's all I saw."

"Did you report this to security?"

"They don't listen to us, so we've stopped talking to them."

We thanked him and asked him to send in the next employee.

An hour later we'd gone through everyone and told Levy and Michels not to bother coming.

Nikki called on our way back to the station. "I got a match. The blood belongs to a Santos Garcia. I'm texting you his photo now."

6

The team sat around the investigation room table.

I compared the photo of Carlos Garcia with the ones from the manager and found a match. "Well, look at this," I said holding up my cell phone. Carlos Martínez and Santos Garcia were either twins or the same person.

"May I see?" Michels asked.

I handed him my phone.

"Dude has the same tattoo on his chest. Or at least it looks like it," Michels said.

"I'll get a BOLO out on Martínez, Garcia, and Perez," Levy said.

"Thanks."

"Great, now go have a talk with Mr. Perez," Bishop said. "He might have something to tell us."

"You want us to tag along?" Michels asked.

"Might as well," Bishop said.

~

PEREZ LIVED in Roswell off Highway 9 near Holcomb Bridge Road. With Levy and Michels following, Bishop jumped on 400. Traffic came to a complete stop just before exit eight.

"Looks like an accident," Bishop said.

"There's always an accident somewhere on 400. Flip on the strobe and scoot to the side. We can get off here."

"I was just going to do that."

After traffic nudged forward a few feet, Bishop angled his vehicle to squeeze in. The guy on the back end of the opening attempted to push us out, but Bishop persevered. "Can you believe the nerve of that guy?" he asked. "We could be en route to a murder scene."

"More than likely, he thinks we're going for donuts or coffee," I said.

"We do have those often, but I've never used my strobe for that." He turned right at the bottom of the ramp.

"Whatever."

"What? It's true."

"I've been your partner long enough to know when you're lying."

A flash of bright red heated his neck and face. "I'm not lying."

"Yes, you are. Want to know how I know?"

"How?"

"Every time you lie your neck and face turn red. Like right now."

He glanced in the rearview mirror. "Oh, hell. Fine. I did it once during my first year. I just wanted to see how it felt, and you know, live the stereotype."

I laughed. "You live so many stereotypes without even trying."

He narrowed his eyes at me, then quickly focused back on traffic.

We passed a dealership for almost every make of vehicle in business. The Jeep dealer I took my Jeep to was on Highway 9, along with the rest of the dealerships not on Mansell Road. We passed them all before making it to the small community where Perez said he lived.

Perez's house siding was a faded white and missing paint in several places. Newspapers stuffed into the windows acted as shades. The lawn was overgrown with weeds and had a dirty plastic baby pool near the sidewalk. "That's it," I said.

Bishop passed it and parked three doors down. Michels parked behind us.

The smell of cigarette smoke grew stronger as we walked up the home's broken concrete sidewalk. I needed a mask by the time we got to the front door.

I stood to the right while Bishop angled to the other side and knocked on the door. Michels and Levy stood behind the dying shrubs just off the porch. Our lack of department-issued uniforms didn't hide the fact we were law enforcement. The gun I carried on my side when not wearing my belt left no one guessing, which was always a risk when approaching a home.

A young girl, maybe eight tops, cracked the door open. She peeped at us with a single eye. "Hola?" She reached Bishop's waist.

He crouched down and spoke to her calmly. "Hi. Do you speak English?"

She shook her head and closed the door.

Bishop knocked again. That time, a teenage boy opened the door just a bit more than she had. "No Inglés."

Bishop stuck his foot inside the door before the kid could close it. "Diego Perez."

I jumped in and told him we were looking for Perez. "Estamos buscando a Diego Perez."

"He's gone. Left yesterday."

"You do speak English," Bishop said.

The kid's shoulders curled inward as he nodded.

"Do you know where Mr. Perez went?" I asked.

"No."

"Did he say he was coming back?" I asked.

"No. He took all his clothes."

"Are you related to Mr. Perez?" Bishop asked.

"Cousins. My mom and his mom are sisters."

"Is your mom here?" I asked.

"She's home."

By home, he'd meant El Salvador. "His mother?"

"Same."

"What about Santos Garcia? Does he live here?"

His brows furrowed. "I don't know him."

"Carlos Martínez?" I asked.

"Carlos was here for a few weeks, but he left yesterday, too." He leaned against the doorframe, his confidence growing from his laid-back posture. "What did they do?"

"We've just got some questions for them," Bishop said. "Do you know any of their friends or other family in the area? Maybe a girlfriend?"

"Carlos got a girl in Cumming, I think."

"You know her name?" I asked.

"No. But he had me take him to her work once."

"And where is that?"

"The Carniceria Hernandez."

"You know where that is?"

"Somewhere that way," he said, pointing toward Alpharetta.

"Do you know what she looks like?" he asked.

"Long black hair."

That was helpful.

He handed the kid one of his cards. "If they come back, or you hear from them, please tell them we'd like to talk to them."

"They won't be back, but okay."

I FOLLOWED up with the Kelleys on the way to the girlfriend's work.

"Do you think they're connected? Have we been targeted for some reason?" Kelsey Kelley asked.

"Is there something connecting your families that might cause reason for targeting?" I asked.

She hesitated, but then answered no.

"Are you sure?"

"I don't see how it could be connected, and I really shouldn't say anything."

"Yes," I said. "You really should."

She exhaled. "Like I said, I don't think it's anything, but the Blahuts are the ones that invited us to the party."

"The swinger party," I said for confirmation.

"Yes. They hosted it at their house a few months ago, but like I said, we turned them down."

"Thank you." I filled Bishop in after ending the call. "Blahut flat out lied. They're the ones that invited the Kelleys to a swingers party a few months ago."

"Maybe he was embarrassed."

"You're always giving people the benefit of the doubt."

"It's my nature."

"He lied, Bishop. He wasn't embarrassed. He just didn't want us to know."

"You think these could be connected to the parties?" he asked.

"I don't know, but now we have reason to look into it."

THE CARNICERIA HERNANDEZ was situated in Cumming, close to the bustling intersection near the Forsyth County Jail and courthouse. Cars stopped, often blocking traffic to drop off people at the courthouse, and pedestrians passed by on their way to both the jail and courthouse. Forsyth County's massive jail provided money for the county by renting cells to *guests* from other counties. If I had been a civilian resident of Forsyth County, I would have been anxious about the influx of criminals coming into town, but I didn't think the government cared. They wanted the money.

Levy and Michels stayed in their vehicle while Bishop and I went inside.

Three lanky, bearded fellows in jackets and beanies entered the store before us. I'd noticed them when we arrived in the parking lot, and although they didn't seem to be up to any trouble, I was suspicious. I was always suspicious.

The aroma wafting through the air was tantalizing: tangy cilantro and cumin, onion, and beef filled my nostrils, making my stomach grumble desperately for whatever owned the smells drifting from the back of the store.

Bishop pointed to the small café along the back wall. "These places have authentic Mexican food. It's the best stuff I've had in the states."

"I'm suddenly starving."

"We'll grab something on the way out."

A young Latina woman worked the checkout counter. She'd twisted her black hair into a bun on the back of her head. I made a mental note of the small almost diamond-shaped birthmark on the right side of her neck.

We showed her our badges. "I'm Detective Ryder and this is Detective Bishop. We're with the Hamby Police Department." Her eyes shifted from side to side. I checked both areas but saw nothing. "We're looking for Carlos Martínez's girlfriend. Are you her?"

"Si."

Thank God. Lenny used to say finding people without having their name was like looking for a needle in a haystack. As if Lenny, a Polish Chicagoan born and raised in the city, had ever seen a stack of hay, let alone searched for a needle in it. "What's your name?"

She dropped her head and stared at the dirty countertop. "Rosy." Her voice was barely a whisper.

"Do you speak English?" I asked.

She mumbled, "Yes."

"Rosy, what's your last name?"

She mumbled, "Lopez. Am I in trouble?"

"No, but we'd like to talk to your boyfriend. Do you know where he is?"

She shook her head in such large, stiff swings her hair fell out of the clip. She quickly twisted it back into place.

"When was the last time you spoke with him?" I asked. "Was it less than four days ago?"

She set her eyes onto mine. "Two days ago. I don't know where he is now. He said he was going to be gone for a while."

"Do you have a cell phone?"

"Yes."

"Does Carlos?"

"Uh-huh."

"May I have it?"

She gave me the number.

"Rosy, did you see Carlos two days ago or speak to him on the phone?"

"I saw him."

"Did he seem nervous or agitated then?"

The three young men in beanies stepped up behind us. Bishop turned to them and said, "It's going to be a while."

"Oh, man," the first one said. They set their items on the counter and said they'd be back in fifteen, then headed to the back of the store toward the mesmerizing smell.

"He was mad, but he wouldn't tell me why. Are you going to arrest him?"

Bishop raised an eyebrow.

"Has he done something we should arrest him for?" I asked.

"He is here to help his mother and six brothers and sisters. He sends most of his money back to her. He keeps a small amount for himself. That is all. He works two jobs. It is hard. He is very tired."

Working two jobs, making what I guessed was less than average pay, and sending it all home to El Salvador would exhaust and frustrate me as well. It wouldn't drive me to invade homes and steal money, but it might for Martínez. "Do you know his friend Diego Perez?"

She pressed her lips together. "I do not like Perez. Pedazo de mierda. Piece of shit."

Bishop cleared his throat. "What makes you say that?"

"He is a bad man. He sells drugs and does other bad things."

"What kind of other bad things?" Bishop asked.

She shrugged. "I do not know. Carlos doesn't want to upset me. I tell him not to hang around with Perez, but he does. Carlos stayed with Perez for a while, but Perez left town. I do not know where he went."

"But you know he's gone?"

"That is what Carlos told me."

"Do you know Santos Garcia?" Bishop asked.

She glanced around the small store and whispered, "He is Carlos. He was kicked out of the country, but he came back as Carlos last month. His family needs the money. They are very poor."

"Do you have a picture of him on your phone?" I asked.

"Si."

"May we see it?"

She swiped through her photos and showed us a picture of her and Carlos. I snapped a photo of it for verification.

"Which name is his real name?" I asked.

"Santos Garcia."

A woman with three small children walked in. The children scrambled toward the restaurant in back while the mother yelled in Spanish for them to behave and not touch anything.

"What did Santos do that got him deported?" I asked.

"I do not know." She straightened a small display of mints on the counter. "I am sorry. I cannot tell you anything more. I have to get back to work."

"Just one more thing." I handed her my card. "This is my cell phone. Call me if you hear anything you think I should know, okay?"

"Si."

Levy and Michels leaned against Michels's department vehicle. "Get anything?" she asked.

I held up my small note pad and wiggled it. "We know where Jimmy Hoffa's body is."

She laughed. "Wouldn't that be the get of the world."

I laughed. "Meet us back at the department?"

"Sure thing," Michels said.

As we pulled out of the parking lot, Bishop said, "You're not calling Santos, correct?"

"Yes. I'm going to tell him who we are, why we want to talk to him, and ask him to come to the station, and bring Perez if he can."

Bishop chuckled.

I called Judge Nowak, my friend, a former Chicago resident, and an avid Cubs fan, on the drive back.

He answered on the second ring. "Detective, a pleasure as always. Is it safe to assume you need a warrant?"

"Yup. We have two home invasions and blood from one of the scenes matches a former employee, but he's gone MIA. We have his cell number, and I was hoping you'd give us a warrant for the cell phone company. Please, and thank you."

He chuckled. "Can you prove he's involved?"

I pressed my lips together while figuring out the best answer to that question. "We know his blood is at the scene of the likely route out of the community, and it's honestly all we have right now, judge."

He groaned, mumbling something I couldn't understand. "Name?"

"Carlos Martínez or Santos Garcia."

"Not a citizen?"

"According to his girlfriend, no."

"Is this one person or two?"

"It's one person with two names. One of them was arrested, left the country, and returned as the other."

"When do you need it?"

"ASAP?"

He exhaled into the phone. "I thought that would be your answer. I'll have it to you as soon as possible."

I gave him the details and then called Bubba. "I'm texting you a photo to run if you have time. Also, can you ping a number for me?"

"Got a warrant?"

"Should be here within the hour."

"What's the number?"

～

BUBBA ALSO TOOK the liberty of running the photos of both our double identity guy and Diego Perez through the system. He confirmed Martínez and Santos Garcia to be the same person, which we all knew would be the case. Martínez had no record, Garcia had been tagged in another town, but we found nothing to confirm he'd been kicked out of the country. It was possible the tag spooked him, so he bolted. Nothing came up for Diego Perez. When Nowak got the warrant to us, Bubba put the wheels in motion. While we waited, we asked Levy and Michels to run the other employee names through the system and see what they could find.

An hour later we met back in the investigation room.

"We ran checks on every other employee name," Michels said. "Nothing."

"I'm not sure how I feel about that," Levy said. "Those places usually hire cheap labor that doesn't stick around. I've seen them pick up workers waiting outside their trailer parks."

"I asked the manager if they ever did that," I said. "He said no, but I'm not sure I believe him."

"I don't know if I would either," Michels added. "And if they do, we could be SOL."

"We're not *shit out of luck*. We've got Carlos Martínez or Santos Garcia, whatever we're calling him, to start, and we'll find Diego Perez through him. If they're involved, one of them will talk," Bishop said.

Bubba slammed through the door, hitting the doorframe with his shoulder in the process. His black-framed glasses dropped off his face. "Damn." He tossed the file to me and grabbed his glasses off the floor. He was breathless and bounced on his toes. "He's moving fast, but I got the last three days of activity."

Bishop's eyes widened. "Anything in Mayfield?"

"Sorry," Bubba said.

"It's not your fault."

I tapped the address into my phone's GPS and then stood. "Let's go." I smiled at Bubba and patted his shoulder as I walked past him. "You're freaking amazing."

"Thank you, detective. If I get a change, I'll let you know."

The other three detectives echoed my appreciation as they followed me out.

"I'm driving," Levy said.

Michels acquiesced without a fight, disappointing Bishop. "You're just giving in without even trying?"

"I'd prefer she drive," he said.

We walked up to our vehicles. "She must be a hell of a good driver," Bishop said.

"Better than him," Levy said.

Bishop opened his door. "That's not our situation."

"Whatever," I said. "We all know the truth."

Michels laughed. "Nope. Not touching that one."

I flipped him the bird.

～

THE PHONE COMPANY TRACED MARTÍNEZ/GARCIA'S whereabouts to a trailer park off Atlanta Highway in Cumming. I contacted the Forsyth County Sheriff's Office asking for a possible assist and gave them the location, saying we'd be there within half an hour.

It ended up being more like thirty-five minutes because of traffic.

Bishop pulled into the drive and veered to the right to miss hitting a handful of men.

"Day workers," I said.

"Yes," he said.

Some of the men stared at our vehicle while others were head down into their phone screens.

Bishop slowed to a stop and rolled down his window. "Evening, gentlemen."

The ones who'd watched us turned away, and the men on their phones ignored us completely.

He rolled up his window. "They hurt my feelings."

I shrugged. "You look like a cop," I said.

"And that's a bad thing?"

"Not to me."

The trailer park had seen better days. The main strip, still gravel, traveled to the end of the property with smaller gravel roads splitting off in both directions. Dilapidated and abandoned trailers, mixed in with clean and maintained ones, lined the street. Clothing lines spattered with mixed sizes of clothing hung in front of some trailers, while the others filled their nonexistent yard with kids' toys or trash. "To think this is better than where they're from."

"Have you ever been to Mexico?" he asked. "Or El Salvador?"

"Turn right. No. Have you?"

"Went with the ex-wife to Mexico once. Most of the areas are fine, but in some places there were small huts and shacks along the sides of the highways and off small gravel streets where their living conditions are no better than the homeless camps in San Francisco or Portland. It's not like that everywhere, but it was awful to see."

"I can't even imagine." I pointed to the last trailer on the left, just two trailers from where we were. "There." I scrutinized the trailer. The three small windows on the front and right side were covered with Snoopy sheets. "Can't tell if anyone's inside."

Bishop stopped, then kicked the car into reverse to park further away from the home. I contacted the deputy from FoCo as well as Levy and Michels.

"Snoopy sheets," Bishop said. "Please tell me there's no kids inside."

"I would if I could."

"I hate this part of the job," he said.

So did I.

We all exited our vehicles. The two FoCo deputies took the far back corner of the trailer while Levy and Michels took the side with the window. I stood on the right side of the door while Bishop stood on the left.

He knocked, waited a few seconds, then knocked again. "Hamby PD. We're looking for Carlos Martínez," he said loudly.

The Snoopy sheet on the right window moved. I caught the eye of a child, but he quickly pushed the sheet back. "A kid," I said. I knocked on the door, said hello and asked if he'd open the door. "Hola amigo, ¿puedes abrirnos la puerta?"

Feet pounded on the floor inside, and seconds later the door opened a crack. The little boy stared up at me with sad eyes. He glanced at Bishop and backed away from the door. I crouched down to his level. "¿Habla usted Inglés?"

"No."

Michels, Levy, and the Forsyth deputy had stepped aside. We didn't want to scare the kid.

I showed him the photo of Santos Garcia on my phone and asked him if he'd been there recently.

He nodded.

When I asked if he was still there, he said he'd left to get something from the store across the street and that he was also getting a candy bar for the boy.

"You got a candy bar in your car?" I asked Bishop.

"Was just thinking about that. Hold on." He jogged back to his vehicle while I made small talk with the boy.

Bishop returned with the double Snickers and handed it to the child. I asked him if Garcia was nice to him. When he said yes, I thanked him and asked him not to say anything to Garcia about us being there. I asked him to hide the candy from him, too. He ripped open the wrapper and shut the door.

"You can't expect a kid to hide candy," Bishop said. "If Garcia shows up, he's going to see that and know someone was here."

"And we'll be ready."

7

Trailer parks lacked hiding spaces, and law enforcement vehicles shone like a diamond. We moved our vehicles across the street and waved at the day workers as we returned on foot.

The six of us positioned ourselves around the trailer and out of view of the small gravel parking area. Bishop and I waited on the right side with our weapons in our hands. The others took positions on the other side. Garcia pulled up in an older model green Ford Explorer and shut off the ignition. As he stepped out of the vehicle, I heard Rosy's voice through the speaker of his cell phone.

"Shit," I said.

Garcia whipped his head back and forth, his body spinning on his heels to examine the area behind him.

"He knows we're looking for him," Bishop whispered. "You ready?"

"Yup."

"Let's roll." He stepped in front of the trailer, gun up and aimed toward Garcia. "Santos Garcia—"

Garcia didn't give Bishop a chance to finish his sentence. He spun around again, tossed his phone onto the ground, and took off like a bullet in the opposite direction.

Bishop shouted, "Son of a bitch," and rushed after him. I passed my partner as the two deputies, Levy, and Michels followed behind.

Michels was closest, his arm just out of reach of Martínez's shirt. "Stop," Michels yelled. "You're under arrest."

Garcia didn't care. He shot through the alleyways, tipping trash cans and anything he could to put distance between us. He reached the end of the alley, veered right, and attempted to climb the low barricade. It was no more than four feet tall, yet Garcia made it look like scaling Mount Everest as he tripped and tumbled back down to start again. I was sure he wouldn't manage to get over it, but he did, eventually, and vanished from sight.

"Where does this go?" I asked one of the deputies.

The taller of the two answered. "The back lot to the building next door. It's empty. The lot is fenced in back, but the front's open."

"He's heading for the road," I said. "Put out a call!"

The deputy did as I'd asked.

The quickest way back to the road was to climb the wall. Weaving our way between trailers would slow us down.

I climbed over and spotted Garcia near an old van. He disappeared behind its other side, and I couldn't tell if he'd stopped or kept running. "That way," I shouted.

The rest of the team rushed ahead, leaving Bishop and me taking up the back. At the van, we split into teams of two and headed in the three different directions.

The layout of the lot was a simple, almost a perfect square with the building at the front. Garcia was fast, but what we lacked in speed, we made up for in numbers. Unless the guy gained some amazing speed in the last few minutes, we had him.

I caught up to the two deputies.

"We have a cruiser in pursuit," the taller one said.

"He can cut through across the street," the other deputy said.

Just as we got to the front of the building, two sheriff cruisers blasted their sirens and whipped right onto another road. "We've got eyes on him," one of the cruisers said. "He won't go far."

Michels kicked it into high gear. He raced across the street, nearly getting hit in the process, and disappeared behind an abandoned and rundown tire store. Cars sped down the street, leaving no room for us to cross. When one finally slowed to turn, we rushed across just as Michels gained momentum on Garcia.

Garcia whipped his head around, and seeing Michels coming at him, threw a tire in his direction. Michels managed to jump out of the way and the tire rolled by. Garcia scrambled up a mound of discarded tires and onto a closed dumpster. He lifted a foot to climb over and froze. Two German shepherds jumped up on the other side of the fence. Garcia freaked, slipped backward, and tumbled off the dumpster.

Michels withdrew his weapon and pointed it at him. "Hands behind your back!"

Stunned, Garcia slowly turned over. The dogs' barks grew louder.

Levy caught up, dropped and cuffed Garcia, then read him his rights.

Blood dripped from his nose, and the left side of his chin was split open. "I need an ambulance," he said. "I'm hurt."

I examined his wounds. "You'll be fine."

Bishop took down the deputies' names for the case file and thanked them for their help. Given Garcia was our bust, and FoCo was only on assist, we took custody of our suspect, and escorted him back to the Hamby Police Department.

AN OFFICER PROCESSED Garcia while the four of us met with the chief.

"We have probable cause," Bishop said. "It's a solid bust."

"I wouldn't call it solid," Jimmy said. "But it's better than reasonable suspicion."

Someone knocked on the chief's door. "Come on in," Jimmy said.

"We have a Mr. Wallace, a resident from Mayfield here. He's got video from the night of both invasions," a young male officer said. "What should I do with him?"

I glanced at Michels.

He shrugged. "Everyone we talked to swore they didn't have anything."

I smiled at the officer. "Escort him to interview room two. We'll meet him there."

He closed the door behind him as he left.

Michels immediately began defending himself again. "We didn't miss anyone."

"It's a wealthy neighborhood. You probably talked to several who didn't understand how their cameras work or even where to access the information," Jimmy said.

"He's right," Bishop added. "We'll meet with the resident and then check on Garcia. Maybe letting him sit and sweat a while will encourage him to talk." He looked at Michels and flicked his chin up and down, then jerked his head to the right. "Let's plow."

We walked into the small conference room. I noticed the change and grinned. Jimmy had had someone take a few of the department recognitions and awards from the main lobby and hang them in the conference room to soften its sterile appearance. The cement gray walls, oblong metal table, and uncomfortable metal chairs trumped any difference the awards and recognitions might have made.

"Mr. Wallace, I'm Detective Rob Bishop and this is my partner, Detective Rachel Ryder." He pointed to Michels and Levy and introduced them as we all sat. "I understand you have video from your home security system for us?"

Mr. Wallace was an older gentleman, upward of Bishop's age. His gray hair had receded enough for him to comb hair from his right ear across the top of his head. If the wind blew, those strands would rise and greet us with a wave. His soft smile lines made him appear kind. He had a natural upward curve to his lips, unlike my permanent frown, and his eyes were ocean blue. His face was cleanly shaven, and I wondered if he'd done that himself or went to a barber.

He reminded me of a grandpa, and I instantly liked him, which was rare.

"I do. Please, call me John. Two officers came to our house the night of both invasions," he said. "But I was out of town and my wife doesn't know how to work the security system. She just assumed it didn't record." He opened the laptop he'd brought. "I've downloaded the files, but I did keep them in the security company's cloud if you need that for evidence or something."

"Thank you," Bishop said.

He spoke as he retrieved the videos. "We live on Carrollton Court, the intersecting street three homes down from the Kelley home, and two streets from the Blahuts. There are several ways to leave the community, but our home is on an exit road. Word got out about the broken fence near my house, and I thought the men had left through it, but I found this. Either way, if they're coming from either of those homes and exiting through the fence or in a car, they'll have to pass us."

"How did you find out about the broken fence?" I asked.

"Living in Mayfield is like playing that game, operator." He looked at Bishop. "You're old enough to know what I'm talking about."

I suppressed a laugh. Michels had a harder time with his.

Bishop glared at Michels. I could have sworn tiny daggers shot out of his eyeballs aimed at Michels. "I'm aware of the game."

"Can someone explain it to us?" Levy asked.

"Before texting, your ancestors used communication devices connected through the wall to communicate. We called them telephones," Bishop said.

Mr. Wallace chuckled.

Levy rolled her eyes. "Got it."

Bishop snarled at me. It made me laugh. "Mr. Wallace," he said. "You'll have to excuse the detectives. Their generations lack manners." He glared straight at me when he said that.

Mr. Wallace laughed and angled the laptop so we could all see. He hit play. "You'll see them about thirty seconds in."

He was two seconds short. At thirty-two seconds a dark-colored SUV, possibly an Expedition, but I wasn't sure, rolled into view. It slowed as two men dressed in dark clothing and ski masks appeared on the side. I eyed Bishop. There were three men in each home, not two, and neither of the two on camera carried a bag of cash. The vehicle slowed as they approached. The back door flung open, they hopped in, and the SUV left. It hadn't sped out of the camera's view. It just drove off like it was supposed to be there.

"The second one is almost exactly the same," Mr. Wallace said. He clicked to start it.

He was right. Still no third suspect and no bag of cash or jewelry.

"Mr. Wallace, do you have any video showing the hour before each event?" Bishop asked.

"Yes, but it's just cars."

"Can we get copies of those as well?"

"Sure, and I can pull them up now if you can give me access to the internet."

Bishop gave him secured guest Wi-Fi information.

"Here," he said. "Do you want to watch them or just have me download copies?"

"I'd like to see the videos first, please," I said.

The same SUV drove past in the first video. "There," I said. The second one had the same SUV as well.

We thanked Mr. Wallace and walked him out.

"They came in through the main entrance?" I asked. "But there's no record?"

"Because they didn't," Michels said. "If they worked there, they came through the grounds entrance. The one construction companies use."

I hit my forehead with the palm of my hand. "Son of a—why didn't we think of that?"

"I did," Michels said. "Not sure why you didn't."

Levy cleared her throat. "Excuse me?"

"Okay, Levy did. We checked it out, and it's a gated entrance with a pass-code. If you don't have the code, you use the phone on it, and it calls the front gate. And before you ask, no. No one called the front gate."

"Which means our guys were employees at one time or another," Bishop said.

After thanking Mr. Wallace and escorting him to the lobby, we walked the videos to Bubba's office. He stood behind his standing desk pilfering through a bag of potato chips with one hand and tapping the keyboard with the other. It took a minute for him to notice us. "Whoa," he said when he noticed our stare down in progress. "Not intimidating at all. What's up?"

I set the flash drive on his desk. He examined it, then flipped his eyes up to me. "A flash drive? What year is it again?"

"The guy was old," I said. "Like Bishop's age." I bit my lip hard enough to stop myself from smiling.

Bubba's eyes widened. "Ouch." His head shifted toward Bishop. "She just threw you some serious shade."

Bishop narrowed his eyes. "What?"

"Threw you shade. You know, slammed you. Insulted you. That kind of thing."

I rotated on my heels and smiled at Bishop. "But only in good fun."

"Don't worry," Bishop said. "Karma's a bitch."

Bubba stared at Bishop and then shrugged as he looked at me. "I'd like to watch when it happens."

"Nice," I said. "Anyway, we've got two guys and an SUV on four videos. Can you see what you can get for us?"

"Security camera from a home?"

"Yup."

"Those are usually pretty grainy when blown up, but I'll do my best."

"Appreciate it," I said.

~

GARCIA WASN'T happy to see us. The jail nurse had cleaned up his wounds, but the cut on his chin looked like it needed stitches. He sat on the far side of the small interrogation table. We'd purposefully had him placed in the smallest room with only two chairs and a square four-seater table to intimidate him. The room was crowded with four detectives standing in there, but the effect would help get him to talk.

Bishop stood next to me while Levy and Michels took the side. I threw the case files on the table, then crossed my arms over my chest. "Looks like your boo-boos are going to be fine."

His nostrils flared. "Vete a la mierda cerdo."

Bishop coughed.

"Wow f-bombs and pig references. Nice. Does your mother know you talk like that?"

He mumbled something none of us could decipher.

Bishop didn't waste any more time. "Where's the money and jewelry, Garcia?"

His face stayed stoic. "What money?"

Bishop leaned across the small table, his face just an inch away from our suspect. "We couldn't find your immigration papers in your things. Did you lose them?"

He didn't respond.

"Where's the money and jewelry?" Bishop asked again.

Garcia stayed silent.

Bishop straightened and shrugged his shoulders. "So, that's how you want to play this?"

"I want a lawyer."

Bishop dragged his hand down his face, then jabbed his finger at the man. "Hope you had a nice vacation in the states, because you're going back where you came from."

I opened the door, and the four of us walked out. "He wasn't going to talk no matter what we did."

A flash of red traveled up Bishop's neck and covered his face. "We had one job, damn it. One job." He stormed off toward the investigation room.

I exhaled, then said to Michels, "Get him a public defender."

"On it," he said. He and Levy headed in the opposite direction.

I walked into the investigation room to Bishop cussing like a truck driver. "You'd think the son of a bitch would give up his buddies to keep himself in the states."

"Why would he bother? He gets deported, he'll just change his ID and come back." I exhaled. "I can't say I fault him for keeping his mouth shut. God knows what his buddies would do to him."

"What if we offer to protect him?"

"For two home invasions? That's a big ask, and I doubt it's in the budget."

"Mayfield is the wealthiest community this side of Atlanta. If they're unhappy, it'll make us look bad."

"Us or the department?" I asked.

"Yes."

I leaned against the wall next to the door. "There were three men in each home, plus the driver of the SUV. The Wallace videos show only two men running to the vehicle. Garcia's blood is on the fence."

"Yes, but he could have snagged his sleeve on it while he worked for the community."

"He dropped money there."

"I know, but a good lawyer would say we can't put the two together at the same time."

He was right. "They knew about the security cameras, Bishop." I pushed myself off the wall and walked over to the whiteboard, scribbled his name on it, then added a few details. "We need to find out where Garcia went after he left the property. Did the SUV pick him up over there, or did he run somewhere else?"

"He's lawyered up. We'll never get an answer to that."

"No one had security cameras in their back lots in that area." I rubbed my temples, feeling the frustration of an investigation block building in the pit of my stomach. "Maybe we can convince the DA to let him stay in the country if he gives up his buddies?"

"Like you said, God knows what his buddies will do to him."

"But it's worth a shot."

"And right now, it's the only one we've got."

Bishop wanted and needed the win. We all needed the win. The investigation was no different than any other in that respect, but after closing the serial killer case, the home invasions should have been easy by comparison, and they shouldn't have stumped us this way. We were better than that.

I grabbed the landline and dialed Jimmy's extension.

He picked up on the second ring. "Chief Abernathy."

"Got a minute? We're in the investigation room."

"Give me five."

~

"You think that's going to work?" Jimmy asked.

"I wouldn't bet money on it," I said. "It's our only shot. He's not going to give up his buddies. They'll kill him."

"The wire will make him look innocent to them," Bishop said.

Jimmy's head tilted to the side. He squinted at me for a good ten seconds before finally speaking. "So, what you're saying is you want us to walk this guy to his death. Then what? We grab the wire on the way to the morgue?"

"Either of you have any other ideas?" I asked.

"Our only option is to promise this guy we can keep him safe," Bishop said.

"But we can't," Jimmy said.

"What about his family?" I asked. "We can't keep him safe, but we can offer to, I don't know, make sure his family gets out of town safely?"

"We don't have the budget for that, and the DA would laugh in our face anyway. We're riding off a big get with the Anderson investigation, and she couldn't touch that. She'll want a win in Hamby if for no other reason than to make herself look good."

"She couldn't touch that because Anderson was dead. There wasn't anyone left to prosecute," Bishop said.

"Doesn't matter. We got a lot of attention for that, and she wasn't included. She considers that a loss for her political career."

Bishop tipped his head back. "Then now what?"

The door creaked open, and Levy stuck her head in. "Public defender is requesting a meeting."

Jimmy grabbed the door handle as Levy walked away. He turned around before leaving and said, "Good luck. Keep me updated."

A STOUT WOMAN WITH BLOND, spikey hair, probably somewhere north of thirty-five, sat next to Garcia. She wasn't stout in a too-many-donuts way. From the looks of her physique, I guessed power lifter, and without a gun, I wouldn't have wanted to run into her in a dark alley.

I'd chosen to sit while Bishop remained standing near the door. She looked up at us but didn't offer a smile or introduction. "Detectives, my client will admit knowing of one home invasion on the night of," she checked her notes and read off the first invasion. "However, he has assured me he was not involved in that criminal event, and he knows nothing about the second invasion."

I felt my eyes roll in their sockets. I wanted to call bullshit, but we needed to get something from Garcia. "How exactly did your client hear about the first invasion?"

"He works within the community."

"Can you tell us what he heard?" Bishop asked.

She consulted her client, the two of them mumbling in each other's ears. "He heard a home had been broken into and that employees were being questioned."

"Which name is your client's birth name?" Bishop asked. "Santos Garcia or Carlos Martínez?"

The woman's left eyebrow lifted. Martínez's eyes widened. Had he not mentioned his other name to his attorney?

"May I have a moment with my client, please?"

"Absolutely," I said as I stood.

We stepped outside.

"He didn't tell her about his multiple personalities," Bishop said.

"That could be a problem for him. It creates a layer of distrust for his lawyer. She's going to push him to be honest, and that could lead to giving us what we want."

"Let's hope," Bishop said.

The lawyer opened the door. "Thank you."

We assumed our previous positions.

"My client has verified his birth name to be Santos Garcia."

"We already knew that."

"For the purpose of record, I'd prefer we refer to him by his birth name, Santos Garcia, here on forward, please," she said.

"That works for us," Bishop said. "Mr. Garcia has been tagged in our system, having been arrested, however the charges were dropped. For what reason did he decide to go by Carlos Martínez?"

"Mr. Garcia believed he was not safe in this country under his real name. He migrated here claiming asylum from a Salvadorean cartel, however during his initial time here, he ran into some trouble, likely your record, and to maintain his safety once again, he chose to go by Carlos Martínez."

"Now that we've got that settled," I said. "I'm sorry, I didn't get your name."

"Morgan Clayton."

"Thank you," I said. "Let's talk about the home invasions now, Ms. Clayton. We have one on Friday night, and another on Saturday night. What can Mr. Garcia tell us about them?"

"My client was not involved in the home invasions. He'd only heard talk of them through work."

I eyed Garcia. He pushed his shoulders back and stared above my head at the wall. "We can place your client with the money." I didn't mention we only had circumstantial evidence tying him to the crimes.

"May I ask how?"

"His DNA."

She turned toward Garcia and whispered in his ear. He whispered back. When they finished, she said, "Mr. Garcia gave a blood sample under duress. He was told he would be extradited back to El Salvador if he didn't comply. That blood sample will be thrown out of court."

"Ma'am," Bishop said. "Mr. Garcia's file includes a signed affidavit stating Mr. Garcia willingly and knowingly gave his blood."

"Again, under duress."

We'd have to discuss that with the district attorney before moving forward. "Ms. Clayton, what is Mr. Garcia's connection to Diego Perez?" I asked.

They exchanged whispers again. "My client doesn't know any Diego Perez."

Bishop exhaled loudly. "Ma'am, Diego Perez got your client a job with Mayfield. We have confirmation of that and the fact that the two lived together recently. How about we stop playing games? I'd be more than happy to toss his ass in jail and let him sit until he goes to trial."

She consulted with her client. "Mr. Garcia acknowledges your information as correct, however he hasn't participated in any illegal activities with Mr. Perez."

"Does he know of any illegal activities Mr. Perez has participated in?" I asked.

After another quick conversation, she said, "As I said, he is aware of one home invasion, not two, however, he will not confirm or deny knowing anyone who might have committed those crimes." She adjusted her position in the chair. "Now, I don't believe you have anything solid enough to arrest my client, so I'd like him released."

Bishop made a point of moving his sleeve on his right arm and checking his watch. "We'll hold him for the allowed forty-eight hours. Perhaps that will give him some time to consider telling us what he knows for a lesser sentence and no deportation."

Oh, wow. He went there without any approval from the district attorney. That was a bold move, and very risky, especially for Bishop. I was impressed.

IT WAS AFTER TEN, and we were all hungry and tired. Michels and Ashley asked if we wanted to grab dinner, but Levy, Bishop, and I opted to go home instead.

"I hear my leftovers calling me," Bishop said as we all walked to our vehicles.

As I opened my door, an officer rushed out of the department's back entrance. I eyed Bishop. He shut his door. "Here comes overtime pay," I said.

Breathless, the officer said, "Detectives, we've got another home invasion. Ambulance is already en route."

"Any injuries?"

"Yes, sir, but that's all I know."

"Thanks," Bishop said. He looked at me. "Looks like Garcia's been replaced. I'll drive."

"Ditto," Levy said to Michels.

We all jogged over to our department vehicles.

8

Four Mayfield security guards paced the entry just outside the main entrance to the community, while three stood inside the small building attached to the gates. Bishop showed his identification and confirmed Levy's and Michels's as well.

"Thank you, detective," one of the guards said. "Ambulance just arrived about five minutes ago."

"Thanks." He nudged his vehicle toward the gate as it opened.

We parked in front of the home. I did a quick visual assessment, looking for any similarities with the others and snapping photos with my cell phone as always. Bishop, Michels, and Levy hurried to the door.

Unlike the others, the home sat on a double lot, so any visual from the neighbors on its side would be limited at best. As for shape and size, aside from a different façade, every home in the community had similar features. Double-doored front entrances, large front porches, and multicar garages. The third home was bigger than the others and had an extra three-car detached garage. And no security cameras or digital doorbell.

I jogged up to the front door, making room for the paramedics to carry a stretcher with a man out. "Who's injured?"

"Both the husband and wife. She's doing okay. It's the husband who took the brunt of it.

Wife says he was hit in the head with a gun, kicked, and beaten. My guess is he's got a couple broken ribs and is going to have a bitch of a headache in the morning."

"Thanks," I said. I slipped on my booties and a pair of latex gloves and checked the doors before going inside. They were thick, so kicking them in would have been hard, but not impossible. The lock was broken, no, more like smashed in, and much of the lock side of the frame was destroyed. Whoever did the damage used something other than a foot.

A cursory check of the main room told me the scene didn't match the others. The layout was similar, an open concept, with the kitchen, living area or formal room, and dining room, all visible in one scan. A woman sobbed into her hands on one side of a white leather sectional. A young girl, maybe seven or so, cried quietly beside her. The other side of the sectional had been detached and turned on its side. Two leather chairs across from them had been knocked over, paintings and photos on the walls and bookshelves were scattered on the floor with the glass smashed, and knickknacks from the shelves appeared to have been thrown around the room.

I noted duct tape, not zip ties, hanging from two dining room chairs. The kitchen looked like a tornado had spiraled through it. Cabinets opened, dishes broken in pieces on the floor, the refrigerator knocked over.

Why was the invasion more aggressive than the others? What did the victims have that the robbers wanted?

I walked back to the woman and child. Bishop had crouched down and was talking to the young girl in his soft, fatherly voice. She sniffled as she nodded, then wiped the tears on her face with her Taylor Swift pajama top sleeve.

The woman looked at Bishop. A purple and blue bruise had begun to form on the side of her mouth and another one under the opposite eye. Her lip had bled. When she noticed me staring, she used an ice bag provided by a paramedic to cover her injuries.

Bishop stood. "Ma'am, this is my partner, Detective Ryder."

She nodded at me but didn't say anything. The little girl lifted her mother's arm and curled herself around her. The woman looked back to Bishop and asked, "What hospital are they taking Tyler to?"

"I'll have to check, but usually it's North Fulton. Ma'am, we'd like to ask you some questions about what happened here tonight. Do you think you can answer for us?"

"Yes. I'll try. Can you tell me if it was the same people who broke into the other two homes? We have security in the community. They were supposed to be watching. How could this happen?"

"Criminals can be very savvy, ma'am," Bishop said. "May I have your name, and your daughter's name?"

She sniffled. "I'm Amber Morgensen, and this is my daughter, Alyssia. My husband is Tyler."

Levy and Michels came down the stairs and pulled us aside. Bishop told the victims to sit tight.

"The safe is up in the bedroom. If there was anything in it, it's gone. They destroyed the room," Michels said.

"If you think it's bad down here, wait until you see the bedroom. They had to be looking for something."

"Maybe they got greedy and thought there was more money hidden somewhere," Levy said.

"Anything's possible. I saw Nikki walk in and out just a minute ago. I think she's getting her things. Ask her to start upstairs, please."

"Will do," Levy said.

Bishop and I returned to the victims.

Mr. Morgensen was being attended to by the paramedics while Bishop asked him questions. Mrs. Morgensen was in the middle of describing her husband being beaten to Michels, with her daughter clinging to her side.

I didn't want the little girl to have to relive the trauma, so I offered her an out. "Mrs. Morgensen," I said. "How about I take Alyssia upstairs? I bet she's got a toy or something she'd like to have. Would that be okay?"

"Yes."

I reached my hand out to the girl. "My name's Rachel. Can you take me to your room?"

She had put her left pointer finger in her mouth to chew on and nodded.

"Great," I said in a happy voice. I pointed to the booties covering my shoes. "What do you think of my booties? I think they're silly."

She let out a small giggle.

"Sometimes it's fun to be silly. Would you like to wear a pair?"

"Yeah," she said.

I removed some from my bag and put them on her tiny feet. I had to tie them in knots at the front of her ankle to keep them from slipping off. "These are perfect. You've even got a fashionable knot. How awesome is that?"

"Really awesome." She grabbed my hand and led me to her room.

I walked on her right to block her from seeing the mess inside her parents' bedroom. Thankfully, her bedroom hadn't been touched, and it was the perfect little girl's room. "Wow, Alyssia. This is beautiful."

The room was truly beautiful, and every little girl would have loved to have it. Pink walls with butterflies and dragonflies painted randomly throughout, a large four-poster bed draped in white and pink tulle, a window bench with a butterfly-patterned cushion, and the same antique, French provincial bedroom furniture my parents still used in their bedroom, but in pristine shape. Stuffed animals covered sections of the floor and hung from the ceiling in a pink net sack. My childhood bedroom and my adult one paled in comparison.

"Thank you," she whispered. "The bad men came in here. Did they take my toys?"

"I don't know. Why don't we have a look around, and you tell me if anything looks different?"

She walked slowly around her room, checking the net bag, and counting the stuffed bears lined up against the window seat. "One, two, three, four, five, six, seven." She glanced at her bed. Her shoulders curved inward.

I stepped toward the bed, crouched down, and faced her. "Were you asleep when they came in?"

She nodded, then put the same finger back in her mouth.

"I bet that was scary."

"Daddy told me to go downstairs with the man. I didn't want to, but Daddy said. He said Mommy was down there and to go to her."

"I would be scared, too. Was the man mean to you? Did he hurt you?"

"He just took me to Mommy."

"Did he say anything?"

She peeked at her bed. "Can I get Barry?" She pointed to a white bear on the far side of the bed.

I leaned over and got him for her. "Barry?" I asked as I handed her the bear.

"Barry the polar bear, silly." She smiled and pointed to her shoes. "He wants a pair of silly booties, too."

"Well then, let's get them on him." I whipped out another pair and tied them over the bear's feet. "How's that?"

She giggled. "Now we're all silly!"

Kids were so resilient, and it never ceased to amaze me. I hoped the trauma would be just a blip on her life radar and not cause any permanent issues, but we never knew the long term effects the victims carried with them.

She leaned into my leg. "Is my Daddy dead?"

I crouched down and looked straight in her eyes. "No, sweetie, your daddy isn't dead. I promise you that. He's going to be just fine before you know it." I hoped I wasn't wrong, but from the looks of him when they carted him out, and barring any unforeseen circumstances, I didn't think I was. "I bet you'll get to see him tomorrow."

She hugged me.

Two people beaten and a trashed house. The violence was increasing, and if we didn't catch the men, someone could wind up dead.

Tick tock. Tick tock.

WE ARRIVED BACK at the station around three thirty a.m. Time always flew by at crime scenes, and we often got our second wind, but there were some that rubbed our emotions raw. The Morgensen invasion was one of those.

"There was four hundred thousand dollars and some jewelry in the safe. I'll write up what pieces later. Tyler Morgensen sells commercial real estate." Bishop said. He rattled off the name of the company and then flipped the page in his pocket-sized notebook. "The wife is a stay-at-home mom. They don't keep company files at home, and other than golf and tennis, they don't spend much time with the Kelleys or Blahuts."

"Is he having an affair with anyone?" Levy asked.

"Not that he'll admit to."

"No problems with anyone at work?" I asked.

"He works with his father and sister. Small business."

"Maybe his sister wants him?" Michels said.

"Doesn't fit the crimes," I said.

"Just tossing it out there," he said. "Wife was pretty shaken. She didn't have much to say."

"Who called it in?" Levy asked.

"The husband. His cell was on the counter. He dragged the chair over and used Siri," Bishop said.

I yawned.

"We'll need a report for when the chief arrives," Bishop said. "Let's go home. We can hit the ground running again after some shut-eye."

"Sounds like a plan," Levy said. She yawned, then added, "Anyone want some liquid fuel for the road?"

Six eyebrows raised in response.

"What? I don't want anyone falling asleep at the wheel."

Two hours later I pulled into my garage and shut the door behind me. Inside, I removed my equipment, checked my weapon, and set everything on my dining room table, other than my weapon, which I locked in a drawer. I unlaced my boots, pulled off my socks, and as Lenny always said, let my puppies breathe.

My beta fish Louie eyed me from his glass castle. He must have been starving. I crawled off the couch and shuffled a few steps over, then dropped some pellets into his castle and chatted at him while he ate.

"You should have seen the girl. Alyssia is her name. Isn't that pretty? She had these adorable brown curls that spiraled to her waist. I'd give my right arm for curls like that."

Our conversations were normally one sided, but I didn't mind. While I talked, Louie swallowed back pellet after pellet, then swam around in a tummy-full celebration. When he finally tired out, he swam into his little cave to go to sleep.

I sat on the couch to destress before going to bed, and the next thing I knew, my cell phone rang. I popped up from the couch and patted my trunk coffee table searching for my phone. The old-fashioned phone ringtone blasted through the room and vibrated in my brain. I finally found my phone, saw it was Ashley, and swiped to answer. A groggy, "Hey," slipped from my lips.

"I'm sorry. Did I wake you?"

"Yeah, but that's okay." In a fog, I didn't even consider it could be about Kyle. "What's up?"

"Well, for starters, you should be. It's after eight. Justin's already at the department."

I glanced at my watch. "Crap!" I stumbled off the couch, tripping over myself as I raced to my bedroom. With no time to shower, I put her call on speaker and stripped off my clothing from the night before. "I fell asleep on the couch. I need to run. Can we talk later?"

"It's about Kyle."

I froze. "What? What's going on? Did you hear from him? Is he okay?"

"He's okay. I didn't talk to him, but one of our agents got word from him. He gave me a message for you."

"From Kyle?"

"Yes." She giggled. "He said, 'Stop worrying.' Does he know you or what?"

Relief soared through my veins, and I felt as though I could finally breathe again. "Did he say anything else? Do you know where he is?"

"All I know is he got word to one of our agents saying things were wrapping up, and the arrests would be made in Atlanta, and to tell you to stop worrying."

I closed my eyes and exhaled, waiting for my heart to stop beating through my chest wall. "When did he make contact?"

"I'm not sure, but I think late last night or early this morning."

Knowing things could change quickly dulled my relief, but I still clung to it with every inch of my soul. "Thank you, Ash. You have no idea what that means to me."

"Oh, I have an idea. Now, get to work before Jimmy gets on you. Justin says he's in a mood lately."

"Right. Thanks," I said and disconnected the call.

Bishop called as I drove to the department. "Sleep in?"

"I'm sorry. I sat on the couch, and I was out. I didn't even realize I'd fallen asleep until Ashley called and woke me up. I'm five minutes out but I'm stopping at Dunkin'. Have you talked with Garcia yet?"

"Nope. I thought we'd let him sit a while and then you can do it. Might be easier to get him to talk that way. Amber Morgensen is already here. I'll wait for you."

"No. Go ahead and start. Going to Dunkin', remember? Need one?"

"Hell yeah. Get our regulars. For Levy and Michels, too."

"Geez, talk about breaking the bank. Not for Jimmy?"

"He's not here yet," he said. "Hurry."

I called Savannah and got her voice mail. "Hey, is everything okay? Call me back."

LEVY'S EYES widened when I handed her the coffee. "God, I love you."

"Good because you're buying lunch later. I want Chipotle."

"Done." She flicked her head toward the opposite side of the pit. "The Morgensen woman is here for her interview. Husband spent the night in the hospital, but we can talk to him there."

"Can you and Michels interview the husband?"

"Sure."

"Great. Meet us back here."

Bishop made calls to the golf course's former employees while I interviewed Amber Morgensen.

"They were so rough," she said. "Why did they have to hurt me? The other wives weren't hurt."

"Do you believe the break-ins are connected?" I asked.

"Of course they are. A group of terrible men are breaking into our homes. They beat up my husband, hurt me in front of my child, and tore our room apart. How could they not be connected?"

I asked her about her relationships with the other victims, and she assured me they were all close friends. Everyone had given me a different answer. Some people viewed friendships differently than others.

"Did your husband have any important papers at home? Maybe insurance policies or investment summaries?"

"Yes. We keep everything at home. Did they take those? Do I need to close our credit cards and notify our banks?"

"I would do that," I said.

Tears welled in her eyes. "This is just awful. Why us?"

"Mrs. Morgensen, are you a part of the swingers group?"

She blinked and her face quickly morphed from busted to confused. "Swingers? Dear God, no. Do you think that group is the reason for the break-ins?"

I raised an eyebrow. "You just said you weren't involved. How do you know who's involved?"

"People talk," she said. "And excluding us, of course. Maybe that's it. Maybe they were targeting the people in the group and were misinformed about us?"

"Who would misinform them?"

"I don't know the answer to that," I said. "Do you know if any of the couples from the previous robberies are involved?"

"I really couldn't say."

I asked her several more questions, but nothing got me any closer to identifying the reason for the break-ins or a connection to Perez and Garcia.

My work phone rang as I watched her walk to her vehicle. "Detective Ryder."

"Detective, this is John Wallace. I met with you regarding the Mayfield break-ins."

"Yes, Mr. Wallace, what can I do for you?"

"I saw you all at the Morgensen home, and I took it upon myself to check my security tapes. The SUV didn't pass, but a white van did. I don't live close enough to the Morgensens to see who got in, but I thought you'd want the recording."

"Yes, that would be great. May we come by today to get it?"

"Actually, I'm headed in your direction. I can drop it off. I'd like to discuss something while I'm there as well. Is now a good time?"

Any time was a good time when it came to evidence collection. "Yes, sir. I'll meet you at the front desk."

"I'll see you in ten minutes then."

I jogged to the investigation room to let Bishop know. "Wallace has something to discuss with us. He'll be here in ten. And Mrs. Morgensen says they're not part of the swingers, but I'm pretty sure she's lying, too."

"Thefts and murders because of a swingers group?" Bishop said. "This is finally getting interesting."

"It's either love, sex, or money," I said. "Every time."

I MET Mr. Wallace and walked him back to the conference room.

"I read about you, detective," he said as I reached to open the door.

I pulled the door open slowly. "You did?"

"You and your partner were the detectives who brought down the local government a few years back." He smiled. "Very impressive."

"Just doing our job."

"And I appreciate it. I mentioned something I wanted to discuss, could we talk now?"

"Sure."

He greeted Bishop and Bubba then sat at the table and placed the flash drive on it. He stared down at it and cleared his throat. "As you know, Mayfield is a wealthy community, and wealthy people don't always play by the rules."

"We're well aware of that, Mr. Wallace."

"I believe you are. Much like your initial investigation, there are residents in my community who," he cleared his throat again. "Like to exchange intimate partners."

"You mean couple swapping? As in swingers?" Levy asked.

"We all knew this was coming," Bishop mumbled.

"Yes, ma'am," Mr. Wallace said.

"And you think this has something to do with the home invasions?" I asked.

"I can't say for sure, but I believe the Kelley and Morgensen couples have participated in the exchange program. I'm not sure about the others."

Poor guy, his cheeks reddened every time he said exchange, and I doubted he could bring himself to say swinger. He was a dying breed. "Mrs. Kelley mentioned this," I said. "She said she was asked, and they chose not to participate." I hadn't believed her, but I wanted to see what Mr. Wallace had to say.

"She is lying," he said.

"What makes you think that?"

"A recent event was held at my neighbor's home. I recognized their cars."

"It's possible they went and then changed their minds," I said.

"That is true," he said. "I can't tell you how long their car was there."

"When was this event?" Bishop asked.

"Two weeks ago, Saturday. There were ten cars parked along the side of the road. The only reason I recognized the cars was because they were parked in front of my house. When someone in the community has an event, their guests are supposed to park in the small parking areas throughout the community, not on the street. I reported it to security, but they said it was all residents, and the rule was only for guests."

"That's a runaround for sure," Michels said.

"Yes, it was," Mr. Wallace said.

"Is there anything you'd like to add?" I asked.

"No. But if I learn anything, I will, of course, be in contact."

Bubba sent the video to his email and printed out a photo of the van. "It's blurry. I doubt I'll get anything from it."

"I'm sorry I couldn't help," Mr. Wallace said.

"No, you have helped. We appreciate it."

He stood. "You have been kind."

"Thank you then. We appreciate your help."

"I moved into a gated community to feel secure in my home. Times are changing, and I thought the added security would be beneficial, but it appears to have proven otherwise."

"We'll get this figured out, Mr. Wallace. I promise." I walked him out and thanked him again.

Back in the investigation room, Bishop said, "John Wallace is the Gladys Kravitz of Mayfield."

I laughed. We'd discussed the *Bewitched* character before. He must have had some weird crush on her when the show aired. "He is not. He's a very sweet man. Reminds me of a grandpa."

"My grandpa smoked a pipe, wore overalls, and loved a good glass of moonshine."

"Mine gambled his retirement away and ended up in a nursing home," I said.

"I don't know how to respond to that," Bishop said.

"Most people don't." I tapped my pencil on the table. "Kelsey Kelley admitted to being asked to a swinger party a few months ago but denied being at the one by Wallace's home."

"Where was the one they went to?"

"The Blahuts'."

"The Blahuts. Damn. But they claimed they weren't involved."

"They lied."

"It's looking more and more like this has something to do with the sex parties after all."

LEVY AND MICHELS set the Chipotle containers on the investigation room table, but they had nothing more to report from their visit to Mayfield.

I filled them in about the swingers group.

"What's with these rich people and their little sex clubs?" Levy asked.

"Don't ask me. I'm neither rich nor a sex fiend," Bishop said.

"I think they're bored." I pointed my pencil eraser at Bishop. "I got that impression during our first investigation."

"That I'm not a sex fiend? I hope so."

"No, and gross. I'm talking about them being bored. I got that impression during that investigation. Geez."

"I was on patrol then," Michels said. "I didn't like you a whole lot back then. You kept calling my mustache a porn 'stache. That pissed me off."

I had done that. "It was a porn 'stache. Google 70s porn stars and look."

"I am not googling porn mustaches. I'll be inundated with dick pics, and Ashley will think I'm a perv and dump me." A smile stretched across his face. "Maybe I need to have a look at her Google history?"

Hearing Ashley's name reminded me of Kyle's message. "Don't you dare hurt Ashley. She's the best thing that'll ever happen to you, and she's a lifesaver."

He held up his palms. "I won't."

Bishop eyed me with his eyebrow raised. "A lifesaver?"

"Another agent got word from Kyle. I think he might be home soon, and he asked the agent to tell me to stop worrying."

Bishop's lip twitched. "Damn if that boy doesn't know you."

"Whatever. About the swinger thing. It's the only thing connecting the couples. We need to move on it."

"Go where the investigation takes you," Levy said.

"Right, but we need motives," I said.

Bishop dragged his hand down the side of his face. "Maybe one of the couples is short on cash and hired the men to hit their friends."

"I thought the Mayfield residents were all wealthy," Levy said.

"They could be house poor, or their circumstances might have changed," Michels said.

"Or they're greedy," I said. "They could have set the whole thing up. Rig a home invasion, have your cash stolen, and get the insurance."

"That could be why Jared wasn't injured as much as the others," Levy said.

"We need to talk to her again," I said.

"What if someone in the swinger group broke the rules, and the break-ins are payback?" Bishop asked.

"Or someone became obsessed with one of the members and was turned down?" I said.

"Or a spouse got jealous," Michels said.

"Three break-ins. All three couples involved in some way with the swingers group," I said.

"Why don't you two talk to the women again, and we'll talk to the men?" Bishop asked.

"I'll take Levy with me," I said. "It'll be like girlfriends having a chat."

~

KELSEY KELLEY SAT at her kitchen bar. Her hands shook as she spoke. "It wasn't like that. We were approached, and initially, we said no, but then Jared . . ." Her voice trailed off, and she sniffled. "Obviously things haven't been good between us lately, and he thought it would, you know, spice things up. I just figured, why not."

"Even though you knew he was having an affair?"

"I thought it might make him jealous to see me with someone else, but I couldn't follow through."

"Was this the Blahut party?"

"No. It was the Turners. Xavier and Stacey."

"Can we get their address and number?"

She blushed. "Okay." She tapped onto her phone and then sent me the contact via text message.

"How long were you there?" Levy asked.

"An hour, maybe a little less."

"Did your husband participate?"

"No. Just like the other one, neither of us did."

"Tell me more about the Blahuts' party," I said.

"What's to tell? Nothing happened there, either. Jared was all for it, and would have done it on his own, but apparently the rules say couples only. We left before they exchanged keys and anyone visited the room."

"The room?"

"It's a bondage room or something. I'm not sure. I haven't seen it, and I don't want to."

We hadn't seen that when we were at the Blahuts' home. "Where is the room?"

"There's a secret door behind the bookcases. It goes to a room walled off from the basement. Alan had it custom designed." She blanched. "I really have no desire to see it."

"Was there someone paying particular attention to you or your husband?"

"If you're asking if the other couples whose homes have been invaded hit on us, no. They didn't. We were all just drinking and talking."

"Was anyone upset you backed out?"

"I don't think so. Why would they be? Do you think someone at the party broke into our homes?"

"We're just covering our bases," I said.

Back in our vehicle, Levy asked, "Do you believe her?"

"I think so. What about you?"

"She was pretty disgusted about the room, so yeah."

We contacted Lisa Blahut, who said we could come by.

We sat on her large sectional. "Lisa, we've been hearing more about this swinger thing," I said. "They've been linked to you and your husband."

Her eyes widened. "Excuse me? We told you, we aren't those kind of people."

"What about your secret sex room?"

She furrowed her brow. "What secret sex room? I don't know what you're talking about. We don't have a secret sex room."

When someone babbled on, they were usually lying. "Would you allow us to look behind your bookcases?"

"Those?" she asked. She pointed to the ones anchoring the fireplace.

"Do you have any others?"

"Just those, but they're built-ins. There's nothing behind them except a playroom, and there's certainly no secret door to that."

"May we?"

"Go ahead," she said.

Levy and I attempted to move the bookcases and checked every inch of space but couldn't find anything that might open them.

"Are you satisfied now?"

"You and your husband were at a recent swingers party only two weeks ago. If you're not involved, why were you there?"

"We weren't." She stood and a diamond bracelet appeared on her wrist. It had fallen from under her sweater sleeve. "Obviously someone is trying to involve us in something we aren't involved in, and frankly, detective, I'm offended you're even asking."

I pointed to the bracelet. "They didn't take that?"

Her face reddened. "It was soaking in jewelry cleaner in the kitchen."

Right. "Why would someone lie about you hosting and being at a party?" Levy asked.

Her jaw tensed. "You'd have to ask them." She turned toward the front door. "Now, if we're finished, I'd like you to leave."

Levy tried Stacey Turner's number as we headed to their house.

"No answer."

"Doesn't mean no one's home."

We pulled in front of the home and walked up to the door. After a few knocks, and no answer, we turned to leave.

Mr. Wallace stepped onto his porch and called my name. "They're not home right now. Usually, a car is in the drive. Would you like me to call when they're home?"

"We're good, Mr. Wallace," I said. "But thank you."

∽

"Deny, deny, deny," Michels said. "*Utterly insulting* according to Alan Blahut."

I adjusted my position in my chair in the investigation room. "Blahut's a lying piece of—"

"We get the picture," Bishop said. "But according to them both, they—"

"Are lying," Levy said. She gave them the 411.

Michels's jaw nearly hit the table. "A secret room? I got to see that."

"We couldn't find anything to open the bookcases," I said.

"Lisa Blahut could be making it up," Bishop said. "Which could mean there's trouble in paradise."

"I don't think she's making it up," I said. "And I don't believe she had a diamond bracelet sitting in a bowl of jewelry cleaner on the kitchen counter either."

"Ditto to that," Levy said. "Maybe the Morgensens have something that belongs to one of the other couples, and they hired the guys to make it look like invasions?"

"Then why not hit just their house?" Michels asked.

"Because they don't want anyone to know what it is they're looking for," I said. "Bishop, can you go talk to Mr. Morgensen?"

"I'll give it a shot," he said.

"We'll go to Alan Blahut's work and talk to him about the secret sex room," Michels said.

"Let's sit on that for now. His wife's probably already told him we know about it. Let's wait until we have what we need and hit him with it then."

"Speaking of sweating it out, Garcia's been hanging out in lockup for a while now. Maybe he's ready to talk," I said. "Levy, why don't you two try calling the Turners again?"

"Got it," she said.

I FLIPPED the metal chair around and straddled it, while giving Garcia a big toothy grin. "How'd you sleep?"

He glared at me.

"Ah, I see you didn't sleep well. For what it's worth, neither did I. There was another home invasion last night. They used a van, so you care to tell me why you dropped cash and left blood jumping a fence when you could have gotten a ride with your friends?"

His face hardened.

I smacked my lips. "Oh, you're upset because you've been replaced."

His eyes shifted downward but returned to mine quickly.

Adding the physical moves to my statements made them appear casual but still got the point across. I wanted Garcia annoyed, and that was a great way to do it. "You ever heard that saying, go big or go home?" I pressed my finger to my chin for effect. "It might be an American phrase. I'm not sure." I shook my head as if clearing my thoughts. "Anyway, it means if you want to do something, do it up big or just don't do it at all. Last night your buddies did it up big. They stole thousands of dollars' worth of jewelry and four hundred thousand in cash. Math isn't my best subject, but," I stared at the ceiling. "If we give the jewelry an estimated value, let's say, $30,000, and I'm guessing low, I think the split is around $110,000. Including the driver." I shrugged. "Bet that stings, doesn't it?"

He kept quiet, so I poked the bear some more.

"If that was me they'd just dropped like a hot potato, I'd be pretty pissed off. I mean, they couldn't even wait until you got out? Don't they trust you to keep your mouth shut like you have been?"

The cords in his neck tensed. I removed a piece of gum from the pack in my jacket pocket and offered him one. He didn't budge. "No worries. More for me." I unwrapped it and stuck it into my mouth, talking as I chewed. "What gets me is they trashed the house and beat the shit out of the dude worse than the other guys. Broke his ribs and whacked him over the head with a gun. They even smacked the wife around. Left her with a busted lip and a black eye. There's not a brand of makeup around that'll cover that kind of purple." My eyes scanned his body from across the table. "Maybe you couldn't handle the dirty work like that. Maybe you couldn't go big, so they decided to find someone who could?" I leaned back and grabbed the metal bar across the back of the chair and made a point of chewing the gum loudly like the gumshoe detectives in old movies. I didn't normally do that kind of thing, but it was worth a shot. "I bet you can't wait to get out of here and take back your spot on the team." I smiled. "Listen, Garcia. Here's what I think. Feel free to tell me if I'm right. One of the couples, or maybe just a spouse and not both, approached you and Perez at work. They offered you some cash to break into these homes, grab the cash and jewelry, smack around the husband, then leave. Maybe they offered you a piece of the pie, say, five percent from each hit. You and Perez bring in two others, maybe give them a smaller split, and the couple tells you which homes to hit. Maybe even one of them is the home of the person who hired you. How am I doing so far? And you know, that's all well and good, but now you're otherwise detained, and Perez replaced you. You've been kicked off the gravy train, buddy. You tell me if I'm right, and we'll see what we can do for you."

His face had turned red, and he breathed noisily from his nostrils. I watched them expand with each breath. "I want my attorney."

Bingo!

I stood and smiled. "I bet you do."

BISHOP READ me the riot act. "You can't promise him anything! What the hell were you thinking?"

"Seriously? You're actually saying that to me? You said the same thing to him earlier. Neither of us made any promises. We just left it hanging in the air." I stuffed a dollar's worth of quarters into the pop machine and hit the Diet Coke button. "The assistant DA is on his way here. We'll do our best."

He dragged his hand down his chin. "We'd better get down on our knees and beg."

I grimaced. "Have you seen the assistant DA? He's not my type, and I don't get on my knees for anyone."

He rolled his eyes and charged out of the kitchen muttering, "It's always a joke with you, isn't it Ryder?"

"Always," I yelled back.

9

I tried Stacey Turner's phone again, but it went straight to voice mail, so I read through my notes in the investigation room as I waited for everyone to return. I'd contacted the DA's office, and a representative was on his way, but I wanted updates on what they'd learned, if anything.

Levy and Michels arrived first. "Still not able to get in touch with the Turners," Levy said.

"We will eventually."

Bishop finally stepped into the room. "Assistant DA is in the lobby."

"He can wait a minute. What did Morgensen have to say?"

"Nothing different than his wife. Looks like she talked to him."

"I expected that," I said.

"So did I," he said.

We called for the DA to be sent down.

Zach Christopher, assistant district attorney, walked into the investigation room for the first of probably many times in his career. "Well," he said as he admired our whiteboards. "Look at this fancy setup." He pulled out a chair, opened his bag, removed a portfolio and a pen, and asked, "What's going on? I'm assuming this is the home invasion investigation?"

Since I was the one who contacted him, I provided the limited details we had. "Yes. We have a person of interest we haven't been able to locate and a suspect in custody for the first two invasions. We've attempted to get him to give us names of the other three involved, but he lawyered up. He's asking for a deal."

Christopher was an attractive man in his thirties, and he acted like he knew it, which was a major turn off for me, thus the reason he wasn't my type. His short blond hair framed his face and highlighted his chiseled cheek bones. He spent time at the gym, and his well-fitting suits, which looked expensive, showed that. If I didn't know he worked for the district attorney's office I would have pegged him as a criminal defense attorney. His salary couldn't afford his clothing style, so mom and dad must have a money tree. "He wasn't involved in the third?"

"We already had him." I filled him in on the rest of the details. How he worked for the community, how he stopped showing up, and how we believed the break-ins were somehow connected to the swinger group.

"What's your evidence?"

"For the person or persons who hired him or to connect him to the crimes?"

"Yes," Christopher said.

Nikki showed him her results from the blood test and the inconclusive results for fingerprints on the money left by the fence.

He reviewed the blood test information and looked up at me. "He's undocumented?"

"Yes."

"I'd need more than the blood test. Could we use it? Yes, but a reasonably good attorney could push the under-duress angle, and then we risk a soft judge tossing it. Not to mention the fact that politicians are pushing the governor to stop the tests. We'll need something additional to link him to the crimes first."

"Part of the deal would be giving us the name or names of the people who hired him," I said.

"Does he have a public defender?"

"Yes," I said. "Morgan Clayton."

He jotted down her name and circled it. "Clayton's good. Went to Harvard Law School and knows her stuff. She knows the blood might get thrown out. She's going to base her negotiation on the fact that his giving up the others admits guilt, and she'll want everything dropped."

"Yes," I said.

"And you're fine with him going free on these?" he asked.

"No, but if you offer lesser charges, he might take it."

He leaned back in his chair and stared at the whiteboards. "We can't keep this guy. We don't have enough to make him desperate. Find what you need, and then we'll talk, but for now, he's got to go."

Bishop and I made eye contact. I knew he was thinking the same as me, and it included a lot of cussing.

"They all wore face masks and gloves," Bishop said. "Finding anything is going to be tough."

"That's your job, and not my problem," Christopher said. He stood. "Get me something on the others or a witness who can identify one of them. Anything we can make an arrest with and move forward. If he gives me some names then, maybe he'll get a deal."

Bishop swung the door closed behind him. "I knew the blood wouldn't work."

"I'm sorry," Nikki said. "It's all I could get."

"It'll work, just not as key evidence, and don't apologize. It's not your fault," I said. I studied our limited information on the whiteboard. "We need the SUV and the van. If we can get one of those, we can connect it to the driver and have at least one more person to talk to."

"Except half of those have fake plates or belong to a family with multiple drivers. We'd need something in them to match a person to the crimes," Michels said. "What we need is Perez."

"He's MIA. We've got eyes and ears out for him, but that's about all we can do right now. I'll see if Bubba's working on the vehicle plates. We need eyes on Garcia once he's released. See where he goes, who he talks to. Get whatever you can."

"Got it," Levy said.

"Finally, some decent detective stuff," Michels said, and they left the room.

Bishop cracked his knuckles. "Let's get patrol on the homes. We need to hit them again." He dialed the captain on shift on our landline and explained the situation. He sent two patrol officers to us right away, and one was Officer Gregory.

"Can you two go door-to-door through the entire neighborhood and ask for video? Show them photos of the vehicles. Maybe someone has something to show them casing the community or a better video of the plates." I knew it was a big and tedious job, but it had to be done.

"Sure thing," Gregory said.

"Sounds exciting," the other added.

"I'd also like you to show the victims Garcia's and Perez's photos," Bishop said. "See if they recognize either one."

"Will do," Gregory said.

I clicked the photos on the room's computer and printed out two copies then handed them to them. "If you get anything, give us a call. We'll come out."

"Will do." He glanced at Nikki and smiled.

She smiled back and gave him a small wave.

I cleared my throat. "Nice wave."

Her smile disappeared. "I'll get with Bubba on the videos and see if I can help read the plates."

"Thanks," I said.

"We need to determine all routes from the community to the trailer park where we believe Garcia and Perez live, then pull up the street cameras from the nights of the invasions. I don't think they went home and made pizza, but they could have driven somewhere in that area," Bishop said.

"I agree. We can give them to Bubba and he can check the cameras. Then we need to find Perez."

"Ready to say goodbye to Garcia?"

"No, but it is what it is."

Bishop and I met with Garcia and his attorney.

"District attorney is cutting you a break," Bishop said. "You're free to go."

Garcia smiled. "You got nothing on me."

"We know what you did, Garcia, and we'll get you."

Bishop texted Michels and Levy to tell them Elvis was leaving the building.

～

THERE WERE several possible routes between Mayfield and the trailer park, but only two were direct routes that would have taken twenty minutes or less at the speed limit. Undocumented immigrants rarely drove above the posted limit, and they did their best to fix broken lights on their vehicles to limit the chances of being pulled over. Since Georgia doesn't allow for undocumented immigrants to obtain a driver's license, they risk being detained and deported if pulled over. What they didn't realize was most patrol officers would walk away because they knew the person would just come back, and the amount of paperwork involved wasn't worth their time.

Considering all of that, we had to assume the routes likely taken, if they were heading back to Cumming, would be the two direct ones. I printed out the maps of the first two and the third one just in case. Since the trailer park was in Forsyth County, we had to request the street videos from their sheriff's office. Bishop made the call on speaker phone.

"Sure thing," Deputy Hampton said. "It'll take a few hours, but I can have them in Dropbox for you."

Bishop eyed me.

"Dropbox is great," I said and gave him my department email address. "Thanks for the help."

"Not a problem. Did you file charges on the guy we chased?"

"Unfortunately, no," Bishop said. "But it'll happen."

"Anything else you need from us?"

"Not at the moment," Bishop said. "But we'll be in touch if necessary."

"Great. Just do me a quick favor and send an email with the request. Then we're both crossing our T's and dotting our I's." He gave us his email address.

I typed out the email and cc'd Bishop and Bubba.

～

STACKS OF PAPERS covered Bubba's desk while others lay scattered on his floor. The mess triggered my type A everything-has-a-place issue, and it was hard to resist the urge to clean up.

Bishop examined the mess and laughed. "Did a file cabinet blow up in here?"

"Just working on an idea. If it pans out, I'll share."

"Good luck," Bishop said. "We've got some lights we need pulled up. Can you break away to do that?"

"Right now? I'm kind of on a—"

We stared at him.

"Oh, yeah. Right now." He pushed aside a stack of papers. "Where am I looking?"

I handed him the three maps.

After a quick look, he said, "You call FoCo? Most of the roads are out of our jurisdiction."

"They're sending their videos via Dropbox in a few hours, hopefully sooner," Bishop said, "What, by the way, is Dropbox?"

I thumped my palm onto my forehead. "I knew you didn't know what it was. It's an online file sharing program that lets you attach big files and allow others to view them."

"Sounds too high tech for me."

"Actually," Bubba said as he tapped away at his computer screen. "With respect to privacy and security, it's already an antiquated system. PCloud is more efficient, has far better security, and its dashboard is easy to navigate." He smiled at Bishop. "Though maybe not for you."

"Thanks for the education," Bishop said. "But you lost me at cloud."

The corners of Bubba's mouth twitched. "Cloud is a storage—"

I interrupted him. "Don't. He'll forget what you said the minute we leave."

Bishop shrugged. "She's probably right."

"Got it," Bubba said. "You're here about the old guy's videos, too, right?"

"If you've got them ready."

He angled his screen toward us. "I've just downloaded each of the files into our system, so you can grab them on the computer in the investigation room and pull them up on the big screen if you want. I also downloaded the day before and the day after the first two invasions, the day before the third, and what I could of today so far. Just in case the vehicles show up. I suggest just looking on the computer screen though because the bigger the video, the grainier it gets."

"Okay," Bishop said. "What about the maps?"

"Give me ten."

We headed back to the investigation room.

"What do you think he's doing in there with all those papers?" Bishop asked.

"Hacking into the federal government's computer system."

"I wouldn't put it past him," he said.

I PRINTED out screenshots of the SUV and van to compare to the videos. We started with the nights of the invasions, fast-forwarding and rewinding the videos several times to recheck. Bubba dropped off maps to determine the routes our suspects took after leaving the community to check against our routes.

The first route gave us only two roads inside our county. We located the van and SUV on one of our roads, but they turned different directions before accessing the second. I texted Bubba to ask for videos on either of those.

If they're available, he responded.

Bishop stretched his arms back over his head and tugged his right one toward the chair arm. "We've solved murders, busted serial killers, taken down almost all of Hamby's previous government officials, and even saved your ass from one of Chicago's big time political criminals. This should be our vacation investigation. We should just be calling it in and getting it done."

Petrowski was the corrupt politician from Chicago Tommy had been on the verge of bringing down. To avoid that, he hired a gang member to murder Tommy execution style. I'd promised justice, and I got it. Petrowski lived in a jail cell when I moved to Georgia, but shortly after my move, he swung a deal with another crooked politician and was released. He came for me, but our small-town team took him down. I got the justice I wanted, Petrowski on a slab, with no regrets. "We'll catch these guys. Keep the faith."

"In all our years together, I think this is the first time I'm not the one with the positive outlook," he said.

"Let's check the videos from the day before and see what we find," I said.

My cell phone rang. It was Michels. "Garcia got picked up by a girl."

"Rosy most likely."

"She didn't get out of the vehicle, but that sounds about right. They went to a Mexican hole-in-the-wall off Highway 9 and ate. We didn't want to spook him by going in."

"Good move. What's the restaurant's name?"

"Burrito Mexico."

"Inventive," Bishop said.

"Right?" Michels asked. "Thirty minutes later they got back in the car. He drove to that place in Cumming, Carniceria Hernandez, dropped the girl off, and took the car. We followed him northbound on 400 and lost him in the construction around the light at exit seventeen. We drove around and looked for him, but he was gone. Sorry about that."

"Don't be," Bishop said. "You hungry?"

"What? Uh, yeah. I guess."

"Good. Head back to the Carniceria Hernandez and talk to Rosy and see what you can get. Grab food. We're starved."

Michels laughed. "We're on it."

Our investigation room phone rang. I answered on speaker, and the front desk officer said, "Detective Ryder, I have Deputy Hampton from the Forsyth County Sheriff's Office for you. Line three."

"Thanks," I said and hit the key for line three. "Deputy Hampton."

"Detective, just a courtesy call to let you know I put a rush on those videos. They're waiting in Dropbox in case you haven't checked your email."

"Thank you so much. We appreciate your help on this. Thank your IT person as well, will you?"

"Sure thing."

I called Bubba and asked him to download them. He'd finished in less than a minute. An hour later, after reviewing and rechecking, we found nothing.

Bubba called. "I called IT at FoCo and asked for videos near the trailer park from previous days. I just downloaded them into our system. There are two."

"Damn, Bubba's kicking ass and taking names," Bishop said.

I cringed. "Okay, Grandpa."

He flipped me the bird.

Officer Gregory walked in. He hadn't called us, so I didn't expect any good news from their assignment, but I was wrong.

"We should have called, but it was literally the last two houses we checked, so we just brought them in." He handed me two flash drives. Flash drives must have been the norm for the Mayfield community.

Bishop pressed his lips together. "The well's running dry. Let's hope we get something on these."

I thanked the officers then plugged the first flash drive into the computer and opened it. If it had anything, we'd get it to Bubba. I scanned through several days of video until I finally saw it. The van. It passed the house twice coming from both directions.

"Can you blow that up?" Bishop asked.

"Apparently not." I closed the program and ejected the flash drive. "Let's see what Bubba can do." He opened the door and let me go through before him.

The scattering of files and papers in Bubba's office had given birth to other scatterings of files and papers. I inhaled through my nose and blew it out through my mouth, trying to keep the anxiety awakening in the pit of my stomach at bay. I could chase down a suspect and tackle someone with a gun but working in clutter or a mess hiked my anxiety into overdrive. "Is this all still that thing you're working on?"

"And I'm almost done."

"Will you clean up your space then?" I asked.

He looked up at me through the top of his blue light–blocking glasses. "Does it really bother you that much?"

I made the pinch sign with my thumb and forefinger.

Bishop cleared his throat. "More like makes her want to peel her skin off."

Bubba's eyes widened. "Seriously?"

"It's hard for me to think in a mess." I drew my shoulders in and cringed. "No disrespect."

"No worries. I don't do it often. If I had someone to help, it wouldn't be like this, but budgets and all that."

"We'll put in a good word," I said. I handed him the first flash drive. "The van is on this. Can you have a look? See if you can get the tag?"

"Did you already download it?"

"Yes, but I don't know where it went, and we couldn't see anything." I said.

"Here," he said as he climbed off his chair and walked to the other table across the small room. Normally, he'd scoot the chair, but the mess prohibited it. He tapped on the other computer's keyboard and the videos from FoCo popped up. "Found it and another one. I'll see what I can do, but rewatch them here. It's better than most in the department."

He hit play and walked away. "Good luck."

A few seconds later, I panicked. "Wait. I can't—" I beat my finger onto the enter button. "How do I pause this?"

Bubba rushed over and hit a button. "There you go."

"Can you rewind it and do that again?" Bishop asked.

"Yup." He showed me how to rewind and start over.

"This computer is completely different than the one in the investigation room," I said.

He chuckled.

"There," I said.

He hit the pause button.

"That looks like the SUV in the other videos."

Bubba tapped away on the keyboard and an enlarged image of the SUV appeared. The plate was blurred, but we made out the first three letters. CJF.

Bishop jotted them down. "This is good. This is real good."

"Bubba, can you blow up the video view of the front of the SUV? We might be able to get a look at the people inside," Bishop said.

"I'll do my best." He hurried back to the other computer and repeated the same steps he'd done to expand the image of the SUV. "No. Sorry. Just the second and third letter and number. R3."

"It's something," Bishop said. "And we need something."

"I'll run them, see if I can find anything," Bubba said. He typed the letters into the system.

I examined the files on the floor. "Is this thing you're doing about our invasions?"

"I've put together a program, a rough one, but it's working, to track everything we'd had happen over the past few years. From traffic stops to murders."

Bishop raised his eyebrow. "For?"

"To see if I can find Perez or Garcia mentioned. Maybe we can find a link that way. It's a long shot, and really, I just want to see if the program would work."

Bishop smiled at Bubba. "You're brilliant."

"Yes, you are," I said.

Bubba's face reddened. "Thanks. That means a lot." He smiled. "I'll have the tag information in a few hours."

I glanced at Bishop. "He'll find thousands of those. Is that a good use of his time?"

"I'll narrow it down to SUVs, and we can go from there."

"It's possible it's a stolen tag," Bishop said. "Let's wait and see what we come up with first."

"Got it," Bubba said.

LEVY AND MICHELS returned with our food. It was cold, but I didn't care.

"Rosy finally talked to us," Levy said. "But only briefly. Garcia dumped her after she picked him up. He knows she'd talked to you, and we think he threatened her, but she wouldn't say."

"She was scared," Michels said. "Getting that out of her was tough."

"I'll ask FoCo to keep an eye on the store," Bishop said. "It's right by the sheriff's office, so it shouldn't be hard." He stepped away and made the phone call while I considered our next steps.

My cell phone rang with an unknown number. "Ryder."

A soft female voice with a Hispanic accent whispered into my ear. "Detective, this is Rosy Lopez. I know where Diego Perez is."

~

BISHOP'S VEHICLE crawled slowly down the street. He dropped his speed even slower as a group of adolescents walked down the middle. One of the teenagers twisted his head and noticed us. He tapped his shoulder into the shoulder of the kid next to him and flicked his thumb backward. The kid looked back, but neither of them moved out of our way.

Another kid wearing a dark jacket and blue baseball cap pulled his cap down low, then turned and looked. He wore a pair of sunglasses, so I couldn't see his face, but the way he froze for a second told me that was Perez, and that he was nervous.

He shifted left and forcefully shoved the kid next to him to the ground. The others stopped and stared at the kid while Perez jumped over him, rammed into another kid, and took off running.

"Shit!" I clicked the button to unlock the vehicle and jumped out. Bishop yelled something, but the adrenaline buzzing through my ears drowned him out.

Perez hopped and darted through the yards, avoiding cars and toys as he jumped over shrubs and vaulted over a chain-link fence. A gray pit bull burst through a grouping of trees and was on his heels in a heartbeat. Perez's arms flew into the air, as the dog rushed at him, but he was too fast for it. Knowing I was close behind, he steered left and scaled the fence again, quickly crossing the street. I followed, pumping my arms and kicking rocks up from a gravel driveway.

Perez skirted behind the back of a house.

"Damn it!" I slowed and withdrew my weapon. I pressed my back into the back corner of the home, took a breath, and swung to the right with my gun out. A woman standing on her porch screamed.

"Where'd he go?" I asked.

Her body shook, but she managed to point toward the back yard. Her thick accent and nervous stutter made it hard to understand her, but her directional helped.

"Into the woods or on the left side?"

"The woods," she said. "Si."

I nodded and raced through the yard as I dug my phone out of my pocket and called Bishop. "He's in the woods behind the houses." I was panting, and I could barely get the words out. "I think there's a road ahead of you that will cut back toward the woods. Get Levy on the other side where the woods end. No sirens!" I stuffed the phone back in my pocket without tapping to end the call.

My feet pounded against the dry dirt, crunching leaves and echoing through the woods. I glimpsed Perez darting between trees, but quickly lost him.

I pushed harder, dodging fallen trees and tree stumps. My legs ached and I twisted my ankle as my foot slipped on a thick tree branch, but I didn't stop. I had to keep going.

The woods went on forever.

Perez peered from behind a tree and aimed a gun at me.

I dove behind a tree and smashed my back against it. Sweat dripped down my forehead and burned my eyes.

He fired a shot.

One.

I braced myself, then whipped around and shot back.

Perez fired again.

Two.

If he had a nine-millimeter, he'd have twelve to fifteen bullets before he had to reload. I didn't know if he had another gun, but I did. My nine-millimeter held fifteen rounds, and my Sig, six.

I flung myself toward a nearby tree, crawled behind it, and shot again.

He returned fire.

Three.

Something moved behind me. I turned back, my gun aimed in front of me, and saw Levy move behind a tree behind me and on my left.

That gave us double the rounds. Perez didn't have a chance.

Four.

Levy and I both returned fire.

"It's two against one Perez," I yelled. "You won't win this one!"

Five.

Levy returned fire, then moved to a tree ahead of mine, and fired again. She said, "On the right. I see movement on the right."

Six.

She returned fire.

My heart raced. I flipped around, rushed to a tree to my right, waited, and when nothing happened, moved forward, hiding behind a large redwood tree.

Seven.

Levy returned fire.

If I wanted to stop him I needed to get closer. I crouched down and hid behind another tree.

Eight.

Levy shot again, and I rushed forward, firing off three more shots in rapid succession.

Silence.

Bam! Bam! Bam! Multiple shots ripped through the quiet, and feet pounded through the woods again.

Levy ran beside me. "Who the hell was that?"

"Hopefully, the good guys."

We raced through the small section of woods searching for Perez, but he was gone. We hit the edge of the tree line and stopped, both of us working hard to catch our breath.

Levy tipped her head back and sucked in a breath. "How the hell does someone disappear like that?"

I called Bishop. "We lost him. Anything?"

Before he responded, three patrol officers walked out from another section of the woods.

"Where are you? I'll be right there," Bishop said.

"East side of the woods. You'll see the three squads." I caught my breath and asked the patrol officers why they weren't out searching for Perez.

"We have three squads searching, but Detective Bishop wanted us in the woods when shots fired. We saw him and fired, but he ran."

I'd lost my hair clip somewhere in the woods, and my hair clung to my neck and forehead. I scrubbed the random loose hairs around my hairline back over my head, sticking them in place with my perspiration, then scanned the area around us. "He's gone." I tossed my hands into the air. "We could search this area the rest of the day and not find him."

"He was with those kids. He's got to know someone around here," Levy said.

I asked one of the officers to radio out and see if the kids were still walking.

"They're not," he said after getting a response from another officer. "Looks like they all bolted when Perez started shooting."

"He's definitely still in the area," Levy said. "Nobody can just disappear like that."

I pointed to the groups of people standing on their porches and staring our direction. "Someone's hiding him."

"We could go door-to-door," an officer said.

"Not enough man power. He'll figure that out and cut and run again. We'll keep patrol close, and if there's a sighting, we'll grab him."

"So, what do we do now?" Levy asked.

"We go back to the department and figure out where he'll go next."

I washed my face in the locker room and grabbed a bottled water from the kitchen, then headed back to the investigation room. I stopped just inside the door and watched our team.

Bishop, Levy, and Michels, each in their own space, operated a solemn harmony of dissent. Papers piled everywhere, evidence laid out like pieces of a jigsaw puzzle refusing to fit together. The evidence boards were covered with photos, notes, and clues, pinned up in a desperate attempt to gain insight into the case. Bishop sighed. Everyone was exhausted, bags under their eyes, and their slumped bodies showed the pressure we were all under.

"Okay," I said. "Hold on." I hit the whiteboard with renewed energy. I moved photos of the victims and suspects into a circle, then scribbled swingers group in the middle. The team watched.

"Swingers," I said. I tapped the dry-erase marker into the board. "Right now, it's the only thing connecting our victims. That's not a coincidence. Something happened within that group that pushed one of the members to lose their shit. Two of the couples are stressing out right now. They know one of the three paid someone to break into their house. They may even know who."

"Then we press them for the names," Levy said.

"It's too late," Bishop said. "They all know we're leaning toward the group as the connection. They're afraid of the one who did this, and they might not know which couple it is."

"Right," I said. "There could be multiple issues within the group."

"If they're too scared to give up their sex buddies," Michels said. "How the hell do we move forward?"

"I second that," Levy said. "We can't get enough on Garcia, Perez is MIA, and we don't have a clue about the driver and whether he's the third or there's another person involved."

"They're a dead end," Michels added.

"No. Right now they're the weak link," I said. "Garcia knows Perez replaced him. He's pissed. Rosy picks him up, and a few hours later, she's on the phone telling me she knows where Perez is?" I turned toward the board and wrote *set up Perez* under Garcia's name. "He set him up."

"Can't be," Michels said. "He risks Perez naming him."

"Not necessarily. We show up in the middle of a side street where Perez just happens to be walking with a group of kids? Pretty convenient, don't you think? He'll know Garcia sent us. He'll see that as a warning."

"If Garcia's pissed off, wouldn't he go after Perez himself?" Levy asked.

"Not if he thinks we're watching him."

"Our best bet is Perez," Bishop said. "He's afraid of us, but I'd bet money we're a distant second to his fear of Garcia."

"Right," I said. I pointed to the photo of Perez. "We're going back to FoCo."

"Why? Levy asked. No one's going to talk. They'll be too scared."

"Someone always talks. You just have to ask the right questions."

Twenty minutes later we'd gone our separate ways, Michels and Levy hitting the day workers area near the trailer park and the trailers where we'd first found Perez, and Bishop and I, the hole-in-the-wall restaurants and stores dotting Atlanta Highway.

IT WAS LATE. The sun had set before we headed out, and I couldn't believe the day had gone by that fast. As we walked through the third Mexican restaurant, the smell of cilantro and jalapenos made my stomach growl.

Bishop stopped and narrowed his eyes into mine. "Was that you?"

"I'm hungry." I scanned the small parking area around the restaurant, checking for the SUV or van, and to familiarize myself with the vehicles.

"Not here." He flicked his head toward the entrance. "We'll grab something on our way back to the station."

The place had no lobby, and no one greeted us, so we headed to the bar at the back of the building. Even though we hadn't sat, the bartender smiled, then dropped a cup of salsa and a basket of chips in front of us. "What to drink?"

"Not here to eat," Bishop said. We showed her our badges.

Her eyes widened. Her head shifted left and right as if she was looking for a place to hide.

"We just want to ask you some questions," Bishop said. He showed her the photos of Santos Garcia and Diego Perez. "Do you know these men?"

She studied the photos then took a step back, rapidly shaking her head.

She was lying. "Are you sure?" I asked. "It's important we find them."

She made eye contact with me, then she glanced down at the menus she'd placed on the bar top. "Un segundo." She raced through the kitchen door.

"Oh hell. She's running. Get out back," I said. I climbed onto the bar and took off after her. She slammed through the swinging door into the kitchen. I caught it with my shoulder behind her. A woman chasing another woman didn't faze the kitchen staff. I pushed past a kid carrying a basket of chips and cup of salsa. The food went flying. I grabbed the woman by the back of her shirt as she reached the back door. "I don't think so." I flipped her around and inched closer, forcing her back against the door. "Which one do you know?"

"I do not know them."

"Then why'd you take off? Come on. Don't make me arrest you for interfering with an investigation. Do you know both men?"

"Perez is my brother. The other is Santos Garcia."

"Your brother? Where is he?"

"I do not know. I don't see him in days."

"What's your name?"

"Maria Perez."

"What about Garcia? Have you seen him?"

"No."

"Where do they hang out? A bar, maybe? Another restaurant?"

Tears streamed down her face. "I do not know."

Bishop appeared behind me.

"This is Perez's sister."

"Do you know anything about home invasions in Hamby?"

Her eyes widened. "No." She shook her head rapidly again. "I do not know my brother's things."

"Are you friendly with Garcia?"

More head shaking. "He is dangerous. I stay away."

"Smart girl," Bishop said.

"Maria, where does your brother stay?"

Tears fell down her face. "I do not know. I promise."

"Where do you live?"

She gave me her address. I wrote it and her phone number down on my pad. "If you see your brother, tell him we're looking for him."

"Please, do not say I talk to you. Garcia will—"

"We won't mention your name," I said.

"That was luck," Bishop said in the parking lot.

"No, that was the process of elimination." I smiled. "Yeah, and luck." I called Levy to give the update.

"That should get us somewhere," she said. "Are you going there now? We can meet you."

"She's already called Perez, he's probably not going to be there, but we'll give it a shot," I said.

"Want us to meet you there?" She asked.

"No."

"Okay," she said. "We got the name of a bar in Roswell where people from the area hang out. "Los Zarape. It's off Roswell Road. We'll check it out."

Bishop and I shared a look. "Keep us posted," I said.

MARIA PEREZ LIVED in a ranch home across from the elementary school in Forsyth. Bishop pulled to the side of the road a few homes past it and killed his headlights. Not a single light in the home was on, but there were six cars crammed into the short driveway.

"She's home already," I said. "She must have taken a shortcut."

"How do you know?"

"Because that white Ford Probe was in the restaurant parking lot."

He shot me a look. "I hate it when you do that."

"Do what?"

"Get things I miss."

A head peeked out from the curtain on the window next to the front door, then footsteps pounded quickly away from the window. After a few seconds, a light out back clicked on and off and a door slammed shut.

"Is that—" Bishop asked.

"Son of a bitch! Not again!" I ripped my weapon from my belt. "You go right. I'll take the left." I sped around the left side of the house. It was lit enough by other houses to make out the chain-link fence in front of me. I skidded to a stop and clambered over the barrier, then ran across the backyard. As I scaled the fence, I caught sight of someone in jeans and a dark hoodie advancing toward the left side of a house. I screamed out to Bishop. "He's on the left!"

The back lights of that house lit up, giving me a better view of him running toward the street. The body shape matched what I could recall of Perez. I kicked my pace into high gear, pumping my arms back and forth like an Olympic runner. He made it across the street, lost his footing, and tripped over himself. I pushed my limits, forcing my body to use what little energy it had left before he got up and took off again.

He had rolled onto his side and was holding his knees up toward his chest, rocking back and forth and swearing in Spanish.

I pointed my weapon at him. "On your stomach with your hands behind you!"

He kept his head buried into his knees and swore some more.

"Now!" I screamed.

He rolled onto his stomach and froze.

"Hands out to your sides where I can see them. Now!"

Bishop finally caught up, his breathing short and quick. He aimed his gun at Perez. "Damn. This guy can run."

"I'll cuff him," I said. I stuffed my weapon into its holster and removed my handcuffs. Once I cuffed him, I flipped him over and dropped an f-bomb.

It wasn't Perez.

10

Since we were outside the FoCo sheriff's jurisdiction, the Cumming Police responded to our request for assistance. After explaining the situation to two very big, very annoyed looking patrol officers reminiscent of Buford T. Justice in *Smokey and the Bandit*, they helped us out. Neither however, could muster a smile.

Our bust wasn't even a relative of Perez. When we asked why he ran, he told us his immigration status was in question and he was afraid we were coming for him. We asked if Maria was home, or if he'd seen Perez or Garcia, but he decided it was time to keep his mouth shut.

Bishop's face had yet to return to its pale beige. I was worried the running was too much for him. "Are you okay?"

"Getting there," he said. "I really need to start working out again."

The patrol officers had left and brought our runner with them. I almost felt bad for the guy. The duo Buford T. Justice cops weren't going to just send him on his way, but had he not run, he wouldn't be facing a possible deportation.

"I've called Stacey Turner's cell phone twice. Got voice mail each time."

"Kelsey Kelley told her," he said.

"Exactly. We need to just drop by their house. We should have done that in the first place."

"It's a little late for that," Bishop said. "Let's head to that bar, see what Michels and Levy got."

"I didn't mean right now." Bishop looked like he would fall over from exhaustion any second, and I needed to try to sleep as well. "Levy and Michels can handle it. They'll call if they get something. I'll call and let them know we're going back to the station and then home." I climbed into his vehicle.

"We're going back, too," Levy said. "The bar had a fire two nights ago. It's closed."

"Great. That's not helpful."

LOUIE WASN'T interested in conversation. When I dropped his pellets into his bowl, he snatched one up and swam to hide in his castle. I crouched down and stared into his small world and wondered if he knew there was something bigger and maybe better out there. "Goodnight, Louie."

After a quick shower, I pulled on a pair of sweatpants and slipped one of Tommy's sweatshirts over my head. Both the soft cotton and knowing Tommy had worn it helped me relax. I wrapped my hair in a towel as my cell phone rang. I sucked in a breath when I read the caller ID.

"Ashley? What's going on?"

Her tone was caring but serious, and her voice coarse and thick like she'd been crying.

"He's at Grady. In the Marcus trauma unit. Intensive care."

I stopped breathing. I wanted to say something, but a pain in the back of my throat made it impossible. My heart raced. I ripped the towel off my head. Finally, I forced out, "I'm on my way. How bad is he?" I squirmed out of my sweatpants and into a pair of jeans.

"I don't know. Rachel, you're not family. They won't let you see him. You know that, right?"

"I have his medical power of attorney." I dug my lockbox key out of my drawer and crawled under my bed with my phone on speaker by my side.

"Justin's already on the phone with Bishop. I'll call Jimmy, and we'll see you there." She ended the call.

I crawled out from under the bed, unlocked my lockbox, and stuffed the paperwork in the back of my jeans. I stood frozen in time with my phone in my hand staring down at it, barely able to breathe. My thoughts crowded with images of Kyle lying on a hospital bed attached to God only knew what mixed with memories of Tommy dropping to the ground, a hole in the center of his forehead. "Move, Ryder!" My scream forced my body into motion. I rushed to the bathroom and pulled my hair into a bun, slipped on a pair of running shoes and maneuvered myself into a bra without removing the sweatshirt.

Bishop called. "I'm going now," I said.

"No," he said. "I'm already halfway to your place. Don't even think about getting into that Jeep."

Five minutes later, I climbed into his car, removed the paperwork from my pants, and clutched it to my chest. "I have his medical power of attorney." My eyes filled with tears. I scrubbed them away. "He's going to be all right."

"Kyle's strong, and he's got a lot of people on his side."

My nose had clogged, and it altered my voice. "Do you know what happened?"

"No."

"If you're lying, I swear to God—"

"We don't know, Rachel." He weaved in and out of traffic. The interstate was always backed up. He honked at cars and yanked his steering wheel to the right, then pulled on the shoulder, slowed enough to put his light on his roof, then hit the gas again. "Listen," he said. "I know this is the worst thing a man can say to a woman, but you need to try to relax. You need a clear head for this."

"Kyle is in the trauma hospital. He wouldn't be there if it wasn't bad."

"Not always."

I closed my eyes and focused on my breathing. Bishop continued to weave in and out of traffic until he slowed and exited the highway. I checked my face in the mirror and wiped the tear stains from my cheeks.

"There's a box of tissue in the glove. Cathy keeps it here for her allergies."

"Thanks." I grabbed a tissue and dried my eyes.

He dropped me off at the main entrance to the Marcus trauma unit. I jogged through the electronic doors, read the sign for intensive care, and burst through them.

Three men wearing DEA jackets stood at the nurses' station. I pushed past them and leaned against the counter, waving the papers in front of a nurse's face. "I'm here for Kyle Olsen."

"Are you a relative?"

"I'm his girlfriend, and I have his medical power of attorney." I waved the papers again.

She held out her hand. "Ma'am, if you'd stop waving them, I can take a look."

I shoved them at her. She reviewed the information, made a copy, and then said she'd be right back.

The agents stepped back as Bishop arrived and introduced himself. Jimmy and Savannah, Michels, Ashley, and Levy walked in shortly after.

I bounced on my feet. Where the hell was the damn nurse?

Savannah wrapped her arm around my waist. "Any news?"

"Not yet."

A drug enforcement agent cleared his throat beside me then introduced himself. "Detective Ryder, I'm Agent Tanner. Agent Olsen's contact for the investigation."

Savannah dropped her arm and stepped back.

I pushed my shoulders back and cleared my throat. I'd be damned if I'd cry in front of him. "What happened to Kyle?"

"He's been shot," he said. "But that's all we know. I'll contact Ashley once we have more details."

Savannah held my hand as the nurse returned. "You can go in, but only you. He's this way." She walked around the station counter and tapped a keycard to the pad on the double doors.

The sounds overwhelmed me. The unit buzzed with machines, flashing lights, rushing nurses, and commands from everywhere. I shook my hands to release my anxiety, but it didn't help. The tension and panic in the air thickened as I passed room after room filled with patients.

She stopped five rooms in. "The doctor will be here in a moment. Mr.

Olsen is on a ventilator, but he's conscious. He's on heavy painkillers, and he needs his rest, so we'll need to make this quick."

I couldn't look into the room right away. "Wait. Can you tell me his injuries first?"

"Mr. Olsen was shot in the lung and abdomen. The bullet pierced his left lung. He got lucky with the other, but he did lose a lot of blood. Surgery to remove the bullets was successful, but his left lung needs time to recover, hence the reason for the ventilator."

I swallowed back the lump in my throat. "Thank you."

She nodded and walked away.

The room's harsh fluorescent lights hummed a low and constant buzz that exacerbated the incessant beeping of the medical machines attached to Kyle. It smelled like a mixture of disinfectant and blood. Kyle lay on the hospital bed in a partial sitting position, his eyes closed, the blue ventilator hoses draped over his left arm. I stood on his right, staring at his face. He'd grown a beard in the few months he'd been gone, but it didn't cover his cut lips and black eye.

I placed my hand gently on his swollen and bruised right hand, and whispered, "Kyle, it's me. I'm here." My tears flowed like rain.

His eyes opened, darted around the room and then settled on me.

I tried to smile but couldn't. "Hey."

He attempted to move his hand, but I stopped him. "No. Just stay still." I softly touched his face. "You're on a ventilator right now. Just rest."

His eyes closed again.

Thoughts and questions swirled in my brain. *What happened? Who hurt him? Where was he?* But it wasn't the time.

The doctor walked in. "I'm Doctor Prichard. I understand you have our patient's medical power of attorney?"

"Yes. Can you tell me how he's doing?"

He checked a few of the machines and jotted something on the chart hooked to the end of the bed. "Mr. Olsen arrived via ambulance at 6:41 last night. He was immediately rushed into surgery to remove two bullets. One lodged in his left lung, the other in his abdomen. He was very lucky." He stood beside the bed.

Kyle opened his eyes. "Mr. Olsen, good to see you're awake. I was just telling your friend what happened."

Kyle moved his head up and down as an acknowledgement.

"As I said, he was lucky. Had that bullet to his lung hit a centimeter higher, it would have penetrated the heart." He checked another beeping machine, pressed a blue button on it, and it stopped. He smiled at Kyle. "If everything goes as planned, and there aren't any complications, we'll have you off that ventilator and in a regular room in a day or two."

Kyle nodded.

"Great," the doctor said. He turned toward me. "You can come back tomorrow or stay in the waiting room, but he needs his rest."

No one got rest in a hospital room. I nodded. "May I speak with you in the hall for a moment please?" I looked back at Kyle. "And then I'll come back and say goodbye."

In the hall, I rattled off a list of questions without taking a breath.

"Ms. Ryder, yes?"

"Yes."

"Slow down, please."

I took a deep breath and blew it out. "Yes, sorry. Can you tell me how he got here?"

"As I said, an ambulance brought him."

"Right. Sorry. Do you know where he was?"

"I do not."

I exhaled. "Will there be any long-term damage?"

"He'll have to take it easy for a while, give his lung some time to heal, but if all goes as it should, it won't impair him in any way."

"So, he's going to be okay?"

"Ms. Ryder, no surgery comes without risks. All we can do is keep an eye on him and make sure he's healing."

"What kind of risks?"

"Pulmonary embolism is the most concerning in the days following any surgery, but I suggest you stay positive. It looks like Mr. Olsen is a strong man. Let us do what we can to get him through this."

I squeezed my hands into fists. "Yes, of course. Thank you." I walked back into the room and kissed Kyle's forehead. His eyes opened. "You're going to be fine, babe."

I caressed the side of his face. "I'll let the nurses know I'm staying just in case you need me, okay?"

He smiled and his eyes closed again.

~

I GAVE EVERYONE THE NEWS. Savannah, Ashley, and Levy hugged me.

"I'm staying, but really, you all should go. If something happens, I'll let you know."

Bishop squeezed my shoulder with one hand and dug his keys out of his pocket with the other, and handed them to me. "I'll catch a ride with the chief and swap my car for yours tomorrow."

I gave him my keys.

"I'm staying," Savannah said. She'd walked over and wrapped her arm around my waist.

"You don't have to," I said. "Who has Scarlet?"

"Grandma Abernathy came to watch her. She won't mind spending the day with her."

"Really, it's okay," I said.

"I'm not arguing this." She kissed Jimmy on the cheek. "Text me when you get home."

~

SAVANNAH SAT on the couch of the ICU's waiting room while I stood, chewing my fingernail, staring out the window at the traffic below. I thought I knew the impact of a pulmonary embolism, but I googled it on my cell to be sure. Kyle could die. I couldn't get that out of my head. I turned to Savannah. "Is everything all right with you and Jimmy?"

She looked up from her cell phone. "What? Of course."

"Are you sure? He's been in a mood lately."

"Honey, I'm here for you. Don't you worry about my life right now."

"Do you know what a pulmonary embolism is?"

Her eyes widened. "That is not going to happen."

"The doctor said it's possible."

"Rach, don't do this to yourself."

"Tell me what's going on with Jimmy. Please. I need the distraction."

"Everything's fine, I promise. He's just stressed. Being the chief of police is demanding, and with Scarlet and the baby, he's worried he's going to miss out."

"Miss out on—wait. Did you just say the baby?"

Her eyes brightened. "We haven't told anyone yet, so don't you go spreading it around the department."

I took three long steps to the couch and wrapped my arms around her. It felt strange, the feelings of devastation and worry over Kyle mixed with happiness and excitement for Savannah and Jimmy.

"You're going to squeeze the baby right out of my uterus," she said.

I released her. "How did this happen? How far along are you?"

"Just two months, and I think you know how it happened." She shrugged. "Jimmy's got some serious swimmers."

"Is Jimmy upset about it?"

"Of course not. He's just got so much pressure from the mayor, and he's constantly getting called in at all hours of the night. He already thinks he's not present for Scarlet, and he's worried it'll be even worse with another baby."

"He's a great dad to Scarlet, and he will be to the baby, too."

"I know that," she said. "And deep down he does, too. Please don't say anything. We're not ready to share just yet."

"I won't."

She looped her arm through mine and laid her head against my shoulder. "Sit back and try to get some rest. You're going to need it for when Kyle's released."

She closed her eyes and snoozed while thoughts of the pulmonary embolism kept me awake. I gently disconnected our arms and tiptoed out of the waiting area to the nurses' station.

"No change," the nurse said. "Why don't you try to get some sleep? We'll come get you if anything changes."

I drank coffee after coffee waiting until they'd let me see Kyle.

Savannah groaned and stretched on the couch. "Did you get any sleep?"

"Nope."

"Then why did you let me?"

"You're pregnant. I've called Jimmy and told him to come and get you. You need to go home and sleep."

"I'll sleep when the kids are teenagers." She rolled her eyes. "What am I thinking? Things will only be harder then." She furrowed her brow. "Any news?"

"They said they'd let me know if anything changed."

As if on cue, a nurse walked in. "Ms. Ryder? We've taken Mr. Olsen off the ventilator. He asked if you were still here and would like to see you."

I handed Savannah my coffee and raced out.

I slowed to a strut at his door, forcing myself to pretend I wasn't worried sick. He smiled when I walked into the room. I wanted to climb into that hospital bed with him, and I would have if I wasn't afraid of hurting him. "Hey," I said.

"Hey." His voice was coarse and groggy. "I'm fine."

I laughed. "Right. Yell that, will you?"

"I'd rather not."

"That's what I thought." I pulled a chair over and sat next to his bed, and said, "I love you," while choking back my tears.

"I love you, too," he whispered. "You look like hell. Go home."

"I look better than you." I rubbed his arm. "I don't want to leave you."

"Did you find the people breaking into the homes?"

I blinked. "How do you know about that?"

"I have my ways." His tone changed. "Rach, please. Go home. I'm tired and I know you are, too."

"I will, but I need to know you'll be safe here."

"I'm safe. I killed the kid who shot me."

11

I'd met Bishop at my place late that morning. I had wanted to shower and go to the department, but I'd been given strict instructions from the chief I was not allowed back before three that afternoon. I showered anyway then lay down and crashed before my head hit the pillow. I slept better in those few hours than I had since Kyle left.

I called the ICU on the way to Dunkin'. The nurse connected me to Kyle's room.

"I'm feeling better," he said.

"I'll try to come by later, okay? Keep me posted."

"Rach, close the case. I'm not going anywhere."

I found everyone in the investigation room. As promised, Agent Tanner had followed up with Ashley, and Ashley came by the department to fill us in.

"He killed the guy after being shot twice?" Michels asked. "The man is a god."

"Agent Fernandez saw the whole event play out. He said Russell Carter was about ten feet away from Kyle. He couldn't believe his shots hit him. Kyle went down," Ashley glanced at me. "Sorry."

"It's okay," I said.

"But Kyle was able to grab his gun and shoot Carter as he stood there, maybe processing what he'd done or something?" She took a breath and continued "One shot in the head."

"Damn," Michels said. "That's freaking awesome."

I stared at Michels. "Taking a life is never awesome."

He dropped his head. "I'm sorry. I didn't mean it how it sounded."

"I know."

"Why didn't Agent Fernandez stop him?" Levy asked.

"He didn't have a weapon," Ashley said.

"Fair enough," Levy said.

"There's more," Ashley said. "The shooter was sixteen."

The room went silent. No one wanted a kid to die, even if that kid was a drug dealer. Kids never asked for a rough life, but many were stuck with it anyway. The constant struggle for them to survive drove them to gangs, child trafficking, and drugs. Some broke the cycle, but most couldn't, and many never even tried. The problem was no one had a solution.

"Man, poor Kyle," Michels said.

"Can't even imagine," Levy said.

I could. I'd seen too many dead kids in Chicago.

Bishop patted my hand. "How're you holding up? Get any sleep?"

"I did, actually."

"Good."

"So, what's the update on Perez?" I asked the room.

Bishop answered. "Still MIA. No vehicles at Perez's house earlier this afternoon, but we're planning another stop."

"Any of the Mayfield residents confess?"

Bishop laughed. "Wouldn't that be nice?"

Bubba walked in. "I got news." He handed us each a piece of paper with the van from the video on top and a name, license and registration information, and phone number below it.

"Our van?" I asked.

"Belongs to Nancy Stevens. Reported stolen from Peachtree City six days ago."

I leaned my head back. "Damn."

"Anything on the SUV?"

"Plate matches a 2020 Honda Accord belonging to a man in Alpharetta.

He bought the car for his sixteen-year-old daughter. Neither of them knew the tag was missing."

"We've still got BOLOs on the vehicles," Bishop said. "Can you update them with the tag information?"

"I can," Nikki said.

"Thanks," Bishop said.

Bubba handed Bishop the blown-up photos of the people in the front seats of both vehicles. "I tried to run for matches in the system, but the photos are too blurry, and the SUV has tinted windows."

Bishop handed me the photos.

"One more thing," Bubba said. He handed Bishop a file folder. "I only made the one copy," he said looking at the rest of us. "Sorry."

Bishop scanned the pages and handed them to me. "This is the project you were working on?"

"I found mentions of Diego Perez in six cases across the state, but mostly in Fulton or Forsyth. All within the last two years. They're not arrests, so I can't guarantee they're our Diego Perez, but it's a start," Bubba said.

"And Garcia?"

"Just the one where he voluntarily gave blood."

"Great work," Bishop said.

He handed me the file, and I reviewed it. I agreed, and passed it and the photos to Michels, who passed it to Levy.

"We can run these by Rosy and see if she recognizes anyone," Michels said.

"I'd like to do that," I said. "Try the community and golf managers at Mayfield first," I said. I eyed Bishop. "That work for you?"

"Yep. Jimmy wants to see you though."

I SAT in front of Jimmy's desk and tapped my foot on the floor to control my excitement about his secret.

He watched me closely. I suspected he was analyzing me to determine if I was up for working. "How're you doing?"

"I'm fine, Jimmy. How are you?"

He lifted an eyebrow. "I'm good."

"Good. Glad to hear it. But yeah, I'm good, too. Nothing to worry about."

He narrowed his eyes at me. "Then why are you tapping your foot?"

"I'm ready to get this case closed."

"All right then. I'm asking this as both a friend and your boss, and I want you to be honest. Do you think you can handle things today?"

"Why wouldn't I? Kyle is going to be fine, and we can't close this without everyone helping."

"Okay then." As I left his office, he said, "But if you need to get to the hospital, do it."

"I will." I'd finished my Dunkin' and headed to the kitchen to make myself another coffee.

Our budget didn't allow for high quality brand coffee pods, so, a while back I'd bought a case of Starbucks French roast and hid it in the cabinet over the fridge. I'd been drinking that ever since.

Bishop walked in. "You ready?" He saw the French roast pod and laughed. "I thought we'd stop at Dunkin'."

"We still can. I need all the fuel I can get."

A FOUR-VEHICLE ACCIDENT BLOCKED 400, so Bishop took Atlanta Highway along with the rest of the people heading home from work.

"Do you want to talk about Kyle?" he asked.

Nope. "Did you know this road has seven names?"

"I guess that's a no. Multiple names for a road is normal here."

"I know. There are like what, twenty names for Peachtree Street alone? Why do that?"

"Moonshine."

I laughed.

We caught another red light.

I tried Stacey Turner's cell again, but it went straight to voice mail. "She's avoiding us."

"Who?"

"Stacey Turner. She's either not talking because she's guilty, or she's afraid her house will be next."

"She should be. The crimes are escalating," Bishop said.

"Because Perez took over and upped the game, or because whoever hired them told them to?"

"We need Perez or Garcia to tell us," Bishop said.

"We have a better chance at world peace right now."

"Let's see what Maria and Rosy have to say, and we can go by the Turners' tonight or tomorrow."

Maria Lopez's house was on the way to Rosy's work. We arrived at the house fifteen minutes later. Her white Ford Probe was the only vehicle in the driveway. Bishop passed the house, then looped back around and parked on the opposite side of the street.

"Let's hope she's inside," Bishop said.

"And knows something." I glanced into her vehicle. She'd left her purse on the passenger's seat. "She's trusting."

"Most people are naive enough to be." He removed his weapon from the holster, then shook his head toward the front steps. "Door's ajar."

"And here we go again." We ducked down and carefully climbed up the few porch steps, Bishop going right, and me left. He stayed to the side of the door and knocked, but got no response.

"Shit! Perez must know we talked to her," I said.

Bishop kicked the door the rest of the way open, and we went inside.

A familiar metallic smell filled my nasal passages right away.

Bishop whispered, "Damn."

The door opened to a small family room on the right and a kitchen on the left. We split up and checked both but found no injured person or body in either. The smell grew stronger as we walked down the hallway toward the bedrooms.

Bishop kicked the partially opened bathroom door and checked inside. "All clear." He moved toward the right bedroom. I took the left.

I held my gun out in front of me and pushed the bedroom door open. The thick, metallic smell hit hard and surrounded me. "A body," I yelled and rushed to Diego Perez lying on top of a pile of bloody clothes. His eyes stared at nothing. I checked for a pulse even though I knew I wouldn't find one. He'd been shot in the abdomen and bled out.

Bishop walked in and groaned. "Hell. Guess he's not running anywhere now."

"Look at his eyes."

"Jaundice."

"Just like Dylan Blahut said."

AT LEAST THE Cumming police detectives were pleasant.

"Deceased is Diego Perez," I said. "We can ID him through his employee photo."

The taller detective said, "You were the ones who had the runner from this address yesterday."

"He was a suspect in an ongoing investigation, but we came here to speak with his sister."

The detective agreed. "You're welcome to stick around and see what we find, or we can get the information to you. It's up to you, but we will need photos of the bottoms of your shoes. Did you touch anything inside?"

"I checked for a pulse, but that's it. I'd like to look around the house," I said.

"Anything specific you're looking for?"

"Stolen jewelry and cash."

"Go right ahead."

While Bishop jogged to grab booties from his vehicle, I took photos of my shoes' soles. I'd make sure to get the detective's number and send him the photos before leaving.

Bishop handed me a pair of booties. "You don't think we'll find the money or the jewelry, do you?" he asked.

"No."

"Maria Perez's car is here with her purse inside it. Where is she?"

"That's a good question," I said.

We went separate directions and searched the small rooms. Knowing we could disrupt the crime scene, we touched nothing, then followed up with the detectives who promised to keep us updated on Perez's murder. If a connection between it and the invasions became obvious, we'd work together. I called Levy, Michels, and Jimmy with a quick update.

"Conveniently, no one at Mayfield recognized the people in the vehicle photos," Levy said.

"Call it a night," Bishop said.

I phoned Kyle.

"They said I'll be moved to a regular room tomorrow," he said.

"Good. Unless it's too late, I'll come by in a bit."

"The nurse said you could have five minutes."

"I'll take it."

"Don't. The faster I heal, the faster I can leave. I need to sleep."

I was disappointed, but I understood. "Okay. I'll call you tomorrow." I turned toward Bishop. "I'll give the bar manager a call and see if Maria's there."

"Five bucks says she quit," he said.

He was right.

"Garcia knew Perez would run. He thought we'd kill him," Bishop said. "When we didn't, he did it himself."

"You think he did something to Rosy after she called us?"

"I don't know, but we're about to find out."

BISHOP IDLED into the Carniceria Hernandez parking lot just as a short Latina woman flipped the sign from opened to closed. I jumped out of the vehicle and jogged over, my exhausted legs begging me to stop. I rapped on the door and when the woman turned around, showed her my badge.

She dropped her head and shook it, but she opened the door. "We're closed. You come back tomorrow."

I stuffed my badge back into my back pocket. "Was Rosy Lopez at work today?"

"She is sick. Now I do all the things myself until I hire someone else."

I said thank you and walked back to Bishop's vehicle as I dialed Rosy's number on my cell phone. It went straight to voice mail.

"Rosy didn't quit, but she did call in sick, and her phone's going straight to voice mail."

He shifted his vehicle into drive. "If she's spooked, she's not going to recognize anyone in the vehicle photos."

"Still worth a shot."

Dispatch interrupted our conversation with a call on the radio. "All units, we have a report of a 10-17 with one possible DOA. Suspect has left the residence. Location 312 Mayfield Club Lane. Repeat 312 Mayfield Club Lane."

I responded. "This is Detectives Ryder and Bishop. We are en route. ETA fifteen minutes."

"Shit," Bishop said. He slammed on the brakes, slowed to a near stop, and yanked the steering wheel to the right before missing a turn that would get us to Mayfield.

12

Flashing blue, red, and white lights illuminated the street, casting shadows of the dozens of neighbors on the road. They blocked Hamby PD vehicles like ours from gaining access. Half the department was there, so I jumped out and grabbed two officers to handle the crowd while the others searched the outside of the home.

"They're blocking emergency vehicles. Get them off the road."

"On it," the one said.

"Has anyone confirmed a DOA?"

The other nodded. "Yes, ma'am."

I jogged back to the car, bumping people out of the way and yelling at them. "Hamby PD! You're blocking entrance to a crime scene. Move it!"

It worked. Bishop whipped his car to the side of the street. I met him at his door. "Officer confirmed the DOA."

"Damn."

Levy stood by the front door speaking with a patrol officer, I interrupted and asked the officer to take photos of the area and send them via text. Inside the home a woman bawled and a baby wailed.

Levy put her hands on her waist. "DOA's a forty-six-year-old male. Shot in the leg. Bled out before his wife could get herself untied."

"Jesus," Bishop said. "How many kids?"

"Just the one. Uninjured. She was asleep when it happened. The intruders left her in the bedroom. Wife is with her now."

Bishop eyed me. "Thank God."

She followed us inside. The interior layout matched the basic concept of the others. A large open space, gourmet kitchen, and open dining area. Officers stood beside a deceased man lying in a pool of his own blood. Near the body lay a scuffed-up shoe, its laces undone.

Bishop sighed. "Looks like a struggle," I said.

"Victim wasn't tied to a chair," he said. "Why not?"

"He tried to fight them and got shot," I said.

"One guy against three men with guns? Doubtful."

"You never know."

The paramedics attempted to help the distraught wife, but she refused to give anyone her child.

"Don't you touch my baby!"

Bishop flicked his head toward her. "You take the wife. See if you can get her out of view of the body. I'll start with him."

I approached the woman. She pressed a bloody cloth to the side of her head with one hand and held the baby with the other. I cringed at the burns and abrasions around her wrists. Rope hurt, but either she didn't notice or didn't care. Blood dripped down her hand and soaked into the collar of her pajama top. I glanced over at the dining room and saw the rope lying on the floor next to a toppled over chair. "No zip ties?"

Levy shrugged. "Maybe they ran out? I've tried to talk to her, but she won't stop crying, and she won't let anyone touch her wrists."

"Did you check her head?"

"It's a pretty big gash. Looks like she might have hit her head on something, but I don't think the perps did it."

"Have the paramedics fully assessed her yet?"

"She won't let them. She won't let anyone take the kid."

"Has she said anything?"

"Nothing."

"I'll talk to her." I walked the few steps to her and crouched down in front of her. "I'm Detective Ryder. What's your name?"

She stared at me with red eyes and a swollen, red nose then hugged her baby tight, dropping the bloodied cloth on her white couch. "Miranda Wilson. You can't have my baby."

"I'm not going to take your baby," I said. "She's beautiful. What's her name?"

She sniffled, but her crying had slowed to a simmer. "Lila. We named her after my grandmother."

"Lila is a beautiful name. Miranda, was Lila hurt?"

"She was in her crib. Matt, he promised to do what they said if they didn't hurt Lila."

"We'll get to that in a minute. The other officer said you've got a pretty big cut on your head. Will you let the paramedics look at it?"

"I'm not letting go of my child."

I shifted toward the paramedic waiting beside me. "I'm sure they can work around her, right?"

He nodded.

"Do you have family in the area?"

"My parents. They're in Roswell."

"How about I give them a call and have them come over?"

"Okay," she said through tears.

I pulled my phone from my pocket. "What's their number?"

The baby whimpered.

Miranda Wilson squeezed her eyes shut. "I don't remember, but they're in my phone. It's on the bench in the mudroom."

"I've got it," Levy said.

"She needs stitches," the paramedic said.

She jerked her head away from him. "I'm not leaving my child!"

"We'll ask your parents to take her to the hospital so she's nearby."

Levy returned with the phone and handed it to me. It was locked. "Miranda, what's your parents' last name?"

It was late, and the phone rang several times before someone answered.

"Is this Mrs. Riley?"

"Who's calling please?"

"Detective Rachel Ryder with the Hamby Police Department. There's been an incident at your daughter Miranda's home. She needs medical attention but won't leave her child."

"What happened? What about the baby? Oh, dear God." She must have covered the phone while she spoke to her husband. "Honey, it's Miranda. Something's happened."

The husband took the phone. "This is Richard Riley. What's happened to my daughter and where is Matt?"

I didn't have time to answer his questions. "Someone will explain when you arrive."

"We'll be right there," he said and hung up.

"They'll be here soon," I said to Miranda.

The paramedic tried to wrap a bandage around her head. Miranda shifted her child further to the other side. "You're not taking Lila!"

"No one's going to take your baby," I said. "The paramedic is trying to cover the wound."

"Matt's dead, isn't he?"

"I'm sorry," I said.

"I tried to get to him, but I fell; I couldn't." Her lips straightened and she narrowed her eyes. "They said all they wanted was my jewelry and the money in the safe, but they shot Matt. He did what they said, and the man just stood there and shot him." Tears slid down her face. "I couldn't help him. I tried, but I couldn't get to him in time."

I whispered to Levy, "Stay with her until her parents arrive."

"Will do."

Bishop crouched down and studied Matt Wilson's body.

I squatted beside him. Noticing the two officers blocking her view, I said, "Good move on the officers. She was too upset to try to move."

"Looks like he was shot in the femoral artery."

I surveyed the area. The chair Miranda Wilson had been tied to sat in clear view of where Matt Wilson died. "God, she must have yanked her hands out of those loops. That had to hurt like hell." I gazed down at our victim. "The femoral bleeds out in two to three minutes. Imagine rubbing your hands up and down on that coarse rope while watching your husband bleed out. That had to have felt like forever to her." I sucked in a breath. Our circumstances might have been different, but I understood.

Medical examiner Mike Barron arrived, cranky from being awakened from a sound sleep. "Y'all plan on finding these sons of bitches any time soon?"

"We're working on it, doc," Bishop said.

He studied the body. "Might want to do that quick. Looks like they're stepping up their game. Femoral shot means either the shooter got lucky, or he knows where to shoot." He eased himself down onto his knees, groaning in the process, checked for a pulse, something he always did with dead bodies, and confirmed the death.

"We'll let you do your thing," Bishop said. "We have a home to search."

"Good luck," Barron said.

Levy stopped as I walked to the home office off the main entrance. "Her parents are here. They want to talk to you."

"You know what I know."

"Got it."

Nikki stood to the side in front of the safe taking photos.

"Looks like looters hit this room," I said.

"It's worse than the Morgensens' place." She turned toward me. "They left a bunch of money and jewelry."

"Seriously? They must have been in a hurry." I stepped over file folders and papers thrown across the floor.

I glanced into the safe and then down at the floor. "You think those files were in there?"

"Based on the way they're lying there, I'd say yes. I'll get prints, but if they wore gloves . . ." She had no reason to finish. I knew what it would mean.

I dodged the mess on the floor and walked over to the desk. Papers and files covered its glossy mahogany surface. What were they looking for?

She turned to me and asked, "If this is like the other break-ins, they walked the husband to the safe, right?"

"We don't know if it's the same people."

"I know, but let's say it is. Why come in here, toss everything around, make the victim open the safe but leave the money and jewelry, then walk the victim back out to shoot him?"

"Because they weren't here for the money. They were here for Wilson."

Tick. Tock.

~

I SEARCHED the house for Bishop but couldn't find him.

"Have you seen Detective Bishop?" I asked an officer.

"Outside with the chief," he said.

The crowd had grown and reporters lined the edge of the yellow tape, yelling out questions no one would answer.

I found Bishop and Jimmy by the garage door.

I interrupted their conversation. "We've got a problem. There's cash and jewelry in the safe, and the room's been tossed."

"Perez is dead, and Garcia was replaced. It's possible it's not the same guys," Bishop said.

I disagreed. "You don't think it's convenient that we find Perez dead and another house hit? Garcia's back to work."

"Maybe someone used the others as cover to get something from the office and killed Matt Wilson in the process," Jimmy said.

"No one knows the victims were tied to chairs," I said.

"Could be coincidence," Jimmy said. "And that's why they used rope instead of zip ties."

"It's connected," I pointed to Jimmy. "Watch. We'll find out the Wilsons are part of the swingers group."

Cooke arrived wearing a black pantsuit with a white shirt. She'd either applied makeup and styled her hair for the press conference, or she'd been out already. She nodded at Jimmy, said, "Chief," and then turned toward Bishop. "Catch me up. Husband dead. Wife injured. Baby fine. Money and jewelry taken. I'm assuming we're looking at the same suspects?"

"You two got this?" Jimmy asked.

"Yes," I said. "Go home."

He walked away.

Bishop answered Cooke's question. "We can't verify if anything was taken, but we don't want that mentioned."

"You think this isn't related to the other break-ins then?"

"We're investigating," I said. "We don't know what we know yet."

Bishop cleared his throat. "I'll take this. You go inside and see where we're at with everything."

"Fine." I flipped around and charged to the front entrance. As I stepped inside, my cell phone rang with an unknown number. I hit the screen and accepted the call. "Ryder."

"Rach, it's me," Kyle said. "This is my new number."

"Hey. Why are you up so late? Are you okay?"

"Fine. My partner dropped off my phone earlier. I just wanted to get you the number."

"This late?"

"No. They just moved me to another floor. It's louder than the ICU. I don't know how anyone sleeps in these places with these beeping machines and the nurses coming in every five minutes. I could recover better at home."

Kyle and I had discussed moving in together a while back, but the actual move was on hold until he returned from his assignment. "Which home? Your current one or the one you'll be living in with me?"

"You're still up for that?"

"I could use the help with the mortgage."

He laughed. "Damn, that hurts."

"Sorry," I said. "Listen, I'm at a crime scene. I'll have to go into the office in a few hours, but I'll try to come by this afternoon. Will you be okay?"

"I'll be fine. Is this another break-in?"

"And a murder."

"Go. We'll talk later."

I walked back into the main living area. Barron had already had Matt Wilson's body removed. I snapped additional photos of the blood on the rug. It would be impossible to get all that blood out, and that was too bad. The thing looked too expensive to be from Target. Even if the blood could be removed, I doubted Miranda Wilson would keep it or even stay in the home. Most people didn't stay when a loved one died violently. Watching it happen only made it worse. She'd carry that memory at the front of her brain for the rest of her life.

A woman carrying Lila on her side approached me. "Are you Detective Ryder?"

"Yes. Mrs. Riley?"

She'd been crying. "Do you know who did this?"

"We're working on it," I said. "Is Miranda on her way to the hospital?"

"Yes. We're getting ready to go, too. Please can you tell me what will happen to Matt's body?"

"The coroner will perform an autopsy and when ready, will release the body to the family."

She gasped. "An autopsy? We already know he was shot in the leg. What else do they need to know?"

"Autopsies provide important information, Mrs. Riley, but I promise you, Dr. Barron is very good at his job, and Matt's remains will be well cared for."

She sniffled. "Okay."

"Did Miranda tell you anything?"

"Just that three men broke in. Two men made Matt take them to the safe, while the other one tied her up and left her there. A few minutes later one of the men came out with Matt and shoots him."

"One man?"

"That's what she said."

I handed her my card. "Can you let me know if Miranda stays overnight at the hospital? We'll need her statement."

"Okay," she said. She turned to leave.

"Mrs. Riley, just a few more questions."

"I need to get to the hospital. Miranda will be upset if Lila isn't there."

"Just a few more questions. Do you know where Matt worked?"

"Yes, he's a vice president of claims at an insurance management company. I think it's called Health Administrators or something like that."

"Do you know how much money your daughter and son-in-law kept in their safe?"

"No," she said. "Matt handled their finances. Miranda once said he had promised that, unless he said otherwise, she didn't need to think about money."

Apparently, Matt didn't follow through with that promise.

～

WE ALL MET BACK at the department's investigation room to review what we'd learned, Cooke included.

She stood beside the open door. "I'll need to know if this incident is connected to the others first thing."

"We can't answer that," I said. "Answer without answering."

She narrowed her eyes at me.

"For now, it's best we limit the details of this one," Bishop said.

She sighed. "I thought that's what you'd say." She turned toward the door, then back to us and said, "You all are doing a great job."

"Thank you," Bishop said.

She closed the door behind her.

"Do we know if any jewelry or cash is missing?" Levy asked.

"We'll interview Miranda tomorrow," Bishop said. "Hopefully, she'll be able to check her jewelry, then we'll know if anything was taken."

"She's not going back there for a while, if ever," I said.

"She has to, for the baby's things," Levy said.

"We'll see."

"This one's different than the other three," Michels said. "Maybe the others were meant as distractions?"

"Break-in gone wrong kind of thing," Levy said.

I eyed Bishop. He didn't say anything. "Miranda Wilson's mom said Miranda told her three men broke in, and like the others, two men made Matt take them to the safe, while the other one tied her up and left her there. A few minutes later one of the men came out with Matt and shoots him."

"The guy left her after he tied her up? That's different," Michels said.

"So is the shooting," Levy said.

Michels asked, "Why would they walk Wilson to the office, then turn around and bring him back into the main living area to shoot him? Why not just shoot him in the office?"

"They wanted his wife to see him die," Bishop said. "And they wanted him to know it." He dragged his hand through his thinning hair.

"Then why go through the files?" Levy asked.

"Because they were looking for something," I said.

"All the more reason to think the others were distractions," Michels said.

"What's the worst thing you can do to someone?" Bishop asked.

"I would think killing them would be high on the list," Levy said.

"What about forcing someone to watch someone they love die?" I asked.

"Or die knowing the person you love watched it happen," Bishop said.

"So this is about the wife?" Levy asked.

"It's possible," Bishop said.

"This is all about the swingers," Michel said. "One of the Wilsons hooked up with the wrong spouse, and died because of it."

"We don't know if they are part of the group," Bishop said.

"They are," Michels said. "I guarantee it."

Bishop checked his watch. "It's after four. Let's get some rest and regroup in the morning."

"It is morning," Levy said.

He shrugged. "Eight o'clock okay?"

"It has to be," I said.

Michels and Levy agreed.

I DROVE past the Mayfield community on my way home. I turned into the entrance and pulled my Jeep to the side. Two men dressed in black pants and blue jackets stood outside the gate. They weren't the security men I had spoken with before, but looked similar, and wore the same type of clothing.

One knocked on my window. I held up my badge as I hand-rolled the window down. "Detective Rachel Ryder."

He scrutinized my badge then nodded. "If you're here regarding the recent break-in and murder, everyone has left the home for the night. You won't be able to get in."

"My partner and I are leading the investigation. When did your team start?"

"Tonight, ma'am."

"Detective's fine."

He nodded once.

"How many you got here?"

"Ten. Two at the front entrance, four canvassing the community, two at the fence where the one possibly exited, and two at the grounds entrance." He stood straight with his legs slightly separated. He was either former law enforcement or former military.

"You serve?"

"Navy. Two tours in Afghanistan."

"Seal?"

"Yes."

"What about the rest of your men?"

"All military. Another seal, two special forces, and two rangers."

I handed him my card. "My cell's on this. Call me direct if anything happens."

"Will do."

I took a right on Hopewell Road and drove the speed limit. The two-lane road contained several sharp curves that always surprised speeding drivers. The department handled a few accidents on it monthly, but the city had never approved lights. The best they'd done was place *curve in road* signs, but by the time the driver saw those, it was usually too late to slow down.

Raised bright lights came over the small hill behind me. The driver kept them on and quickly closed the gap between us. The engine roared behind me. The bright lights reflected off my rearview mirror, making it hard for me to determine the vehicle. I gripped the steering wheel tighter and my body tensed. Both involuntary reactions on my part. "Chill out," I told myself. It was probably some teenager thinking they drove better than they did. I muttered, "Get off my ass."

The vehicle inched closer. I leaned my foot into the gas pedal. I'd hit a sharp curve in about a quarter of a mile. I rolled down my window, slowed down, and waved him to pass on my left. The small section of road was flat enough to see that the other side was clear.

He didn't pass. I rolled the window up. "Asshole." The bright lights hurt my eyes. I sped up again. The vehicle moved into the middle of the road but still didn't pass. We were closing in on the tight s-curve, and I had two choices. Move my car toward the side of the road and slam on my brakes or put the pedal to the metal and chance the curves. And I had about ten seconds to choose. I figured what the hell and chose the latter.

Bishop always drove so I hadn't gotten to use my defensive driving skills in a while. I was due. I pushed down on the gas pedal and checked my speed. Fifty in a thirty. I knew I could handle the curve at seventy, seventy-five. There was a stop sign about a block up from the curve. If he kept up, and it was clear, I'd swing my Jeep to the right and slam on the brakes. He'd have less time to brake and would either smash into me or go through the sign. Either way, he'd have to slow down, and that would allow the predator to become the prey. If he didn't drop off the side of the road and crash into trees. The vehicle hadn't backed off, so I really didn't have any choice. If the driver made a stupid move like trying to pass, we both were in trouble.

Road rage really pissed me off, but I didn't want a kid getting hurt or killed because he was an idiot. Unlike Chicago, Georgia didn't require license plates on vehicles' fronts, so I couldn't ask dispatch to run a plate check. I could have called it in anyway, but I waited it out to see what they did.

I hugged the center line knowing I'd have more room to correct before going down the steep drop-off if I lost control. The driver of the other vehicle stayed in the center of the road behind me as I upped my speed. "Is this how we're going to play it?" I put additional weight on the gas pedal.

Double fists on the steering wheel, I took the first curve, a tight right, at seventy-six then yanked my steering wheel the opposite direction for the second. My breathing accelerated. I checked my driver's side mirror.

The vehicle didn't swing fast enough. I watched it swerve back and forth as the driver tried to regain control. The brakes squealed. It wasn't going to make the turn.

"Shit!" I slowed but was too far ahead to see it drive off the side of the road. But I heard it. One loud crash, then another, and then silence.

I yanked my steering wheel around, called dispatch, and gave them the location. Flames brightened the area below where the vehicle had lost control. I switched on my hazards, stuffed my cell into my pocket, then bolted from the Jeep to the edge of the road. I shined my flashlight down at the flames.

The SUV was dark colored like the ones in the videos from the break-ins. "Son of a bitch!" I scanned my flashlight around the vehicle and thought I saw someone running through the trees, but I couldn't be sure.

The SUV must have flipped forward as it careened down the hill because the roof had been smashed in. The SUV lay on the passenger's side, the entire front end a crumpled, flaming heap. The driver's side door hung open. I yelled, "Ambulance is on its way," then began a slow climb down the steep drop.

I aimed the flashlight ahead of me. The flames grew, and I worried the car might explode. I jogged down the hill, caught my foot on a thick vine, and fell. My flashlight went flying, and I smacked my head onto something hard. I lay there for a second, my head pounding from the pain. Something caught the thigh of my jeans as I moved to stand. A searing pain pierced my thigh. A stick. Damn, it hurt. It wasn't near my femoral, so I inhaled, squeezed my eyes shut and pulled the stick out. "Fuck!" Blood dripped down my leg and soaked my jeans. I took off my jacket, twisted it into a rope, and tied it around my leg to stop the bleeding. My arms shook.

The puncture pulsed. My head throbbed. Something trickled down my forehead. Blood. I hobbled to the car, sidestepping tree stumps and large branches in the process. "If you can speak, talk to me," I yelled.

Nothing.

"Ambulance is on its way." I reached the vehicle, but it was empty.

I dragged my leg toward the back of the vehicle and read the license plate. It started with CJF. The flames crackled. Something in the engine hissed.

"Shit!" I hobbled toward a tree just as the SUV exploded.

13

Burning gas thickened the air as the flames burned the ground between us. I took off up the hill, the pain in my leg fighting me every inch of the way. Piercing pains shot through my head, and falling and rising loops of sirens made it worse.

High beams lit up the area. I dug into my pocket for my cell phone, but it was gone. It must have fallen out somewhere down the incline. I waved my hands at the officers standing in the high beams, and yelled, "Detective Ryder. No victims in the vehicle, but I think I saw a runner."

"Fire's coming down now. You're hurt," one officer said. He and another officer took off down the hill toward me. They wrapped my arms around their shoulders and grabbed a leg each.

The officer holding my bloody leg said, "That looks bad."

"They escaped, but the roof was crashed in and may have caused some head damage. We need to check the area."

"We'll take care of it," an officer said. The firefighters dragged a long white hose down the hill as three officers ran past us with their flashlights lighting the way.

"Be careful," I hollered.

Jimmy and two paramedics met me at the top. The officers set me on a gurney and the paramedics rushed me to the ambulance.

Jimmy ran beside me. "What the hell happened?"

I wiped the blood from my forehead. "Someone tried to make a point and lost."

"Looks like you lost," he said.

One paramedic examined my head and the other ripped my jeans and worked on my leg. "We need to get her to the hospital," the second one said.

Jimmy stood just inside the ambulance. I looked at him and said, "It's the Mayfield SUV. CJF tag. They were following me."

Jimmy dragged his hand across the right side of his forehead and over his eye. "From where?"

"I stopped back at Mayfield after leaving the department. They must have been watching me. Next thing I knew, the SUV is on my ass with its high beams on, so I hit the gas around the curve. They lost control and went down. I circled back. I think I saw a runner." I patted my pockets. "I must have lost my cell phone when I fell."

"You punctured your leg," the paramedic said. "We're taking you to the hospital now."

I tried to sit up and look at my leg. "It's not hurting as much now. I'm fine."

"It could get infected, and you need stitches over your eye," a paramedic said.

"I've had a tetanus shot. Just butterfly my cut. It'll go back together on its own."

"Ryder," Jimmy said.

"I'm okay, chief. I want to—"

"You're going to the ER." He looked at me. "Keys."

"They're still in my Jeep."

"I'll make sure it's at your place when you get home. I'll have Bishop pick you up."

"He needs to rest. I'll take a cab."

He climbed out of the ambulance.

~

THE ER DOCTOR stitched up my cut, had a nurse clean and bandage the puncture wound, then came back and watched as the nurse jabbed me with three shots, tetanus, antibiotics, and a nonnarcotic pain reliever.

"You're good to go," the doctor said. "But take it easy on that leg, and redress it every few hours."

I asked to call for a cab.

"No need," he said. "There's a police officer waiting in the lobby."

Thankfully, it wasn't Bishop.

The officer wanted to help me to my door, but I pushed him aside. "I'm fine, but thanks. Do you have my keys?"

He handed them to me. "Chief wanted me to tell you to stay home."

I laughed. "I bet he did."

When I got home, I walked inside, got undressed, and fell into bed.

I slept four hours, then showered, and other than my throbbing leg and pulsing headache, I felt brand new. I slipped into a clean pair of jeans, my puncture expressing its displeasure about it, and pulled on a white Hamby short-sleeve polo and my only other Hamby windbreaker. My feet ached from running in my Doc Martens, so I opted for a more comfortable boot.

I stopped at the Dunkin' drive-through first, then headed to the Verizon store near the department for a new phone.

The phone lit up with text messages and voice mails as soon as the rep connected it to my number.

I sent Kyle a text. *Had an incident. I'm okay. I'll try to call later. Love you.*

He responded. *Savannah already texted. Be careful with that leg. Love you back.*

Savannah had texted four times. I called her on the quick ride to the office.

"Are you okay? Do you need anything?"

"I'm fine. I mean, I know you love me, but those calls? Kind of stalker-like, Sav."

"You try having a cop for a husband and one for a best friend. I'm lucky I haven't been committed or had shingles."

I laughed. "I'll make sure to let you know I'm okay the next time some idiot tries to run me off the road."

"Are you going to work?"

"What do you think?"

"You're impossible."

"But you love me."

"How's Kyle?"

"He's out of intensive care."

"Perfect. I'll bring Scarlet by. She loves him."

"I've got some things of his at my place. Some jeans, a few shirts, shaving stuff, that kind of thing. There's a bag in my closet. Can you bring him something to change into for when he leaves? I'm worried he'll get released, and I won't be able to get him."

"They won't let him leave naked, but sure thing. Don't overdo it, okay? Text me later."

"Can't make any promises," I said and disconnected the call.

I MET Nikki in the hall as I hobbled toward the investigation room. "I heard what happened." She eyed the stitches on my forehead. "Are you okay?"

"I'm fine." I pointed to the files in her hand. "That from last night? Anything we can use?"

"I just got them all photographed and noted. I'll check them for prints, and if I find any, run them."

"Where are the other files?"

She opened the investigation room door. "In here."

The smell hit me immediately. A familiar wintergreen that reminded me of my grandfather. "Why does it smell like my grandfather in here?"

Michels laughed out loud. I glanced at Levy. She covered her mouth but laughed as well. Bishop was the only one who didn't laugh. I hobbled over to him and sniffed. "Are you wearing Bengay?"

He exhaled. "I got a crick in my back last night. Don't judge." He gave me a once-over. "You could have just called it in."

"That's not who I am."

"Jimmy said you looked rough. He was right. How's the leg?"

I pulled out a chair and eased into it. My leg hurt. "It'll be fine. Catch me up."

"Why don't you go first?" Bishop asked. "Jimmy said it was the same SUV in the videos?"

I explained what had happened.

"And they took off? They weren't hurt?" Levy asked.

"I don't know, but where they went off the road meets up with a small subdivision, so they could have gone anywhere."

Bubba opened the door. "I found—oh, my God." He stared at me. "I didn't realize it was that bad. Why are you here?"

"It's not that bad, but thanks for the confidence boost. I'm here because we have an open investigation."

His eyes widened. "Okay then. I think I've found something." He handed us each a paper. "Luca Santiago."

I studied Bubba's information. "Didn't we interview this guy at Mayfield?"

Bishop examined the photo and nodded. He set the paper down and went through the file notes from the interviews. "Here." He pointed to a photo. "But he doesn't go by Luca Santiago. He goes by—"

Bubba interrupted him. "Lucas Anthony?"

I tilted my head. "That's obviously not a guess."

"Nope," he said.

"How did you figure it out?"

He handed me another image. "First, I checked the interview list and started going through them by hand. Alpharetta brought him in for a lineup a few years ago."

I compared the photos. "These are great."

"Bubba, you rock," Michels said.

"He does," I said.

"It looks like we need to have a conversation with Anthony," Bishop said.

"I'd also like to go to the autopsy," I said. "Unless he's already finished?"

"Barron's been delayed. He said he'll get to it this afternoon," Bishop said.

"What's the delay?"

"Accident off Birmingham Highway. Sixteen-year-old kid blew a stop sign and T-boned a forty-two-year-old woman. They both died on scene."

"Mrs. Riley was supposed to call about Miranda. Has anyone talked to her?"

"I called the hospital. She wasn't admitted. Michels and I went by the parents' house this morning. She was there."

"What did she say?" I asked.

"She reiterated she had no idea how much money was in the safe, but one of the men carried a bag out, and it looked like something was inside."

"All wore black clothing and ski masks," Michels said. "She did say they all had Hispanic accents. She thinks the one who shot her husband was the leader."

"Let me finish," Levy said. "Miranda said the three men broke in, she heard her husband arguing with them, and came downstairs. One guy grabbed her and tied her to a chair. He told her to keep her mouth shut and she'd live while another guy held a gun to Matt Wilson. He threatened to kill her and Lila if Matt didn't do what he said. The third guy just kind of stood there."

"Interesting."

"It gets better. The two guys took Matt to the office and left the one with her, the one that tied her up. All of a sudden, the two with Matt start screaming at each other in Spanish. The one with her runs in there, the arguing continues, and then the leader guy walks Matt back into the main area. He's got the gun rammed into his back, but the guy who didn't tie her up was right behind him. They yelled at each other in Spanish, then the one holding the gun on Matt walked in front of him and shot him in the leg. He took off through the front door, the second guy following, and then the third guy ran out from the office with the bag. He looked at her, then ran out."

"So, something happened in that office that stopped them from getting what they came for," I said.

"That's what we think," Michels said. "We just don't know why they killed Wilson."

"Other than some home improvement files she had given her husband, she didn't know anything about the papers in the office," Levy said.

"I gave them a list of the jewelry," Nikki said.

"And she said it was all there," Levy said.

"Did you ask her about the swingers group?"

"Claims to know nothing about it."

"Do you believe her?"

"Fifty-fifty," she said.

I turned to Michels.

"Same. Her mother was with her. If she is involved, she probably didn't want to mention it in front of her."

"Speaking of," Levy said. "Her mother was going there to get some of their things, but the wife doesn't think she'll go back." She pointed to a key on the table. "But she gave us permission if necessary."

"Can you two follow up with the homes near the Wilsons' to see if anyone can add anything to the officer interviews last night? Talk to Wallace, too. See if he's got anything on video. You know what to do." He glanced at me. "We'll call the course manager and see if this Luca person's been around."

After everyone else left, I said, "You know he's gone."

"I know, but we still have to check." Bishop handed me a pair of gloves and pointed to the three boxes with Wilson scribbled on them. "Start going through these. I'll call the golf club manager."

LUCAS ANTHONY HADN'T WORKED at Mayfield in months. According to the manager, his mother was ill, and he went back home to be with her.

"Another dead end," I said.

"And no firm connection to the sex club," Bishop added.

"It's there," I said. "I'll talk to Miranda again. I'll get her to tell the truth."

"Right now, we need to go through these files. The men didn't toss the room for shits and giggles."

"Shits and giggles." I read through a file with one-page summaries on various cryptocurrencies and mumbled, "I don't understand any of this stuff."

"I might not know about digital cash, but I know how investing works." He closed a file and moved on to another one. "Whoa. This is big."

"What?"

"The Wilsons are going into foreclosure." He scanned the paper and handed it to me. "They're three months late on their mortgage."

I skimmed the letter then handed it back to Bishop. I walked over to a clean whiteboard and jotted some things down. "What if Wilson needed cash, so he hires Perez and Garcia to rob his friends. They give him the cash, he gives them a cut, maybe lets them keep the jewelry? Then Perez is killed, Wilson finds out Garcia killed Perez and tells Garcia their game is over, but Garcia's worried Wilson will give him up, so he kills him."

Bishop raised an eyebrow. "And left without the money?"

"Miranda Wilson said the men were arguing. Maybe the other guy didn't want Garcia to kill Wilson. They argued, and Garcia did it anyway." I shook the dry-erase marker to draw out more ink, but it was dry, so I grabbed another one. "Or it's one of the other victims. Maybe, like Michels said, someone had issues with the swapping, and wanted Wilson dead, but had the other homes robbed to draw attention away from him or her as a suspect?"

"I like it," he said. He exhaled through his nose. "Garcia thinks he's in the clear, so he decides to get back involved. He talks to Perez and says he wants back in, but Perez's already got someone to replace him, and says no. Garcia kills him, argues with the other guy, then kills Wilson to keep him quiet, too."

I'd been skimming papers as we spoke. "Take a look at this." I handed him a paper with a short list of numbers, all written by hand. "I think they're bank account numbers."

He reviewed the document. "I think you're right." He glanced at the pile of papers in front of me. "Anything else in there? Maybe a general register with a list of names and dollar amounts?"

I laughed. "This isn't the 1930s."

He handed back the paper. I counted how many were on the list. "There's only six. They could be his."

"Where was it?"

"In a home remodeling file." I lightly patted the bandage under my jeans and grimaced. "What if it's Wilson? What if there were supposed to be two more invasions, and these are the accounts where the money is?"

"He'd have himself robbed to make him look like a victim and not the thief," Bishop said.

"But Garcia gets pissed and ends it all by killing Wilson."

He mumbled a long number. "My bank account number is twelve numbers. These are different sizes."

I counted mine in my head. "Mine is nine." We put the rest of the files aside. "Let's see what Bubba can do with them." I dialed Bubba's extension.

I asked if he had a minute when he answered.

"Sure. You still in the room?"

"We are."

"Be right there."

My cell phone rang. Barron's name flashed on my caller ID. I greeted him with, "You haven't started yet, have you?"

"Good day to you, too, Detective Ryder. No. Nikki asked me to contact you thirty minutes before, so that's what I'm doing."

"We'll be there," I said. "But it may be more like forty-five. Please don't start without us."

"The deceased can wait, but I'm not as patient."

"We're just finishing something, and then we'll be on our way. I promise."

"Looking forward to seeing you," he said.

Bubba entered. "What's up?"

Bishop handed him the document. "Think you can figure out what these are?"

He looked at the numbers and nodded. "That's easy. They're bank account numbers."

"We thought the same, but how can you be sure?" I asked.

"Most bank account numbers consist of between eight and twelve numbers, and these look to align with that."

"Can you figure out the account holder's name by the account number?"

"Yeah, I mean, with the bank routing numbers, and we'd need a warrant obviously. Do you have the routing numbers?"

"Not sure yet," I said. I pointed to the stack of files. "We're not finished going through the files."

"How easy would it be to pull up information on a wealth management company?" Bishop asked.

Blahut?

"Very. Which one?"

"Spectrum Group."

"Sure thing, and I'll see what I can dig up on those account numbers, but I won't get anything from the banks without a warrant."

After he left, I said, "Blahut?"

"He's a money guy. Money guys get greedy."

I called Zach Christopher on my way to the morgue.

"Detective," he said. "I understand we have a possible murder victim. Any movement on the investigation?"

"We're working on it." I briefed him on the details, adding, "I'd prefer a warrant for the Wilson bank accounts over permission from the wife."

"I can do that," he said.

"And Blahut's a wealth manager for a company called Spectrum Group. Can we get a warrant for his accounts?"

"Just because he's a wealth manager? That won't fly."

"Someone doesn't handwrite account numbers on a piece of paper and stuff it into a home improvement brochure for no reason. We're looking for information connecting the four families, particularly a match to even just one of the account numbers or any solid associations with Matt Wilson."

"So, warrants for the homes as well?"

"Yes."

"And you think you can find a paper trail doing that?" he asked.

"Hopefully," I said. "Listen, I know it's a long shot, but Bishop and I feel strongly that we're heading in the right direction."

"That's not a lot to go on. It'll be hard to convince a judge." He exhaled. "This is slim at best. Can't you get me anything else?"

"We're working on it," I said.

"Fine. I'll see what I can do."

"That's great," I said. "You've got my number."

14

No one liked viewing an autopsy, even from a window, but being in the room while the coroner performed one was an entirely different story. Bishop put on two masks to prepare for the rank, pungent, sticky-sweet smell of the dead body. I couldn't say I was used to the stench, but I did have a strong stomach. A mixture of blood, decay, disease, sweat, dirty feet, and chemicals piggybacked the stench of death riding on the stale air of the room. Bodies in metal drawers stacked one on top of another were a constant reminder that the next heartbeat could be the last. Death wasn't a fine wine; it didn't improve with age.

Bishop gagged, quickly learning—again—two masks weren't better than one. "Dear God."

Goosebumps formed on my forearms; the room's temperature was colder than usual. "Toughen up, old guy." I'd worn a mask, but only at the request of Dr. Barron. I stepped close to Matt Wilson's body. "This smell is particularly disgusting. Why is that?"

"Body chemistry," he said. "Every body secretes a unique smell buried deep inside the normal smells of death. Sometimes they're stronger than others. This one has a mix of sulfur, blood, sweat, rotting flesh, and cologne." He sniffed the air. "Something musky, I think."

"No need to go into so much detail, doc," Bishop said.

Barron laughed. "It's my job."

"I smell feet," I said.

"Not uncommon."

Matt Wilson's gray remains lay on the table, his body slack from the lack of life inside it. The bullet hole in his thigh revealed torn muscle and severed skin hanging from the bone like a torn flag.

Barron had drawn a blue circle around the wound. He hadn't lied. He wasn't patient. He'd already done a cursory examination of the body. "I found something foreign in his hair." He turned toward the metal cart behind him and removed a small baggie. He handed it to Bishop.

"It's a hair," Bishop said.

"A black one," he said. He pointed to Wilson's head. "His hair is blond."

"The family had blond hair," Bishop said. "Can we run a DNA test on this?"

"Already planning on it."

"Garcia has black hair," I said.

"Most Latino men do," Bishop said.

"I know, but we can see if the DNA matches the DNA he gave voluntarily."

"Right. Christopher said we'd need additional evidence tying Garcia to the crimes if we wanted to use that DNA from before. This would work."

Barron cleared his throat. "Now, after my initial review, and given the bullet found on scene," He winked. "I can say the victim was shot with a nine-millimeter at close range."

"That's what we expected," I said.

"It gets better. The bullet appears to have entered at an angle, which leads me to believe the shooter was standing in front of the victim and aiming down, like this." He walked around the exam table, stood in front of Bishop, and pretended to shoot his leg. "Bang! When I get inside, I'll be able to better determine the distance, but given the damage, I suspect it was at close range." He walked back to the other side of the table and removed a knife from the cart behind him. "Let's see what we find inside."

"Hold up." Bishop took two steps back. "I don't think we need to be here for this." He jerked his head toward the door. "Ryder?"

Bishop barely tolerated the slicing. I couldn't say I was a fan of watching a person be fileted and dissected, but the scientific part of it fascinated me. I smiled at Barron. "Mr. Weak Stomach needs to go. Will you let us know your findings?"

"Already the plan." He shifted his eyes to Bishop. "Rob, I got myself a boar this weekend. Good meat on the thing. I can bring you some loin chops if you're interested." He turned toward me and winked again.

Bishop's face paled. "I'm good, but thanks."

I held the door open for Bishop. "Thanks, Dr. Barron."

"Any time."

As we walked out, I said, "Christopher will use the DNA now that we've got a hair to match to Garcia's blood."

"I agree. Let's see if we can get a match."

I turned back around and opened the door. "Hey, doc? Can we get a rush on that hair?"

"Yes, ma'am."

I tried both Stacey Turner's and Rosy's numbers. Both went straight to voice mail. "Let's run by the Turners' house. I'm worried they need a wellness check."

"I like that."

Stacey Turner answered the door dressed in a silk camisole nightgown and a flimsy short robe tied loosely around her waist. Bishop cleared his throat and stared at the ground. Her voice was deep, and her accent was stronger than Savannah's. "Yes?"

I showed her my badge. "We'd like to talk to you about the recent incidents in the community."

Her eyes widened. She glanced at her robe, and then to Bishop standing there turning redder by the second. She pulled the robe tightly across her body. "Uh, sure. Come on in. I'll get Xavier, and just change right quick." She directed us to the main sitting area. The home's layout was identical to the Wilsons'.

She returned and said, "Xavier will be right up. He works in the basement office. He's a touch on the messy side, and I just can't have that kind of distraction staring at me every day." She sat in an oversized leather chair across from the couch. That thing wouldn't have fit through my front door. "Now, I'm happy to help, but I can't see what benefit I would be to your investigation. It is terribly sad, what's happened to Matt Wilson. He was such a lovely man."

Xavier Turner appeared behind her. He cleared his throat. "Officers. My wife tells me you're here about Matt Wilson?"

"We understand you had a party a few weeks ago, and we'd like to know if the Wilsons attended."

Stacey's shoulders curved inward.

Xavier sat on the arm of her chair. "Just a small gathering of friends, not a party, but yes. The Wilsons were here. Such a shame, what happened to Matt."

"Are you close to the Wilsons?" I asked.

"We're friendly," he said.

Once he'd walked in, Stacey went silent. "Mrs. Turner, are you close to Miranda Wilson?"

"We're friendly as well."

Xavier pulled the invisible leash around his wife's neck tight.

"Yet you invited them to your small gathering of friends?"

"We thought it would be nice to get to know them better," Xavier said. "I'm sorry we won't have that opportunity now."

"Did they leave with different partners?" I asked.

Bishop adjusted his position on the couch.

Xavier smirked. "I'm not sure I understand what you're asking."

The fact that he'd reiterated that contradicted its truth. "I think you know exactly what I'm asking." I eyed Stacey. She wouldn't make eye contact.

"Officer—I'm sorry. I didn't get your name."

"Ryder, and Bishop, my partner. Mr. Turner, we're not here to judge. We're trying to solve a murder."

"A murder you think is somehow connected to our gathering?"

"You mean your swingers group? Yes."

"X, think of poor Miranda. Just tell them," Stacey said.

Good for her.

Xavier's face reddened. His lips settled into a fine, thin line, but he regrouped quickly. "They left together."

"Have you had them at parties before?" I asked.

"It was their first."

"Did they understand the reason for the party?"

"We did not invite people to our homes merely to trade partners, detective, but if the opportunity presents itself, we don't discourage, and yes, we explain the possibilities when we invite someone. It's how the group works. Everyone must approve the couples suggested before they're even approached."

"Understood," I said. "When partners do trade, do you provide rooms, or do they leave with keys?" I watched his wife for her reaction. She looked to him and then to her hands. She'd run out of courage.

"It depends," he said.

"What did the Wilsons choose?"

"There was an incident with Miranda and Lisa Blahut. Not sexual. An argument. The Wilsons left without participating."

"She was very upset," Stacey said. "We haven't talked since, and I just feel terrible about that."

"Who else attended?"

His chest heaved. "I'm not comfortable saying. We prefer to keep the group participants' identities private."

"I'm happy to get a warrant, bring ten or twelve squads here. Your neighbors have been watching everything lately. I'm sure they'll be interested."

He exhaled. "Alan and Lisa Blahut, Jared and Kelsey Kelley, and like the Wilsons, Tyler and Amber Morgensen were invited for the first time."

"They didn't stay," Stacey said.

"Have you had any issues with group members?" I asked.

"Other than the argument between Lisa and Miranda, none," he said.

"Speaking of Blahut," Bishop said. "Do you invest through his company?"

"Spectrum?" He shook his head. "I looked into it, but Alan advised against it."

"He advised against investing through the company he works for?"

"He's leaving. Said the company isn't on the up and up, and he hooked me up with someone online." He raised an eyebrow. "What does this have to do with the investigation?"

"We're just doing our job."

"Lisa Blahut and Miranda Wilson argued," I said. "Maybe a lovers' quarrel?"

"Or jealousy over a hookup with a husband?"

"Turner said they didn't stick around for that, but he could have lied," I said.

"Miranda could have paid Garcia and his goons to break into the homes and then kill her husband."

"And made up the story about the argument," I added. "So she could keep her money and jewelry."

"What about the possible account numbers?" he asked.

"They could be nothing, or she could have put the money in them," I said. "But she doesn't strike me as that aggressive."

"They're the ones that usually are."

Michels and Levy called. "Nothing to report," Levy said. "No one in this damn community has a security system."

We updated them on what we learned.

"Wow, if that's the case, Miranda's a good actor," Levy said.

"What do you want us to do?" Michels asked.

"Go home," Bishop said. "Jimmy's going to flip over our overtime hours."

I wanted to check on Kyle and see if Savannah had brought Scarlet by, but it was late, and I didn't want to wake him. Bishop turned the opposite direction of the station. "Where are you going?" I asked.

To the Carniceria Hernandez. "Maybe the nice lady you met there will have something to say."

The parking lot was empty, and the woman from before was flipping the door sign to closed again when she saw me. She opened the door and sighed.

"She's in the back. She has nowhere to go. I told her she can't stay here and ruin my business."

"We'll handle it," I said.

We walked to the back of the store and walked into the back room.

Rosy shook her head when she saw us. "I can't. He'll kill me."

Bishop closed the door and stood behind Rosy. I stood in front of her, both of us barriers to either exit.

"Perez is dead, but you already know that, don't you?"

"He forced me. He said he would kill me."

"Garcia?"

"Si."

"He forced you to do what? Call us about Perez?"

"He threatened to kill my family."

"Why did he want you to call us?"

"He said Perez would pay for what he did. That is all I know. I didn't know he would kill him."

"You think he did?" I asked.

"Si."

Bishop moved next to me. "What do you know about the home invasions?" Bishop asked.

Her eyes widened. "I can't."

"Yes," I said. "You have to, Rosy. Another man was murdered last night, and we think your boyfriend killed him."

"He will kill me and my family."

"I promise, we'll do what we can to keep you safe from Garcia."

Tears slid down her cheeks. "I heard him talking to someone on the phone before the first one. He said he had three other people to help, and that they agreed to the payment amount."

"Do you know who he was talking to?"

"No. But he sounded American."

"Were they on speaker?" Bishop asked.

"No. No. I heard the man. His voice was very loud. He was very upset."

"What was he upset about?" I asked.

"He said they were supposed to have done it already. That's when Santos said he was ready."

"Did either of them say the words home invasion, or break-in, or Mayfield?" Bishop asked.

"No. The man said to get it done, then Santos threw his phone on the ground. I picked it up. It wasn't his phone. It was a different one."

I glanced at Bishop. "Burner."

He agreed.

"Has he said anything about the invasions since then?" I asked.

"No. He only said Perez screwed him, and he would pay. Then he made me call you."

She bent her head into her hands and sobbed.

I ASKED an office assistant to set Rosy up comfortably in one of the conference rooms while Bishop and I talked with Jimmy.

"You brought me in for a woman involved in a potential murder?" He leaned back in his chair. "And you want to give her protection?" He shook his head. "It's not happening."

I explained what she had told us.

"She can't verify who Garcia was talking to on the phone?"

"No, but he's threatened her, so it's pretty clear," Bishop said.

"What's clear is she's afraid of Garcia, and that's not enough to warrant protection." He leaned forward and dipped his chin toward his chest.

"Chief," Bishop said. "Garcia's involved. And we believe the invasions were setups to cover the real job he was hired to do. Murder Wilson."

"The hair's a match. Bring him in. We don't need a *he said she said* from the girlfriend." He looked me in the eyes. "Let her go. If she gives us something solid on Garcia, I'll put her up in the hotel down the street."

"Chief," I said. "We really need—"

"I know what you need, detective, but the money train's left the station." He checked his watch and groaned. "From now on, unless it's an emergency, don't pull me away from my family."

"Great," I said and charged out of the room. Bishop followed and pulled me into his cubby. "I told you he wouldn't go for it."

I removed the clip on my bun and let my hair fall. It made my lingering headache worse. "She's got to know more." I turned around and walked out of his cubby. "Come on."

We grabbed three waters and met with Rosy.

"We think you know more," I said.

"I don't," she said. "I don't."

A lawyer could drown her statements in reasonable doubt. We needed something concrete, something to convince Jimmy. "I need you to take a moment and think hard about what he said. Did he mention any other names? Locations? Anything?"

"No," she said. Her eyes widened. "He's going to kill me!"

I eyed Bishop then smiled at Rosy. "Give us a moment, okay? We'll be right back."

Outside of the conference room, Bishop said, "We need to know who Garcia talked to before Jimmy will protect her."

"We can't just drop her off at home. Garcia might have someone watching her. We could lead her right to the morgue."

"There's nothing we can do about that."

"We can keep her for forty-eight hours without arresting her."

Bishop exhaled. "We don't even have any possible charges. We have to let her go. We can't help her."

"I can." I opened the door to the conference room before Bishop could stop me.

"No way," Bishop said when I told him my plan. He didn't support it, but he couldn't change my mind. "He'll suspend you for this."

"I'd never get anything done if I worried about that."

He dragged his hand down the side of his face. "Damn it, Ryder. Why the hell do you always drag me into your shit?"

"I'm not dragging you into anything. Go home, Bishop."

❧

I SHOWED Rosy around my townhouse.

"It's so big. You live here by yourself?"

"Well, I have Louie, so I'm not alone."

"Louie?"

I guided her toward him. "My fish." I tapped on the glass, and he swam over. "Hey little guy, this is Rosy. She's going to be staying here. You keep her company, okay?"

"Are you leaving?" she asked. Tears pooled in her eyes.

I exhaled. "I need you to tell me where you think Garcia might be."

Her jaw stiffened. "He sometimes stays with Elisa Ortega. La puta."

The whore? "Where does la puta live?" I had a feeling she'd know the address by heart, and she hadn't let me down.

Her bottom lip quivered. "What if something happens?"

"Give me your phone." I added dispatch as a contact. "If something does, you call them first. You tell them you're at Detective Ryder's townhouse, okay? Then you call me right after. You understand?"

"Yes."

"Do not call anyone, and only answer if I call. Do you understand?"

"Si."

"Okay. Stay here. I'll be right back." I pushed my leg too far running upstairs and limped to my bedroom. I grabbed some sweats and a sweatshirt from my drawer, then snatched my wedding ring from my jewelry box and put it in my safe. I closed my door behind me.

I took the stairs slow and handed her the clothing. "Here. There's a bathroom with a shower upstairs. Sleep in the room across from it, okay?"

"Okay."

"I'll be in touch soon," I said. "Keep the doors locked and don't let anyone in unless they show you a badge. Got it?"

"Yes."

"I'll lock the door. Don't open the garage door for anyone."

"Okay."

Bishop's vehicle blocked me from pulling out of my garage. "I told you not to come."

"Did she tell you anything more?"

"Garcia's got another girlfriend."

He sighed. "I'll drive."

I climbed into his vehicle and clipped the seatbelt around me. "No call from Christopher yet about the warrants isn't a good thing."

"We'll see. We're not his only case." He pulled out of my driveway.

"I know, but this is important."

"He'll call when he has something to tell us."

~

Elisa Ortega lived on the second floor of an older apartment complex off Milton Parkway. One side of her building bordered an old cemetery, the other, a building identical to hers along with several rows of matching buildings layered behind it. Parking lots in front and behind the buildings provided little distance between them. Bishop rolled into a stop directly in front of her building.

"Are you sure about this?" I asked.

"I'm your partner. We're in this together."

"Okay."

The exterior walk-ups to each apartment offered no security. We walked right over to her unit. Bishop knocked.

A short, dark-haired woman with thick black eyeliner and long false lashes answered. She was either pregnant or had a basketball-sized tumor in her belly. When she saw us, she tried to slam the door shut. Bishop was prepared and stuck his foot in front of it.

"He's not here," she said.

"Are you Elisa Ortega?" I asked.

"Santos is gone. I don't know where he is."

"When did he leave?" Bishop asked.

"A few hours ago."

"Do you know where he went?"

"No."

"Did he tell you to say that?" Bishop asked.

She shook her head. "He tells me nothing."

"Did someone pick him up?" Bishop asked.

"No. He took my car."

"What's the make and model?" I asked.

"A Honda Odyssey. It's silver. I don't know the year."

"Is it older or newer?" I asked.

"Older. Has some dents."

"Is it in your name?"

She looked down and to the right.

"Who owns the vehicle?" Bishop asked.

"My sister."

Bishop wrote down her sister's name. "Do you know the tag number?"

"No."

I pointed to her belly. "The baby his?" She blinked. I took that as a yes. I handed her my card. "Miss Ortega, next time you see Mr. Garcia, tell him we'd like to have a chat."

She took the card. Bishop moved his foot, and she slammed the door shut.

"Rosy's better off," Bishop said.

"For many reasons." I led the way down the stairs and back to the parking lot. My leg hurt, but the pain had eased a little.

Just as we reached the front of the vehicle, a flash of light and a pop exploded from behind it.

I ducked down and immediately removed my weapon from its holster.

Bishop yelled, "On the right," and ducked behind the right front of his vehicle. I drew my weapon as I took the left. Two more shots fired. One hit the metal light pole behind me, the ding vibrating in my ears. I moved slowly, stood, and aimed. A second later, a man appeared behind a vehicle a lane over, and aimed his gun in my direction.

I fired off a shot. He dropped to the ground. I ducked down again and waited. Footsteps pounded the pavement as the guy headed toward the cemetery. "Shit! I've got him," I said and took off after him.

I couldn't run far. My leg wouldn't hold up. I yelled for the man to stop, knowing it was totally useless. He'd propelled himself over the cemetery fence without missing a beat. I slowed, then grabbed on to the metal bar and threw myself over. I hit the ground hard, almost losing my footing, but I caught my balance. Blood seeped through my jeans. "Damn it." I tried to catch up with the guy, dodging battered and broken headstones in the dark.

The seconds ticked off like minutes. Where were the damn sirens? Why hadn't Bishop called in the shooter?

I tripped over a small headstone, my leg gave out, and I fell to the ground. I caught a glimpse of the man cresting a hill with a large mausoleum at the top. He paused for a moment then went left.

I'd deal with the pain because I wouldn't let him get away. I could run forward, having to sidestep rows of tombstones, or cut left and run a straight line. I risked losing him either way, but at least going left would allow me to run faster.

I jumped over a freshly dug grave, tumbled into a somersault, and screamed as my wound stretched across my leg. I sucked in a breath and forced myself to get up and run. Tears fell from my eyes. I cut right and darted in between buried bodies before getting my eyes back on the runner. He was close, only two rows away. As he ran the border of graves, I aimed my weapon and screamed, "Stop or I'll shoot."

He skidded to a stop just before an open grave. His arms flailed. He lost his balance, and I thought for sure he'd fall into the empty grave. I hobbled toward him, but he jumped over the hole and sprinted into the darkness.

I skidded to a stop. I'd lost him. "Shit!" Sweat poured from my hairline. I bent forward, gasping for air, then got on my radio and made the call. "Suspect on the loose. Latino male. Five-five to five-eight, approximately 150 pounds. Jeans and a dark sweatshirt. Not sure if it's blue or black. Last seen in cemetery located next to Hamby Apartments."

Dispatch responded, "Ten-four. I've tracked your location." The line fell silent for a moment and then she got back on the radio and requested assistance.

A gunshot ripped through the air. I held my breath waiting for another one or for Bishop to clear himself to dispatch. Instead, a loud ringing screeched from the radio. "Bishop!" I took off running, the pain in my leg nothing compared to the panic in my heart.

BY THE TIME I had Bishop in my line of sight, he had cleared the tone and was providing details to dispatch, then requested a crime scene tech. He leaned against the side of his vehicle. I crashed into the other side and rushed to him. He held a bloody white hand towel over his left shoulder.

"Which way?"

He pointed toward the front of the complex. I flipped around and surveyed the area. Identical apartment buildings facing all different directions provided numerous opportunities for escape.

"Your leg," he said. "Stop. Shooter's too far out. You'll bleed out before you find him."

"I didn't catch the other one either." Breathless and panting, I asked, "What the hell happened?"

He looked like a ghost, pale and clammy from pain and sweat. "Someone shot me."

"No shit, Sherlock." I gently moved his hand from the cloth. "Let me take a look."

"It's only a graze, but damn if it doesn't piss me off."

He was right. A bullet had ripped through his jacket and shirt, grazed the side of his shoulder, and continued its trajectory. "Give me your keys and take off your jacket."

"They're somewhere near the back end. I dropped them when I drew my gun." He laughed. "Heard them hit the pavement, but I had other things on my mind at the time."

I found them near the inside of a back tire. I opened the trunk and removed his trauma kit. Sirens howled in the distance. I ripped Bishop's shirt to reveal the wound. It wasn't as bad as the blood made it look. As I cleaned the small wound, two Hamby patrol officers arrived.

They jumped out of their vehicles and ran to us.

"Your leg," the one said.

"I've got it," I said, "Two shooters. One took off into the cemetery. The other went toward the front of the complex. Watch for a silver Honda Odyssey. Don't know the year but it's an earlier model and has dents."

One said, "We'll be on the lookout, detective," and they headed back to their vehicles as an ambulance siren howled close by.

"Take care of your leg first," Bishop said.

I used my knife and cut the leg off my jeans and wrapped the wound in gauze.

"Peachy," Bishop said.

I swiped a large alcohol pad over his wound.

He whined. "Ouch! That hurts."

"My leg's about to self-amputate and you're complaining about a boo-boo on your shoulder?"

"I feel like an ass. I should have never activated the emergency tone."

"Two men are out there, running loose with weapons. We need our people on alert."

Jimmy called my cell. I put him on speaker. "For the love of God, Ryder, what happened now?"

"We got a lead on Garcia. He's got someone watching us, Jimmy. Two men shot at us. Bishop took a bullet to the shoulder, but it's superficial."

"He needs to go in. It's procedure. Your leg?"

"Bad," Bishop said.

"It's fine," I said. "I'll need a ride." I glanced at Bishop's tires. Two had been stabbed with steak knives. "And a tow truck."

"I'll send both," he said and disconnected.

"Make them take you to an urgent care. You'll get out of there faster. Nikki should be here any minute. I'll stick around for a while, but I've got to get back to Rosy." As the ambulance rolled up, I asked, "Did you get a good look at the shooter?"

"No. He was somewhere over there I think." He pointed between two buildings. "I never saw him."

A department van arrived, and a part-time tech stepped out, not Nikki.

"Shit," I said. "We've got the nerdy kid who can't lift a print to save his life."

The paramedics rushed to me first. "I just need it cleaned and dressed." I pointed to Bishop. "He's been shot."

"Grazed," he said. He watched the part-time tech kid almost fall over from the weight of his equipment bag. "Nikki's probably maxed on overtime, so we get Harold."

The paramedic poured antiseptic onto a cloth and pressed it carefully over my wound. "Oh," I said. "That stings."

Dispatch disrupted my whining. "All units we have 10-32 with a possible BD." She gave the location.

Bishop's eyes widened. "That's your place."

"Rosy."

15

Patrol vehicles lined my small street. The officer who'd given us a ride to my place pulled in front of my driveway and let us out. A crowd of officers blocked my front entrance, and a group of neighbors stood to the side trying to get a glimpse of the action.

I limped over to nosy neighbors and showed them my badge. "This is a crime scene. I need you all to back off." When no one moved, I yelled, "Now!"

I heard one man say, "Cop that lives there needs to move the hell out."

Apparently, I was a hit with my neighbors.

Bishop cleared the way to my front door. Rosy Lopez lay on my small porch with a hole in her chest. He turned to me, hung his head, and shook it.

Three paramedics worked on her, one covering the bleeding while the others administered CPR. Rosy lying there was on me. She knew it would happen, but I'd convinced her I'd keep her safe, and I failed. Her death was my fault.

Bishop grabbed my arm and pulled me toward the garage. "Don't go there, Rach. Just don't."

I shook him off and rubbed the tears in my eyes with my sleeve. "Why not?" I smacked my hands into my chest. "I did it! I caused this!"

A paramedic yelled, "We got a pulse!"

Thank God.

The paramedics rushed her off to the hospital. When Michels and Levy arrived, they delivered a message from Jimmy. Bishop was to go to the hospital, and they couldn't let me anywhere near the scene.

Levy escorted me to the other side of my garage. "You okay?"

I pressed my back against my metal garage door and closed my eyes. Reporters had begun arriving, but I ignored their questions. "No. I need to know what happened."

"I can't, Rach."

Taylor Cooke charged over. "What happened?" She looked at me. "This is your place?"

"Detective Michels and I are handling this," Levy said. "Give us a chance to get our bearings, okay?"

"What about you?" She asked me.

I took a deep breath and said to Levy, "My Jeep's at the station."

"On it." She whistled for an officer.

VISITING HOURS WERE OVER, and Kyle was asleep. The nurse at the desk looked me up and down and raised an eyebrow. "You okay?" The ripped jeans and blood stained down my leg bothered her.

I showed her my badge. "I'll be fine."

"I'm not sure about that. Let me take a look at you."

"May I see Kyle first, please?"

She pursed her lips. "Five minutes, but don't wake him. If he does it on his own, fine."

"Thanks," I said and dragged myself to his room.

I stared down at him. His bruises had begun to lighten to a greenish, baby-puke color. They'd removed all the tubes and wires connected to him except the one attached to the saline bag. I brushed my hand against the side of his face.

His eyes opened, and he smiled. "Hey." He squinted. "You look almost as bad as me."

"It's been a day."

"What happened to your leg?"

"It's a long story." I smiled. "For another time. Did Savannah come by?"

"I can't believe how much Scarlet's changed since I left. Oh, she brought my things. Thanks for that."

"I didn't want them to send you home naked."

He scooted to the right side of his small bed. Kyle stood just over six-two. He was lean, but muscular, and his broad shoulders didn't leave a lot of space on the bed. "Crawl up here."

"The nurse said five minutes."

"Don't worry. She loves me."

I bet she did. I crawled onto the bed and jerked away when he groaned. "Did I hurt you?"

"No, no. I'm fine." He lifted his arm, and I nestled my head against his side. "Tell me what happened."

I closed my eyes and completely relaxed for the first time since he'd left. "I'll tell you in a minute."

∿

The nurse nudged me awake. "I'll let you stay here," she said. "You've got to let me look at your injuries."

I sat up "Okay."

She handed me a pair of scrubs. "They're not all that sexy, but they're clean. Take a shower. Come get me when you're ready. I'll have a look, and then let you get back to business." She wiggled her finger at Kyle. "Not *that* kind of business."

Kyle smiled. "Yes, Nurse Ratched."

She winked at him and left the room.

The dried blood on my leg turned the small shower floor red. I stood under the water until it ran clear again. I used the shampoo and soap Savannah had brought for Kyle, then dried off with the hand towel hanging on the rod. It hurt to bend down and pull the pants over my leg, but I did it.

My cell phone dinged. It was from Jimmy. I hoped it was about Rosy, but it wasn't.

Eight AM. My office.

I walked out of the bathroom and looked at Kyle. "I'm in trouble."

"What did you do?"

"A possible witness was shot at my place tonight. I don't know if she made it. I wasn't there."

"Why was a witness at your place?"

"I thought she'd be safe there."

"Who just texted you?"

"Jimmy."

"Call him."

He answered on the first ring. "What the hell were you thinking?" He wasn't on speaker, but Kyle could hear him anyway.

"I was thinking she needed protection."

"She's in a medically induced coma because of that protection, Rachel."

My jaw tensed. He was right, but he didn't have to rub it in. "I didn't have any other option."

"You defied a direct order." He breathed loudly into the phone. "Tomorrow morning, eight a.m. My office. I'm serious, Ryder. Don't be late." He ended the call.

"He's not happy," Kyle said.

I cringed. "Nope, but I deserve it. I screwed up." I texted Levy and asked if it was okay for me to go home.

She responded right away. *Yes. Call Bishop. He has news.*

I woke him. He answered on the third ring. "Christopher called. He got the warrants, but not for any bank accounts. Just the homes."

"That's good news," I said.

"You screwed up, Rachel. Jimmy's pissed."

"What about you? I'll make sure he knows you weren't involved."

"But I was."

"I'm sorry."

"It's fine. He got on me for not going straight to the hospital, but that's it so far."

"I'll be in at eight," I said.

"Be prepared. The shit's gonna hit the fan." He ended the call.

"Tell me," Kyle said.

I exhaled and told him the story.

"Jimmy could fire you for that."

"He won't do that. He needs me."

"Don't walk in with that ego tomorrow. It won't go over well."

"I know. I know I screwed up, and I take responsibility for it."

"That's great, but it doesn't erase the fact that a woman is fighting for her life right now." He held my hand.

I used his brush to work the tangles from my hair and let it hang down my back.

"May I make a suggestion?" he asked.

"Of course."

"When you see him tomorrow, be humble."

Humility wasn't one of my finer points.

～

ROSY'S BLOOD stained my brick porch and hit me like a sucker punch to my gut. I stared down at it, remembering exactly how Rosy lay there lifeless as the paramedics fought to bring her back.

Because of me.

The fact that she was alive was something, but when I'd asked Kyle's nurse if a medically induced coma meant something positive, she'd said things could go either way, and without knowing the situation, she didn't think offering a medical opinion was appropriate. I took that as bad news.

I'd hoped for her to ease my guilt, but the truth was, nothing would. I'd done what I thought was the right thing, but good intentions didn't make it okay.

I walked back to the garage, unlocked the door to the inside, and hit the garage door button to close the big door.

They'd left on every light in the house. My frying pan and a mixing bowl sat on my kitchen counter, and an unopened bottled water next to the stove. Rosy had wanted to cook herself something, but all I had was that half-eaten bag of carrots. Is that why she was on the front porch? Because she was hungry? Was she going to the store, or had someone come over, and she answered the door? Was there a struggle? I hadn't been able to check her fingers or hands for signs.

I knew they could have followed us, yet I left her there, defenseless. I stared down at the pan in the kitchen. I lived near the quaint oldtown area of Hamby, walking distance from stores and restaurants. She must have thought she'd be safe walking to get groceries. I put the pan back under the counter, wiped down the mixing bowl, and placed it on the shelf.

Knowing the comfort my shower provided, I decided to take another one, and stripped out of the blue scrubs Nurse Ratched had given me. She'd cleaned and redressed my wound, then taped plastic over the bandages to help prevent bleed-through.

The shower felt good, but it didn't relieve my guilt. I knew I wouldn't sleep, and there wasn't enough time before I had to meet with Jimmy anyway.

Savannah called at six. "You okay?"

"I could be better," I said. "Is Jimmy home?"

"No. He went in early." She blew a breath into the phone. "He's going to drop you to records. Please don't tell him I said that."

I laughed. "Records? You've got to be kidding. That's a total waste of my skills."

"Just let him do what he has to do. Once he cools off, I'm sure everything will be fine."

"I appreciate the notice," I said.

Less than an hour later I was at the department, walking through the pit to my cubby. The officers sitting at desks stopped and watched me. One cleared his throat and shook his head.

Word traveled fast when you screwed up as bad as I had.

Jimmy stepped out of his office. His face and neck were all red. He pointed to me. "You. In here. Now."

I took a deep breath and walked into his office. "I know you said—"

He stood behind his desk with his arms crossed. "No," he said, cutting me off. "You don't get to give me excuses. You housed a potential witness in your home." He spoke through a clenched jaw and gritted teeth. "Your goddamn home, Ryder." He dropped his head and shook it, then said, "Not only have you set the city, yourself, me, and everyone associated with the damn investigation up for a lawsuit, you've jeopardized the integrity of the entire case, and now we've got a woman in a coma on our dime."

"I didn't have another choice."

His cold eyes glared at me. "Don't try and blame this on me—"

I interrupted him. "I'm not. I'm just saying—"

He shoved a pointed finger toward me. "You defied a direct order. You're lucky I don't fire you for insubordination." He grabbed a paper off his desk and waved it at me. "You're working records indefinitely."

Savannah had been right. I laughed. "You can't be serious."

He flung the paper at me, but it landed on the edge of his desk. "I sure the hell can. I've let things slide because you're a good detective. But this? I can't look the other way." He ran his hand over the top of his head. "Jesus, Ryder, what the hell were you thinking?"

"I was thinking she needed protection and that was my only option."

"No." He dipped his head back and groaned. "You almost got a woman killed because you wanted to keep your damn close rate high."

I clenched and unclenched my fists. "I'm supposed to close cases, that's my job. This isn't about my numbers, Jimmy. She needed protection."

He pointed to the door. "Records. Go."

"I'm not working records. We're in the middle of an—"

"*We* aren't in the middle of anything. You're in records. It's not up for discussion."

I crossed my arms and hitched my hip to the left. "That's a waste of time, and you know it. Write me up, put me on desk duty, I don't care. But I'm not working records."

The cords in his neck stiffened. He pinched the bridge of his nose then balled his fists. "You don't want records? Fine. Hand over your weapon and your badge. You're suspended indefinitely."

Heat flushed through my body. "What? You can't do that."

"Yes, I can."

"Jimmy," I said.

He steeled his eyes at me. "Weapon and badge, now."

I'd crossed the line before, and he'd been mad, but never once had he officially reprimanded me. "Come on, just—"

"Don't make me throw you in a cell, Ryder."

"You know what, chief?" I yanked my weapon from my belt, dropped the magazine and set it on his desk, then cleared the chamber, letting the bullet pop out and fall to the floor, then set the gun on his desk, too. "Screw records, and screw your suspension." I unclipped my badge and dropped it beside my weapon. "I quit."

I couldn't work an investigation from records or on suspension, but as an everyday citizen, I sure as hell could work it on my own.

I DROVE to Mayfield and waved to the gate staff as they opened the gate. The Kelleys', Wilsons', and Morgensens' streets were devoid of city vehicles, but both Bishop's and Michels's vehicles and the tech van sat in the Blahuts' driveway.

I called Bishop. "Hey, how's it going in there?"

"Where are you?" His tone was curt and annoyed, and worse than when we had talked earlier.

"Outside the Blahuts' house."

"Go home, Ryder."

"Jimmy called you."

"You quit on me, *partner*."

My chest tightened. "He was going to—"

"Go home. I've got a job to do." He disconnected the call.

I tossed my phone into the passenger's seat. "Damn it." I'd let my ego and my anger get the best of me without even thinking about Bishop. I deserved his anger, but it wouldn't stop me from finding Matt Wilson's killer.

16

"Yo, Detective Rachel! Long time no talk. How the hell are ya?"

"I'm fine, Joey. You still living in your mom's basement?"

"Hell yeah, I'm her baby. It'd break her heart if I moved out." He laughed.

"More like her wallet."

"Dude, I pay my share. I bought groceries last week. And pizza. Now, I know you're not calling to shoot the bull, so what do you need?"

I'd busted Joey several years before for a misdemeanor but let him go when he agreed to be my confidential informant. Joey was Bubba's evil twin. He could work a computer like a madman, and did it all, most of the time, on the wrong side of the law. I'd used him many times while working for the Chicago PD, and a few times in Hamby.

"I've got a list of account numbers and some names. I need to know if they're connected."

"Bank account numbers? You got the routing number?"

"I do not."

He made a popping sound with his lips. "You're talking people's names, right?"

"Yes." I gave him the Blahut and Wilson names and addresses.

"Might take me a few days. How many account numbers you got?"

"Only six."

"Six? Make that at least a week."

"A week? I can't wait that long. I'll have two Lou Manati's gift cards texted in five minutes."

"Make it three, and I'll do my best."

"Will do, and I need this ASAP. Thanks, Joey."

"Hey, detective?"

"Yes?"

"Why can't your computer guy do this?"

"He can, but it requires a lot of work around, and we don't have time." And he was no longer *my* computer guy.

"Capiche. Talk soon."

I'd parked in front of the Blahut home and was leaning against the passenger side door of my Jeep when two patrol vehicles arrived. I eyed Gregory as he headed toward me.

He pressed his lips together. "Ms. Ryder, I've been told to kindly ask you to leave." He blew out a breath. "And if you don't, I've been ordered to bring you in."

Ms. Ryder. Got it. I was no longer in law enforcement, no longer a detective. Just your average citizen hovering near a home. "Bring me in for what?"

He exhaled. "Loitering, for starters."

"Try again, officer." I laughed. "My standing here leaning against the side of my vehicle doesn't warrant a justifiable and reasonable alarm or immediate concern for anyone's safety." I glanced down at the road then back up at Gregory. "And I'm sure as hell not a threat to the safety of this road." I knew the laws like Billy Graham knew the Bible.

His shoulders lobbed up and down. "Listen, I'm not saying this because I want to, and I really don't want to bring you in, so can you please just leave?"

"You going in to help with the search?" I asked.

He straightened his shoulders. "Yes, ma'am. Once you leave."

I pursed my lips. "Gotcha, officer." I flipped my keys in my hand and strolled around the front of my vehicle like I didn't have a care in the world, even though I really wanted to call Jimmy and tell him where he could stick it.

I drove to North Fulton Hospital to visit Rosy, but the gatekeeper nurse outside of the intensive care unit wouldn't allow it. My looks forbade me from lying and saying we were family, so I asked her what she could tell me.

"You're not married to her brother? Maybe a distant cousin?"

"No, but she was shot at my house. I just want to know what's going on."

"I'm sorry, ma'am, but if you're not a relative, I'm not allowed to disclose any information regarding her condition or treatment."

I leaned into the nurse's station. "I understand you've got procedure, and I can respect that, but I've been working the investigation that got her shot. I'm the reason she's here, and I need to know if she's okay."

She raised her eyebrows and sighed. "Did you say you're her sister-in-law?"

"Yes."

She whispered, "This can get me fired."

I knew that risk well. "I appreciate it."

"The bullet nicked her heart. She's had extensive internal bleeding, and three transfusions."

"Is she going to survive?"

"She's not out of the woods yet, but we're hopeful."

I exhaled. "Thank you. Thank you so much."

"Just go find the person who did this and get him off the streets."

"I'm working on it," I said.

I got in my vehicle, but I couldn't just sit around and wait for Joey to call me back, but I also didn't want to call or visit Kyle because he'd ask me how things went with Jimmy, and I didn't want to upset him while recovering.

I took a left out of the hospital, turned right into the Starbucks entrance, and pulled through the drive-through. I picked up my coffee, and then parked on the side of the building.

I removed my second BUG—backup gun—from its magnetic holster below my steering wheel and stuffed it into the back of my pants. While working, that Glock 27 was usually stuffed into my boot, which made driving uncomfortable. I left my other Glock, a 26, in its holster beside the 27s.

A woman could never pack too much heat.

I finished my coffee and checked Bishop's location on my phone. If the team had started with the Blahut house, it was unlikely they'd be done with the others.

This person is not sharing their location, flashed on the screen.

"Seriously?"

I headed home to figure out my next move.

THREE HOURS HAD PASSED, and Joey hadn't called back. I sat on my couch and sent him a text asking him how much longer it would take. He responded with a snarky comment about Michelangelo not painting the dome in one day.

A while back I'd had an unwanted guest and installed the Ring digital camera system around the exterior of my home. I'd put cameras above the garage, on my front door, and back deck. Since I lived in the end unit, I'd also placed them on the front and back sides of my unit.

I'd willingly given Levy my Ring account information so she could view the videos from Rosy's shooting. I thought I'd see them at work, but obviously, that didn't happen.

I pulled up my account on my laptop and watched the videos from each camera.

She'd collapsed angled toward the garage, so I assumed she'd planned to cut through my driveway to get to the sidewalk. Whoever had shot her had been somewhere near the street but out of my camera's view. But that didn't mean it was out of my neighbor's view.

My community included one hundred townhomes attached in groups of threes, but I didn't know a soul there, and I'd never even casually spoken to any of my neighbors. I'd lived by the *keep out of my business, and I'll stay out of yours* rule, but it was time to introduce myself. I knocked on my neighbor's door.

The man who'd wanted to get me out of the community the night before answered. He wore a pair of dark jeans and a T-shirt under an open bathrobe. He hadn't shaved in a few days, nor had he brushed his hair. Or if he had, he'd chosen the messy look, but he didn't wear it well. "What do you want?"

"It's nice to formally meet you, too."

He rolled his eyes. "That person who got shot. Did they make it?"

"Yes." I didn't provide any additional details. "And that's why I'm here." I pointed to the camera above his door. "I'd appreciate seeing your videos from last night."

"I already sent them to the old guy. Can't you just get them from him?"

Bishop would have been livid to know he'd referred to him as the old guy. "Detective Bishop is a little busy trying to catch the guy who shot her, and I don't want to bug him."

He huffed and yanked his door open for me to enter. "Come on in."

The builders in Georgia weren't all that original. We shared the same layout. Front entrance into the main living area, the small dining area on the right, and the kitchen next to that. A path from the front door led to a bathroom, then two bedrooms, and the master up a set of stairs. Nothing hung from his walls. No pictures, no paintings, nothing. He was obviously a no-frills kind of guy.

His dining room table served as a desk. "Have a seat." He sat in front of a laptop, pulled on a pair of glasses from the top of his head, and tapped away while talking. I never understood how people could do that. "You're Rachel Ryder, right? You caught that serial killer."

Catching a serial killer had made local and national news. "It was a group effort."

"But the others aren't my neighbor. I read about you."

Here it comes, I thought.

"A drunk driver killed my wife. There isn't a day that goes by without me wishing I could kill the bastard." He glanced up at me. "How did it feel to kill your husband's murderer?"

I wasn't sure how to answer that. "You find the videos yet?"

"Sorry. I'm sure that's hard to talk about."

"Yes."

He angled the laptop toward me. "There's four. One from the front door, one on each side of the garage, and one where my place connects to my other neighbor's place." He grimaced. "I got their approval for that."

"No judgment from me."

"I put them in after that handyman got killed at your place."

I didn't bother responding. I clicked on the first video from the front door and increased the speed to get through it faster. There were two entrances into the community. One at the back and one up front near where we lived. Our road could be accessed from both. The video showed nothing.

The video on his garage angled my direction. It was clear as well. That meant the person who shot Rosy did so from the right side of my building and wasn't close enough to be in the front camera view.

No vehicles passed my unit in either direction. It reaffirmed what I'd suspected from my videos. The shooter either walked up the right side of the road or stopped and shot from their vehicle, and then left the way they came.

I hit gold with the third video. The silver Odyssey. I'd been right. It pulled up next to the neighbor on my neighbor's other side, a man jumped out, shot Rosy, then got back in the van. Whoever was driving kicked it into reverse and sped away. "You heard the gunshot, right?"

"That and tires screeching, but by the time I got to my door, the van was gone."

Of course, he'd checked his camera. "Were you the one who called it in?"

"Yes, ma'am."

"Is there any way to blow these things up from the video? I want a better look at the guy."

"Not from the program itself, but I have a trick." He turned the computer back in his direction, tapped a few keys, then rotated it back to me. "He's blurry, but you can see him."

I examined the photo. The man was too short to be Garcia. "Can you print this out in this size?"

"Sure thing. I already did it for the old guy though."

"That's okay. We're working different angles."

"Got it."

Joey called as it printed. "I'm sorry," I said to my neighbor. "I have to take this."

He handed me the paper. "No problem."

I whispered thank you and skirted out while answering Joey's call. "What do you have? I need to get back inside so don't start rambling just yet." When I got inside my place, I grabbed a pen and paper. "Okay. Shoot."

"These are bank account numbers. They're at three different banks, and the interesting thing is, they were all created on the same day." He gave me the bank names. Three of the biggest in the state, if not the nation.

I jotted all that down. "When were they created?"

"May 22, 2022. Can't tell whether they were done online or in person."

"How much money is in each account?"

"Can't tell."

"Recent activity?"

"Nope."

"Opening deposit amount?"

"Can't tell that either. It's easier to hack the government than it is a bank. Okay, full disclosure, I was only able to pull the first six numbers from each account number. But because of their open dates, I'm ninety-nine percent sure I've got the right accounts. If you need exacts, you'll need to do it the right way. I can't get that."

That was the first time Joey couldn't get me what I needed. "You're slacking," I said jokingly. "How many accounts at each bank?"

"Two. Even split."

"And you can't get me the names on the accounts?"

"Not yet, but now it's just pissing me off, so I will. It'll take a while, but I will."

"Okay. What about Spectrum? Can you connect them to this?"

"Nope. Spectrum's a solid wealth management company with good ratings. When I tried to create a fake account for their program, it only took me so far before I had to speak with a *highly qualified wealth manager*. So, I can't tell you how their process works for setting up accounts."

"What about the names?"

"You probably already know the Blahut dude works for Spectrum, but like I said, I can't get anywhere on their site. Other than that, I don't have anything yet."

"Okay, do what you can. I really appreciate this."

"You can't use this stuff in court, right? I'm not gonna have to like, testify or anything?"

"Use what stuff?"

"Gotcha," he said and ended the call.

Three different banks, each with two accounts with the same deposit amount created on the same day. Why did Wilson have the numbers hidden in a home improvement file?

Was he laundering money? He'd be stupid to use only three banks to clean it, and even more stupid to open them on the same day. But I couldn't rule it out. White collar criminals thought they were smarter than everyone else, and their egos often led to their demise.

I contacted the Cumming detective handling the Perez investigation. "Detective, this is Rachel Ryder." I purposefully didn't refer to myself as Detective Ryder or mention Hamby PD. "I'm calling for an update."

"Detective Ryder," he said. "I just spoke to your partner. He gave me the information about Rosy Lopez, and that's appreciated, but like I told him, no one's talking. You know how these things work."

"Understood. You've got my cell. Can you call me if something breaks?"

"Sure thing," he said.

At least Bishop hadn't told him not to talk to me.

I tapped my pen onto the pad of paper, then flipped to a fresh page and brain dumped. Four home invasions escalating in items taken and/or physical contact. Three of the couples involved in a sex club. Two possible suspects worked for the community where the invasions occurred. One of them dead.

Fourth invasion included disrupted files, cash and jewelry still in the safe, and murder.

I wrote down the victims' names and jobs, added Xavier and Stacey Turner, Garcia, Perez, Mayfield, the baby momma, Rosy, the Odyssey minivan, and the SUV. I noted what we knew under each name, studied it, then drew circles around Lisa and Alan Blahut.

They both lied about being involved in the swingers group.

Lisa had lied twice.

They hosted a swingers party.

Lisa and Miranda Wilson argued at the Turners' *gathering*.

Alan Blahut told the Turners not to invest with Spectrum and gave them another name.

Xavier Turner also said Blahut wanted to quit his job.

I hadn't confronted Lisa Blahut about her argument with Miranda Wilson, nor had I personally followed up with her husband about his lie. Other than those, what was I missing?

Money and sex. Could it have been that easy?

Yes. If Matt Wilson's murder had anything to do with money, odds were, Alan Blahut was involved. If I got lucky, something in their files would link them, and I'd still check the other victims' files for links as well.

If Matt Wilson's murder was because of an issue in the swingers group, someone would eventually talk. As far as I knew, no one had gone back to talk to Miranda Wilson privately, so she wouldn't have known I'd quit.

I dialed Mr. Riley's landline.

Mrs. Riley answered. "She's getting by," she said. "She's asleep at the moment. Have you found out who murdered Matt?"

"The team is working very hard to make that happen. Has she said anything more about what happened?"

"I'm sorry, no."

"That's fine. Do you know anything about your daughter and Matt's relationship with the other couples whose homes were broken into?"

"I think she's played tennis with some of them, maybe? You'll have to ask her when she's awake, or you could come by again tomorrow?"

"That would be great," I said.

BISHOP SHOULD HAVE BEEN DONE with the searches and back at the department, but it was later than I'd thought, and it was possible Nikki hadn't even started entering the files into the system, so the chance of the team reviewing them was slim. I called Bishop to check, but it went straight to voice mail. I sent him a text, but he didn't respond.

I couldn't sleep, and I couldn't just stand around hoping Bishop would call. I sent Kyle a message. *Are you still awake?*

He called. "Hey. Things going okay?"

"That depends."

He sighed into the phone. "What happened?"

I avoided his question. "It's late. Why are you awake?"

"It's a hospital, remember? Now, tell me what happened with Jimmy."

"He tried to stick me in records, so I quit."

"You're not serious."

I cringed. "Records, Kyle, and it was indefinitely, by the way."

"You messed up. You take your punishment and move on. You don't quit." He paused.

"Talk to him, Rachel. Fix it."

"He's not going to change his mind, and I won't waste my time in records. I've got too much experience for that."

"You want to close this case?"

"Yes."

"Then eat crow and talk to him."

"I can close it without a badge."

He exhaled. "Don't pretend to be naive. You'll compromise their investigation, and you know that. Just go back to the station in the morning and apologize."

I said I would, but I wasn't sure that was true.

"On a happier note, they're releasing me in two days."

"Really? I'll be there to get you."

"I know. I'm tired. I need to try and sleep, and so do you. Talk to him in the morning, okay?"

"Okay."

17

I'd just cleaned and redressed my leg and changed into sweats when someone rang my bell. I checked the camera.

Bishop.

I hobbled over, unlocked the multiple locks, then swung the door open, and hobbled back to the couch.

Neither of us said anything. I leaned back and set my feet on my wood trunk coffee table. "Well? Come on. Let me have it. It's late, and I want to go to bed."

He unclipped his gun from his belt and set it on my dining room table. "Why the hell did you quit?"

"Because I'm an overreactive, egotistical idiot."

He blinked. I'd surprised him.

"He dropped me to records, Bishop. That set me off."

He sat on the other side of my small leather sectional. "He had to do something, Rachel. The entire department knows you messed up. If he didn't, he'd lose their respect, and everyone would hate you for being favored."

I hadn't considered that. My shoulders slumped. "Doesn't matter. What's done is done. What about you? Did he reprimand you?"

"Not officially."

"That's good. I'm sorry. I shouldn't have put you in that position."

"No, you shouldn't have, but I'm your partner. I should have stopped you."

"You couldn't have. You know that."

"Then I should have reported you."

"Did Jimmy say that?"

"There are rules, Rachel. You're not exempt from following them, and neither am I. I knew better."

"Did he write you up?"

His cell phone rang before he could answer. "Hold on." He answered the call on speaker. "Bubba, what's going on?"

"Nothing. Just wanted to give you an update about the account numbers."

"Shoot."

"Do you know how many banks there are in this state? Thankfully, most of them are branches, but it's still going to take some time to get through them all."

"Go home," Bishop said.

"I am. Just wanted to give you an update." He cleared his throat. "Should I tell detective—your former partner?"

Bishop narrowed his eyes at me then shook his head as if he'd lectured me nonverbally. "She's no longer part of the investigation."

"Right. That sucks," Bubba said. "See you tomorrow."

"Thanks for the update," he said and ended the call. He set his phone on my table.

I bit my bottom lip.

"What?"

"I had Joey look into the numbers."

He held a palm toward my face. "I don't want to know."

"Okay. I think you were right. Blahut's involved. Did you go through any of the files?"

"Nikki's still got to enter them into the system."

"What about the rest of the Wilsons'?"

"We were one man down, so we were a little busy with the searches."

"The secret room, did you find it?"

"If it's there, the cabinet has to move electronically, and we couldn't find a controller anywhere."

"Was Alan there?"

"At work."

"It's probably there. Did Christopher get a warrant for his office?"

"Not enough for the judge to approve it." He ran his hand over the top of his head. "Rachel, Jimmy hasn't even filed your voluntary termination papers. Go talk to him. Don't make me train another partner. I finally got you how I want you."

I laughed. "Yeah, and Santa's real." I leaned my head back. "Fine. I'll talk to him."

I TOSSED and turned all night, thoughts of approaching Jimmy and the connections between the Wilsons and the other members of the swingers group. I got nowhere with either, but Kyle and Bishop had pricked a small hole into my ego, and it had slowly deflated to nothing.

It was past eight the next morning, and I knew Jimmy would already be at the department, so I called Savannah.

She answered on the first ring. "Are you okay?"

"My ego's a shriveled balloon by my own doing."

"You're a hotheaded Chicago girl. You let your emotions get the best of you."

"Cops can't do that," I said.

"You're only human, and you wanted to protect that girl. Jimmy knows your intentions were good, he's just angry at the way you handled it."

"Do you think I can wipe the egg off my face, and get my job back?"

"Don't you dare tell him I told you this, but he hasn't even announced your departure or set up your exit paperwork. He wants you back. The both of you just need to cool off."

"Okay." I had already showered and was half dressed when I called her. "I'm going in. It's either going to be fine, or one of us will need bail money."

"If I don't hear from either of you in a few hours, I'll be the one needing bail money." Scarlet screamed in the background. "Great. I've got to go. I don't care what you two need to do, just fix it. Now." She disconnected the call.

Well, okay.

I decided to talk to Jimmy first, but job or no job, I was going straight to Miranda Wilson after.

All eyes were on me again as an officer escorted me through the pit. The gossip train had taken off at lightning speed when Jimmy and I argued. Termination papers or not, word had gotten out. I knocked on his closed door.

"It's open."

My sweaty hand slid on the door handle. Jimmy sat behind his desk with Bishop sitting in a chair on the other side.

Bishop gave me a slight nod. "I'll give you two a minute."

I gripped the back of the chair Bishop had been sitting in and worked up the nerve to nail shut my ego's coffin. Jimmy crossed his arms over his chest. I cleared my throat. "Savannah's upset."

The corner of his mouth twitched. "That's an understatement."

"Any word on Rosy?"

"They're going to try to bring her out of the coma today."

I rocked back on my boot heels. "Thank God." I stared at the ground for a moment until I summoned the nerve to look him in the eyes. "Listen, Jimmy." I stared at the aging gray carpet. "I might have over reacted." When I looked back up at him, he was smiling.

"You might have? Think again."

"What happened to Rosy is my fault. I take full responsibility. You were right, I defied a direct order." I rubbed the back of my neck. "God, this is harder than I thought."

"Apologizing?"

"And eating crow."

"It's not something you do often," he said.

I stepped around the chair and dropped into it. "Nope." I pressed my lips together and let a breath out slowly. "I'd like to rescind my resignation."

The corners of his mouth twitched. "Anything else?"

"Yes. Please let me work the case."

"You put the entire city at risk of being sued. That includes everyone on your team. Rob. Levy. Bubba. My family."

"I know."

He leaned forward and rested his forearms on the table. "I had to tell HR what happened, but I didn't tell them you quit, just that I had sent you home for the day."

"I understand. What happens next?"

"We met with the city attorney. Rosy is an undocumented immigrant. Theoretically, she can take us to court, but she risks being deported if she does."

"I've got money. I can pay her medical bills."

"We've got insurance for that, but there has to be an official reprimand, Rachel. I can't just let you walk away from this."

I gripped the chair's wooden arms. "What are you going to do?"

"I can put you on desk duty, drop you down to records for an undetermined amount of time, or write you up."

"Do I get to pick?"

He leaned back and drummed his fingers on the arms of his chair. "If we do this, I need your word you won't color outside the lines again."

I cringed.

"Come on, Rachel."

"I'll do my absolute best to color within the lines." I exhaled. "But I'd prefer desk duty over records. That way I could go through the files from the searches."

"You'd drive everyone crazy sitting in the pit all day. I already wrote you up. It's in your permanent file. No raises for a year. But Rachel, two more strikes and you're out."

I limped over and hugged him. "Thank you."

"Don't let me down."

I released my grip on him and leaned against his credenza. "I'm sorry for putting you in a tough position, but more than that, I'm sorry I hurt you."

"Was that hard, too?"

"Not as hard as I thought."

He smiled and then pointed to my leg. "You need to let that heal."

"It's fine. I need to call Savannah. She threatened me with bodily harm if I didn't."

He stood and reached out his hand. "Welcome back, detective."

"Thank you, chief." I opened the door and went straight to Bishop's cubby.

~

"Bubba will confirm they're account numbers and connect them to the banks," Bishop said. "He should be able to find out the deposit amounts, too. Christopher covered all bases with the warrants."

"Can I give him a little push in the right direction? It'll save us some time."

His eyes widened. "Are you trying to get yourself into records?"

"I won't tell him anything. Just lead him where he needs to go." I motioned for him to follow me. "I'm not coloring outside the lines."

"What?"

"Nothing."

He grabbed a file and followed me to Bubba's office.

Bubba had earbuds in and was singing along, poorly, to a song I didn't recognize. He couldn't hit a note or stay on tune.

Bishop tapped him on his shoulder and startled him. "Oh, sorry!" He smiled at me. "Are you back?"

"I am."

"Awesome! It's not the same around here without you." He glanced at Bishop. "Uh, it wouldn't be without you, either."

Bishop grunted.

"How's the account number search going?" I asked.

"Slow, but we'll get there."

"Where'd you start?"

"I started with Georgia-owned banks first. They're smaller, so it will be easier to get through them."

"Do me a favor, look into these next, okay?" I wrote the bank names down on a sticky note.

"Sure? Is there a reason?"

"Just testing a theory," I said.

"Got it. I'll get with them now."

"Thank you."

Bishop and I grabbed coffees in the kitchen.

"I told Mrs. Riley I'd be by to see Miranda this morning."

He held up his file. "Good. I did another quick search through their files and found a few things."

"I'd like to go through them all after we talk with Miranda."

"Sounds like a plan."

WHILE WAITING IN THE DUNKIN' drive-through, Bishop asked the question he hadn't wanted the answer to before. "What did Joey tell you about the numbers?"

"How do you know it was Joey and not my outstanding detective skills?"

"Because your computer skills are almost as bad as mine."

"Good point. He said he pulled up the numbers but could only see a portion of them."

"That doesn't help."

"I wasn't finished. All the accounts were opened at three banks, and all on the same day."

"The ones you suggested Bubba check."

"Yes," I said.

"Same amount deposited?"

"Don't know. He can't get that."

"And we never had this conversation."

"Never."

MIRANDA WILSON'S parents lived in Cumming, near the Gwinnett County border. Miranda answered the door holding her sleeping baby in her left arm. If her drooping sweatpants, oversized sweatshirt, and hair tied in a messy bun didn't show her exhaustion and grief, the dark circles under her eyes gave it away.

She whispered hello and smiled down at her child. "The baby is finally asleep. Come on in. I'll just put her in her crib."

She showed us where to sit while her mother walked in with a tray full of pastries. My stomach growled. When had I eaten last? I couldn't remember. I thanked her and helped myself to a sticky cheese Danish and a napkin.

"I'll let you talk in private," she said and walked away.

Miranda returned. She glanced at the tray of sweets and sighed. "My mother. She's always feeding people."

Bishop picked up a coffee cake muffin, broke off a piece, and stuck it in his mouth.

"We appreciate it," I said. "Sometimes we're so busy we forget to eat."

"Have you found the person who killed my husband?"

"We're working on it," I said. "We do have some questions for you."

She tilted her head. "The other detectives already asked me questions."

"This is follow-up."

"Okay."

"Money and jewelry were taken from each home invaded prior to yours."

Her expression went blank. "Okay?"

"There was $350,000 and jewelry in your safe."

"Yes, I know. But I can't tell you how much money they stole because I don't know how much was in the safe before they broke in."

"But you believe they took some?"

"Of course. Why wouldn't they?" She wiped her eyes. "What's going on?"

"Miranda, we can't be sure they took any money."

Her eyes widened. "What are you saying? Why did these men break into our house then?" She gasped and covered her mouth with her hand. Tears fell from her eyes. "Matt! They wanted to kill Matt!"

"We're still trying to figure out what happened," I said. "Did you know he had defaulted on your mortgage? He hasn't made a payment in three months. Your home's going into foreclosure."

"That's impossible. Matt would have told me."

Bishop removed a copy of the foreclosure warning from his file and handed it to her.

She skimmed over it. "I don't understand. How could this happen?"

"We were hoping you'd know," I said.

"I don't. Matt didn't tell me."

He handed her the page with the account numbers. "Is that Matt's handwriting?"

She examined the numbers. "Yes. What are these?"

"We believe they're bank account numbers. Our team is looking into it right now."

Her mouth opened slightly but no words came out right away. "I don't understand what's going on. Why would Matt have that many bank accounts?"

"We've yet to determine if they're his," Bishop said. "Were you close to the Blahuts?"

She looked the other way and nodded. "They're our friends. Alan and Matt play golf." She sniffled. "Or they used to. And Lisa and I, we have become closer over the past year. Why do you ask?"

"Did Matt ever say Alan invested your money?" I asked.

"He hasn't said, but they were talking about investing the last time we saw them."

"Where was that?"

"Uh, a get-together, I think."

"At a neighbor's?"

"Yes."

"What did they say?"

"I don't know. Lisa and I were talking. I wasn't paying that much attention." She looked at Bishop. "Are these from yesterday? Did you find anything else?"

"We're still going through the files," he said. "Though I did find a few investment statements." He removed them from his folder and handed them to her. I had reviewed them on the way over. "Are you familiar with the investment company Merit Investments?"

"No."

"If you look through them, you'll see the investments have improved each month for the past year," he said, "but last month's statement shows a cash-out of $500,000."

"Five hundred thousand dollars? Why would Matt take out that much money?"

"We're not sure."

"Well, I know he wouldn't take it out to spend it. Maybe he wanted to pay down our mortgage?" She dabbed her nose with the tissue. "I'm sure he didn't want me to know we were in foreclosure, so he probably took out the money to pay off the mortgage."

I doubted that. Based on the paperwork, the five hundred K would have only put a small dent in it. "So, he hadn't made any major purchases recently or talked about making any?"

"Matt was very good with our money. That's why I don't understand why he would let the house go into foreclosure."

She flipped through the statements. "Wait, I think this might be the company they were talking about." She looked at Bishop. "Have you talked to Alan about it?"

"Not yet," Bishop said. "Mrs. Wilson, can you think of anyone who might have had an issue with Matt?"

She stumbled over her words. "I don't know. Matt is a good man. He does volunteer work. We go to church. Why would someone have a problem with him?"

"Was he having trouble at work?" I asked.

"No. Not Matt. Everyone loves him."

The living often turned the dead into saints but most people weren't that high on the totem pole when alive.

"What about the swingers group?" I asked. "How did they feel about him?"

Her eyes widened.

"Miranda, we aren't here to judge you, but we need to investigate every angle possible to find who killed Matt."

"We weren't involved in that." Her earlobes reddened. I raised my eyebrows, but Bishop and I said nothing. The silence made her uncomfortable enough to shift her sitting position. She cleared her throat. "It's not how it sounds. Yes, we went, but I couldn't. I thought I could, but when we got there, I just couldn't. I'm so ashamed."

"What did you and Lisa Blahut argue about?"

"Nothing to do with Matt or Alan. I'd already said no, and she was trying to change my mind. It made me angry. I told Matt I wanted to leave, but he brushed me off. Alan was showing him something on his office computer."

Bishop side-eyed me.

"You've been to two parties then?" I asked.

"Like I said, just the one at the Blahuts'."

"According to Stacey Turner, things became tense between you and Lisa Blahut at her house."

Her eyes shifted between Bishop and me. "Lisa and I are still friends. It was just a misunderstanding. I don't know how this can possibly have anything to do with the group or our financial situation." Tears fell down her cheeks. "You've made a mistake. The papers are wrong. Matt would never default on our mortgage, especially when he had the money to pay it."

"Thanks for your time," I said.

"Wait a minute." Her hand shook as she wiped her face. "You practically just accused our friends of murdering my husband. What am I supposed to do now?"

"My suggestion," Bishop said, "is to keep your distance, keep our conversation between us, and let us do our job." He stood.

"That's it? You just want me to sit here like nothing's changed while you go around making accusations that have nothing to do with my husband's murder?"

"No," I said. "We're going to go around and find evidence to catch your husband's killer, regardless of who it is."

18

In the car, Bishop said, "That wasn't at all awkward." He drove past the Blahuts' house. "I couldn't tell if she was lying about Lisa Blahut or if she was telling the truth. Her emotions were all over the place."

"I'm not sure," I said. I studied the statements from Merit Investments. "But I don't get a *pissed off husband killer* vibe from her."

"Neither do I. She's genuinely upset he's dead."

"Wait a minute." I removed the account number list from my file and compared it to one of the Wilson statements. The statement number was two numbers longer, but otherwise it was a match. I checked the other numbers against other statements and they matched the same way.

Bishop slowed the vehicle and moved to the side of the road. "What?"

"The numbers on the Merit investment statements almost match the ones on Matt Wilson's."

"Almost?"

"The statement numbers have two additional numbers at the end."

"A tracking number of some kind?"

"Maybe. Xavier Turner said Blahut recommended some online guy for his investing. Think it could be Merit Investments?"

"That's what I'm thinking. Check the website, see what it says."

I scanned the statements. "There's just a company logo on the statements. No contact information."

"An investment company with no contact info on their statements?" Bishop asked.

"That's fishy."

"Let's see what Bubba can dig up." He answered on the second ring. "Hey, can you run a check on a company for us, please?"

"Sure. Name?"

"Merit Investments, and that's all I have."

"No website?"

"Nope. No contact info at all."

"Interesting. I'll do what I can and get back to you."

"Thanks," I said.

Bishop sang, "It's beginning to look a lot like Blahut, everywhere we go," to the tune of the popular Christmas carol.

"Right. He slams his current company and gets his special friends to invest with an online-only company."

"He doesn't want them to know it's him."

"Because he's scamming them," I said.

"And Wilson found out, so he murdered him."

"Maybe Blahut shows him Merit's investment record, and he dumps his entire savings into it, maybe even using his mortgage money because of the big returns. He gets the foreclosure threat, and needs his money, but can't get in touch with the guy, so does a little digging and figures out it's Blahut," I said.

"Blahut gives him the 350 K; Garcia and his men leave it at the house."

"If we're right, Blahut's got to be pissed they didn't get the cash."

"Pissed and worried we can track it back to him. We need to talk with the other victims and find out if they've invested with this Merit company," he said. He made a U-turn at the stop sign. "And since we're already here—"

My cell phone rang. "It's Kyle." I clicked to answer. "Hey. I'm so sorry. I should have called. Everything's okay. How are you feeling?"

"Good enough to be released. Just got the paperwork. Nurse said it would be about an hour."

"Wow! That's early. Bishop and I are in Mayfield. I'll have him bring me back to the station and head straight there."

"See you soon," he said.

I tapped the end call button and smiled at Bishop. "He's coming home."

"I'll drop you off and head back here to talk to the Kelleys and Morgensens. We can meet back at the station to go through the files."

KYLE SAT on the small chair in his room. He'd changed from his thin hospital gown into a pair of bluish green scrubs. He smiled when I entered. "I hear this is all the rage."

I raised an eyebrow. "The color suits you. Didn't Savannah bring you clothes?"

"These were easier to get on." He pushed himself to stand, then dropped an f-bomb, and eased himself back into the chair.

Kyle wasn't easily angered, but pain frustrated him. That and his physical limitations would keep him off the job for a while. Whether he liked it or not. I rushed over to him. "Let me help."

He smiled. "No. I can do it. You should have seen me pull on this shirt. Took me fifteen minutes, but I did it."

"You can walk around naked at my place if that makes you feel better. I won't mind." Our place. It was going to be our place. "Our place."

"About that." He'd finally managed to stand. "I'd like to hold off on moving in."

My heart dropped and settled like a brick in my gut. "Why?"

"Because I don't want you and our friends doing all the packing and moving. It's my stuff. I should be the one getting it to *our place*."

A wave of relief carried my heart back to where it belonged. "But you are planning to stay there until you're better right?"

"If you'll still have me."

"Wouldn't have it any other way." I kissed him on the cheek. "I'll find the nurse."

The hospital required Kyle be wheeled out in a chair. Since walking more than a few steps at a time had him near tears—he'd never have admitted that—he didn't argue. I met him at the entrance and helped him into my Jeep. It was a climb, and he winced multiple times.

"I'm so sorry. We'll take your truck from now on."

"I think getting into my pickup will be harder than this. It's okay. I'll feel better every day."

I asked him about what happened on the way home.

His smile disappeared. He stared out the window. "He was a kid. We already had our guys, and then this kid walks in and shoots my partner. I'm along the opposite side of the wall, so I don't see any of it. Kid sees me first. I still can't figure out how, but he shoots. I drop to the ground. My partner tried to shoot him, but he missed. He was lucky he could even stand. His shots distracted the kid, but only for a second. He was coming toward me with the gun aimed at me. I had no choice."

"It sounds like you didn't. You were shot four times in the chest. How were you able to move?"

"Adrenaline is an amazing gift."

"It is. What about your partner? Is he going to be all right?"

"Yes. He was in the ICU with me."

I crossed over the highway to take the exit for 400 north. "Why didn't Tanner tell me that?"

"You're not a relative."

"I'm not your relative either?"

"You're on my paperwork as my emergency contact. That gives them permission to talk with you."

My heart melted. "You're my emergency contact as well."

"The kid was only sixteen."

"I'm sorry."

"He wasn't even a part of the investigation. We have no idea why he was even there. Probably needed to pass the kill test to get into a gang."

I didn't know what to say. The wrong place at the wrong time was how a lot of people ended up dead. Call it fate or whatever, there was just no explanation to ease the pain for the loss. And the kid was a loss for Kyle.

It was after three by the time I had Kyle settled in, fed, and on the couch with the remote in hand. I headed back to the office with the promise of bringing home something that didn't remotely resemble hospital food.

Bishop hadn't called. I called him, but his phone went straight to voice mail. I sent a text asking for him to call me, and then called Levy.

She and Michels had been in court in Roswell all morning. She didn't know I'd un-quit. Her words, not mine. "Thank God. I wasn't looking forward to being the only female detective."

"Been there. It's not a picnic, but you would have been fine. Are you heading back to the department?"

"Yes. ETA fifteen."

"Have you heard from Bishop?"

"Phones were on silent all day, but no missed calls or texts. Why? What's up?"

"Nothing. He was going to follow up with the Kelleys and Morgensens." I explained our theory.

"Are you getting a warrant?"

"We've got to go through all the files still."

"Need some help? Michels and I are free now."

"Sounds great. See you there."

BUBBA CAUGHT me as I passed by his office. "I can't find anything on that company. Are you sure the name's right?"

I handed him a statement. "Yes."

"Weird."

"Maybe not." I updated him on our theory en route to the investigation room.

His phone dinged with a notification just as I'd finished. "Oh, I've got something. Be right back."

Levy and Michels sat at the table going through the files.

"If Blahut wanted Wilson dead, why rob the other people, let alone himself?" Levy asked.

"Cash and cover. Having himself robbed takes eyes off him." I pictured Lisa Blahut's jewelry. "The night they were robbed, Lisa Blahut had on her wedding ring, and later, the diamond bracelet she said was soaking in cleaner."

"The robbery was fake," Michels said.

"Then the wife knows?" Levy asked.

"Blahut took a beating. He made sure it looked real. I don't know if she knows."

"Garcia's guys would have taken her ring," Michels said.

"Not if Blahut told them not to," Levy said.

"We need to connect Blahut to Merit Investments or get Garcia to give him up."

"I don't see that happening," Michels said. "Garcia's getting paid. He won't cut that money tree."

"He might if he thinks Blahut gave him up." I checked my watch, and texted Bishop again. "Where the hell is Rob? He should be here."

Bubba returned a few minutes later and confirmed what Joey had told me. "All the accounts are checking account numbers, opened on the same day, and each with a $100 deposit."

"Do they belong to Merit Investments?"

He tweaked his head to the side. "Nope. John Hagar, and they're all personal accounts."

"Who's John Hagar?" Nikki asked.

Bubba shrugged.

"Were the accounts opened online?" I asked.

"Nope. Cash deposits in person."

"Do you have their transaction history?"

"There wasn't any. They were opened May 22, 2022, and have moved since."

"Call the banks and see if we can get video from that day. We need to see what John Hagar looks like."

"Will do," he said and left the room.

I checked my phone in case I'd accidentally silenced my ringer, but there was still nothing from Bishop.

～

BISHOP STILL HADN'T MADE contact an hour later. Something was wrong. I checked my text messages to him, and all had been delivered, but none marked read. Bishop had his phone to show messages as read when he read them. "Something's up," I said. I checked his location just in case, but he hadn't allowed me access again. I contacted dispatch.

"Yes, detective?"

"I need a 10-20 on Detective Bishop, please."

"Sure thing." She got on the radio and called for Bishop. He didn't respond. "Let me check his vehicle." A few seconds later she got back on the radio and requested assistance in the same area where the SUV had run off the road while following me.

I looked at Levy and Michels. "Bishop's in trouble. Let's go."

19

Bishop's vehicle sat at the bottom of the same curve where the SUV had landed. I stared down at it as fear and anger overwhelmed me. "Garcia's got him."

Jimmy threw his flashlight on the ground. "Sons of bitches. Where was he last?"

"He dropped me off at the station and was going back to talk with the Morgensens and Kelleys again."

"Get over there."

I jogged to my vehicle, the pain in my leg forcing me to slow down, but I still made it to the Kelleys' in less than ten minutes.

Kelsey Kelley answered the door. "Detective?"

"When did Detective Bishop leave your place today?"

She blinked. "Today? He hasn't been here."

"Are you sure?"

"Yes, I'm sure. I've been home all day." She narrowed her eyes. "Is everything okay?"

"If he comes by, please have him contact me. His phone is apparently dead." Sweat beads covered my temples. I wiped it with the back of my hand. "It's important I get in touch with him."

She blinked. "Yes, of course. Can I get you something to drink?"

"No, thanks. Do you invest with Merit Investments?"

She raised an eyebrow. "The company Alan Blahut's going to work for? I think Jared was planning on putting in something, but I don't know if he has. Why?"

I ignored her question, said thanks, pivoted around, and jogged back to my car.

I checked the Morgensens next.

"Your partner?" Amber asked. "I'm sorry. I haven't seen him since he was here with the warrant."

"Do you invest with Merit Investments?"

"My husband handles our investments. Her neck tightened. "What does this and our personal files have to do with the break-in?"

I didn't have time for her. "Thank you," I said and left.

I checked the Wilsons' place in case Bishop had decided to take another look around, but he wasn't there.

Had Blahut figured out we were on to him? There was only one way to find out.

Lisa Blahut answered the door. I blurted out my question without a greeting.

"No," she said. "I haven't seen him." She stared at the ground and then her eyes trailed up my body. "Are you okay?" She stepped into the doorframe.

"Is your husband home?"

"He had to go on a business trip this morning. It was a last-minute thing."

I bet it was. "Where did he go?"

She blinked. "New York City. Why?"

"I'd like to talk to him." I pulled my phone from my pocket. "May I have his cell phone number?"

She rattled off his number and I typed it into my contacts. After I finished, I swiped through my photos and pulled up Santos Garcia. "Mrs. Blahut, do you know this man?"

She looked at the photo then held her arms crossed over her chest. She rubbed her shoulders but wouldn't look at me. "I don't think so." Her head shifted back and forth. "I'm sorry. I need to go. I have an appointment."

"One more thing."

She'd already closed the door halfway. "Yes?"

"When is your husband leaving Spectrum?"

She blinked. "He's not leaving. Why would you say that?"

"Oh, I'm sorry. I thought he mentioned it the night of the break-in."

"I doubt that," she said. "Now, I really must get going." She closed the door before I could say goodbye.

Lisa Blahut appeared genuinely surprised when I asked about her husband leaving his job. If her husband was responsible for the break-ins, I didn't think she knew. I called Jimmy for an update.

"The vehicle is empty, and so far, Bishop's nowhere in the area."

"What about his radio? Maybe if fell off during the crash?"

"We haven't found anything around the vehicle."

"If he was able to get out, he would have called dispatch," I said. "Jimmy, he wasn't driving. He never made it back to Mayfield. I think we're right about Blahut. He's behind this, and he's got Bishop."

"Damn it. I'll put officers near the house. Where are you now?"

"On my way to Garcia's baby momma's apartment. If Blahut's got Bishop, Garcia's doing his dirty work."

I DROVE out to Elisa Ortega's apartment complex and banged on her door. "Police! Open up."

She opened the door slowly, leaving the chain lock loose and hanging but still connected. She stuck her face in the small opening. Her left eye was swollen and purple. "He's not here."

"Did he do that to you?"

She looked at the ground.

"Elisa, let me in."

She closed the door. I heard the chain unlatch and clink against the doorframe, then the door opened. I pushed her to the side—gently, then stepped in and closed and locked the door behind me. "Where is he?"

"I don't know. He came here. I wanted my car back, but he said it's gone.

He told me it was stolen. I know they were here when you were. I hear the shots. I told him I knew."

"And that's when he hit you?"

"Si."

"Did you know Rosy was shot? She's in the hospital. She almost didn't make it."

Her eyes filled with tears.

"Elisa, if you know where he is, I need you to tell me. We've got two people dead, one barely hanging on, and a missing cop. I need to know what you know."

She sobbed into her hands. "My baby. He said he'd kill me and my baby."

"He won't," I said. "Come on Elisa, do you know where he is? Does he have my partner?"

"I think so, but I'm not sure. I'm afraid."

"I know you are. Please, my partner's life is at stake."

"His brother works on cars at a warehouse. He tell me if I ever disrespect him, he'd take me there and kill me. He takes others there. He said he makes people pay there."

"What's the address?"

She knew where it was, but not the street address.

"Let me make a call." I dialed Jimmy's cell and told him what I knew.

"That's down the street from the department. I'll get our men there."

"She needs protection, Jimmy. He's already beaten her, and he's threatened to kill her, and Jimmy, she's pregnant."

"I'll send a patrol to get her. Don't leave until they're gone."

"Thanks." I stuffed my phone back into my pocket. "There is a squad car on its way. I need you to grab some things and put them in a bag. We're going to keep you safe."

"I . . . I'm due in a week." She cried again. "I can't handle this. My baby. He will hurt my baby."

"I promise we're not going to let that happen." I followed her to the bedroom. "Does anyone else live here?"

"Santos, he pays the rent. He stays sometimes."

"So, he has a key."

She stuffed some personal items into a bag.

"Has he said anything about any home invasions recently?"

Her cheeks blushed.

"Elisa, if you know something, you need to tell me."

"He didn't, but he gave me this." She opened the top drawer of her dresser and removed a small box. Inside was a pair of diamond stud earrings. "He said they were for the baby."

"I'm going to need to take them."

"Si."

A loud knock on her apartment door startled us both.

"Let me," I said. I drew my weapon and looked through the peep hole. It was a Hamby patrol officer. I opened the door. "Take her to the department, and don't let anyone that's not law enforcement near her, you understand?"

"Yes, detective."

"Thanks."

I explained the next steps to Elisa and hightailed it back to my Jeep. I called Jimmy on the short drive to the warehouse and let him know I was on my way to the warehouse.

"We've got SWAT en route. What's your ETA?" he asked.

"Five minutes. Garcia gave her diamond stud earrings. We should be able to link them to one of the victims."

"Lock them up," he said. "And don't come here in your vehicle." He explained where he wanted me.

"On my way."

I dropped my vehicle off at the department. The entire patrol lot was empty. Jimmy had gone balls to the wall for Bishop. I just hoped it wasn't too late. I asked Nikki to tag the earrings and rushed down to weapons for additional magazines.

"I need you to sign them out," the officer said.

"I'm good for it," I said. I grabbed the loaded magazines and stuffed them into my front pockets as I headed out.

I jogged behind the buildings, spotting officers scattered in between and behind the buildings leading to the warehouse. I found Jimmy wearing his Kevlar vest at the building across the street from the warehouse. I caught my breath. "What's the status?"

"He's in there," Jimmy said. "They've got him chained to a metal pole."

I saw the ambulances and fire trucks waiting just out of view.

My heart raced. "Is he okay?"

Jimmy looked into my eyes. "He's still alive, but that's all we know."

Heat rushed through my body, kicking every sweat gland I had into high overdrive. "Then what the hell are you waiting for? We need in, now."

"You know how this rolls. Building owner gave us the codes for the fire alarm and keyless entry. Plan is to set off the fire alarm. It automatically unlocks all doors. The alarm will distract them, SWAT goes in. Bishop walks out alive."

I imagined what it would be like to take out Garcia. One bullet. That was all it would take. "No way in hell are they leaving me out of this, Jimmy. Bishop's my partner. He needs me."

"He needs you alive."

I bit back my tears, turning my head to the side so he couldn't see. My body shook uncontrollably. "I can do this. I am just as good as any SWAT member, and you know that."

"No, you're not, and even if that was the case, this is theirs."

I dropped my head and breathed. I didn't give a damn what SWAT said or wanted. I was going in. Bishop would have done the same for me, and I couldn't let him down. I should have been there with him. I should have stayed with my partner.

"I know that look," Jimmy said.

"Who's running this?"

He exhaled. "Rachel."

"Who's running it, Jimmy?"

He pointed to a tall man at the end of the building where we stood. "Major Spencer. Big guy with the black hair. Tell him I okayed it." As I ran toward him, he said, "Don't make me regret this."

I waved my hand in the air to acknowledge hearing him. "Major Spencer." He looked at me but didn't speak. "Detective Rachel Ryder. That's my partner inside. What can I do?"

"Stay over there," he said pointing to where I'd just come from.

"No. Hold up," I said. "I have information about at least one of the suspects inside, and I can help."

He looked at me and scowled. "Go ahead."

"I believe Santos Garcia, a suspect in a multiple home invasion and murder investigations is—"

He stuck his hand in my face. I wanted to smack it away. "I know about the investigation. That's not my problem. My problem is getting your partner out safely."

My body stiffened. He was wasting precious time arguing with me. "I know the drill. We need Garcia alive. Tell your team."

"Can't do it."

"Just tell them and let me handle Garcia. Your men can work the rest of the scene."

"That's not how this works, detective, and you're not part of my team, so you're not going in."

I breathed in deeply, forcing myself to stay calm. "My chief is good with me going in. What else do you need?"

He eyed me up and down. "We've got this handled, ma'am."

My blood boiled. I stepped closer to the man, his beefy chest taking up my visual space. I looked up at him and said, "That's my partner in there. I'm going in whether you like it or not. You can either tell me where to go, or watch me walk away, but either way, I'm going in. And don't try to tell me you wouldn't do the same."

He smiled. "Your chief said this would happen."

I kept my eyes focused on his.

"I'm already going against my better judgment and letting you in. I know who you are, and I know your record. Consider yourself lucky."

He exhaled. "He's on the southwest corner of the building. It's a chop shop. Three vehicles nearly block him from view. We've got ten men ready. You want in? You position on the southwest corner. There are two men there already. One steel door, and a blacked-out window. Follow their lead. You go rogue, and get hurt, it's on you."

"Tell them to apprehend."

"Not happening, detective."

"Then I'll just have to get to him first," I said and ran toward my position.

Bishop was in that building, and God only knew what they'd done to him, or if he was still alive. If he wasn't, Garcia would pay. I wasn't about to lose another officer on my watch.

CONCRETE BLOCKS, with only a few windows where we could look inside, limited our view. But the building was new, about thirty feet tall, and with windows meant to let in light about twenty-five feet up. The SWAT drone could see inside and prepare us for what we were going to walk into.

I made it to the two SWAT members. One recognized me from our serial killer investigation, but I didn't recall his name.

"Don't worry about your partner," he said. "We'll make sure he's safe."

Major Spencer got on the radio. "Drone shows LEO moving and strapped to pole. Three men with him; two behind, one in front. All armed."

The ten men and a sniper replied with copy that, in position. My heart raced. Santos was very likely the front man, which meant he could see SWAT and shoot Bishop. I needed to get in there first, and I had to do it without him seeing me.

"Tell Major Spencer Garcia won't hesitate—give me that." I yanked on the one man's radio. "Major Spencer, this is Detective Ryder. We go in at once, Bishop's dead. I'll go first. I can get him talking. Distract him."

"Fire alarm and quiet entry is our plan. Stand down, detective."

"Major, you set off that alarm and Garcia will panic. Bishop can ID him. We're at risk of a femoral artery shot. The ambulance is too far away to get here." Why the hell hadn't they put paramedics closer? "I respectfully request I go in first with entry code access." I glanced at the building behind us and saw the sniper. "I'll keep the sniper shot as open as possible."

"Thirty seconds and we sound the alarm," he said. "Don't screw this up."

If there was a god, he'd just given me a miracle. "Copy that."

One of the SWAT members entered the entry code and the door beeped as it unlocked. Damn it! Garcia would hear that. I pushed the door open a crack. Garcia was about fifty feet from me, and angled left. He couldn't see me, but if I wasn't careful, his men could.

There were three vehicles in various stages of being stripped on my side. I dropped and crawled, checking the scene at every break. Bishop was alive. They'd chained his wrists above his head, and his legs just under the knees. The area smelled like sweat, motor oil, and blood. Knots of fear and anger hardened my gut. An imaginary clock ticked off the seconds in my head.

Tick. Tock.

Time was running out. I had no choice but to go for it. His men would shoot. He would shoot. It would take his attention away from Bishop. SWAT would come in and take them down. It was a risk, but it was my only chance of saving my partner.

Sweat covered my chest and back, the stress and vest only making it worse.

Tick tock.

I stood with my gun aimed straight at Garcia. "Drop your weapons."

Garcia turned and aimed his gun at me. His two men did the same. Shots fired, pinging the vehicle in front of me. One whizzed by my head. I waited for their slight pause to stand and shoot again, but the alarm blasted to life and drowned out the sound of their bullets. The high, rhythmic pitch hurt my ears. SWAT rushed in, guns up and engaged. I only had one chance. I shifted between the vehicles, stood, and just as the alarm stopped, aimed my weapon at Garcia, and fired.

20

A shot screamed through the air and ripped right through the skull of one of Garcia's men. He was dead before he hit the ground. The second man shuffled to the left and then to the right, shooting his gun in all different directions, dodging bullets from all directions. A bullet hit his right shoulder. He jerked back and froze. I knew the look. The rush of adrenaline paused just long enough for him to feel the burst of pain setting fire to his shoulder. His gun slid out of his hand and fell to the ground.

SWAT was all over them within seconds.

I rushed to Bishop. He was breathing, but his face was almost unrecognizable. "Rob, it's me."

He tried to speak, his whisper rough and impossible to understand. I glanced around for the keys to the locks but couldn't find them. I turned toward the men running around and yelled, "We need a bolt cutter over here! Now!" I wiped my tears from my face. "We got you Rob. You're going to be okay."

Hamby officers hurried into the building.

"Where the hell is that bolt cutter?" I screamed.

Jimmy, Michels, and Levy raced to Bishop.

Michels blanched. "Holy shit!"

Major Spencer jogged over with the bolt cutter.

Michels and Jimmy held Bishop's arms while Spencer cut through the chain around his wrist. Once it was removed, they slowly guided his arms down. Levy and I supported his legs. They were heavy and dense, like Scarlet felt when she slept in my arms.

Jimmy yelled, "We need a paramedic over here!"

Four paramedics rushed toward us. A SWAT member yelled, "We've got three injured, one dead."

The paramedics separated, two to Bishop, one to Garcia, and the last one, after he checked the pulse of the dead one, to the last shooter.

Someone yelled, "We're losing him!"

I whipped around to see a paramedic pressing his palms into Garcia's chest. "Oh, no. No, no, no, no, no!" I pushed Levy out of my way and ran to Garcia while screaming at the paramedic. "Don't let him die!"

He pressed into his chest again, sweat pouring down his face. "Take over! I need the defibrillator!"

I positioned myself on Garcia's side.

"On three," he said. "One. Two. Three!"

I put weight on my hands and administered CPR. "Don't you die on me Garcia! You hear me?" Blood covered the ground beneath him. The paramedic had cut open Garcia's shirt and wrapped a thick towel around the wound. "This is bleeding through," I said. "We need pressure!"

The paramedic returned. "It's not going to matter if we don't get this guy's heart beating again." He held up the defibrillator paddles. "Ready?"

I raised my hands. He shocked Garcia, and I checked for a pulse. "Nothing."

He shocked him again. I pressed my fingers into his neck. "Oh, thank God!"

Another paramedic appeared. He took care of the wound as I tried to wake Garcia. "Santos! Santos, can you hear me? Santos, wake up!"

His eyelids fluttered.

"Who hired you?"

He opened his eyes and looked at me but I had no idea if he understood what I was saying.

"Who hired you?"

He eyelids fluttered again.

"Santos! Who hired you?"

He coughed and muttered, "Blahut." He coughed again and blood reddened his lips. His eyes rolled back, and his body went limp.

"Santos!" I checked his pulse and put my hand over his mouth. "He's not breathing!"

The paramedic pushed me aside. "We've got this."

Garcia's blood had soaked my pants and covered my shaking hands. I watched the scene around me in slow motion. A stabbing pain pierced my stomach. The room began to spin. "I think I'm going to be sick."

Levy crouched down by my side and kept me upright. "I've got you."

I took three deep breaths and the nausea passed. "I'm okay." I pushed myself up. It took a second or two to steady myself. A paramedic rolled Bishop's stretcher toward the door with Michels jogging by his side. My breath caught in my throat. "He has to be okay, Lauren."

"I know, Rachel. I know."

Jimmy stood beside me. "Someone call Cathy. They're taking him to Northside. She'll want to be there."

"I can do it," Levy said. "She needs some air."

He touched the side of my arm. "How're you holding up?" He looked me over. "Your face is bleeding."

I wiped my hand across my cheek. "It's just blood from my hands."

"What about your legs?"

"It's Garcia's. I'm fine," I said. "I don't think Garcia's going to make it. He needs to live. He gave up Blahut. I want that bastard." I glanced over at him just as the paramedics lifted the stretcher onto its wheels and hurried to the door.

"We'll get him," he said.

"Do we know who the dead guy is?"

"Lucas Anthony," Jimmy said. "Checked his wallet."

Levy returned. "Cathy's on the way to the hospital," she said.

"Good," he said. He flicked his thumb toward me. "Get her out of here."

"Sure thing, chief." She placed her hand on my shoulder. "Let's get you cleaned up."

We headed back to the station. "I have some extra clothes if you need them."

"I've got some in my cubby." I'd left an extra pair of clothes and shower items in my office, so I grabbed them and headed to the locker room. "I won't take long."

She washed up in the sink near the showers. "Hold on. What're you planning?"

"I'm planning to shower and change." I peeled off my bloodied clothes, walked behind the shower curtain and doused myself under the hot water. My puncture wound burned. Garcia's blood had soaked through my jeans onto my thighs. I'd need a run of tests, STDs, AIDS, Hep C, the standard. It wasn't the first time, and it wouldn't be the last.

"And that's it?"

"For the immediate future, yes."

"Okay, but whatever you're doing, I'm in."

"I know."

"I'll clean your boots. They've got blood all over them."

"Appreciate it."

When she finished, she said, "I'll be in my cubby."

"Thanks."

I lifted my face toward the water, closed my eyes, and relaxed as it ran over my skin. Bishop looked bad. They'd probably beaten him for hours. Where did they find him, and what happened? How did he end up in that warehouse and his vehicle smashed at the bottom of the hill?

I finished my shower, towel dried my hair and twisted it into a bun, then got dressed. My boots looked brand new. I, on the other hand, looked like hell, and I felt like it, too. I stared in the mirror, the dark circles under my eyes more prominent than before. I needed sleep, the deep, restful kind where I didn't dream and didn't move. Rest would come, but only after we nailed Blahut's ass to the wall.

Levy leaned against the front of her desk chewing on a fingernail but pushed herself off when I walked in. "Garcia didn't make it."

"Damn it. He gave me Blahut. I wanted it on record."

"You've got an undeniable record. Any jury will believe you."

"Let's hope. I need to check on Elisa Ortega. Tell her what happened. Garcia's the father of her kid."

We walked to the conference room where I'd expected they'd put Ortega to wait, but she wasn't there, and neither was an officer. "Damn it." I slammed the door shut and went to the radio room since it was after hours, and the front desk wasn't manned. "Anyone know what happened to our guest?"

One of the chairs turned my direction. "I'm here," Elisa said. Her face was red and swollen. "Santos is dead."

"Yes. Are you okay?"

"I am fine. Now, I can raise my child right. Can I go home now?"

"Not yet," I said. "We want to make sure you're going to be safe."

The dispatch officer spoke. "I've got an officer en route. Chief wants her in a hotel for a few days. She'll be at the Hilton Garden Inn."

"Thanks," I said. I smiled at Elisa. "This will be wrapped up in a day or two, and you'll be able to go home. Okay?"

"Thank you."

Levy and I headed to the investigation room.

"Why are we here?" she asked. "I thought we'd be going to Blahut?"

"Not without more evidence. We need to search these files for the Wilson, Blahut, Turner, Morgensen, and Kelley investment docs, then separate the documents by month, first."

"Got it."

It didn't take long. I grabbed the first from each file and laid them in a row. "See anything interesting?"

"Holy shit. They're all Merit."

"Except the Blahuts'."

"He scammed everyone in that group."

"Friends who sleep together, invest together."

She laughed. "More like are scammed together."

The header included the investment company name. Below that, the date, followed by the account holder's name, account number, and address on the left, then a summary of the month. The summary listed the starting date and dollar amount and the ending date and dollar amount plus the percentage increase or decrease. It didn't list any stock names or anything else related to where the money went.

Alan Blahut had invested through one of the big-name brokerage firms, and their statement provided specific details on each type of investment as well as the name of the company invested in.

"Other than Blahut's files, it looks like someone created a template and typed in the contents." She searched the Blahut files. "No bank statements, but he'd be an idiot to deposit the money into his own account."

"Tell that to Bernie Madoff."

"That's how he got busted."

"After twenty years. And his scam was simple." I held up one of Wilson's statements. "He made fake statements showing—" I set it next to Wilson's next month's statements until I found the only one with a loss. "They've only lost money one month," I said. "And that was almost a year ago. Otherwise, they've gone up, and look," I handed her a statement. "All by ten or twelve percent. The only one that's different is Wilson's most recent one with the $500,000 payout."

She checked the other statements. "The numbers all match," she said. "Except for Wilson's last one."

"And they're all posted on the same day of the month."

I sorted through the Wilson statements again. "There's two Mays. He's missing an April."

We checked the others, and they were the same.

"How do we prove Blahut made these?" she asked.

"He's scamming his friends. They'll testify against him."

"Even if the swinger stuff comes out?"

"Their money matters more than their sex lives."

"I hope."

"Bubba's supposed to get videos from the banks so we can see what John Hagar looks like. Let me text him. Hopefully, he's still awake." After he responded, I typed out thanks and set my phone on the table. "He's getting them in the morning. If we're lucky, we'll be able to tell that our John Hagar is actually Alan Blahut."

"We might be able to get him on a Ponzi scheme, but other than Garcia's last words, none of this proves he killed Wilson."

"We'll prove it. The other guy survived. He'll give him up."

~

I SENT Cathy a text asking for an update on Bishop before leaving the department. She called while I drove home. "How's he doing?"

"He's in bad shape, but he'll be okay. They broke his maxilla. The doctor's got his face in some support contraption. He can speak, but it's hard to understand him, and the doctor would prefer he not. He did, however, tell me to tell you something."

I clicked my garage door opener. "I'll be right there."

"No. He needs his rest."

She was right. "What did he want you to tell me?"

"Lisa."

~

KYLE HAD STACKED pillows behind his back and fallen asleep on the couch. I tiptoed toward him, not bothering to remove my weapon or belt, and kissed him on the cheek.

His eyes opened. "Hey, babe."

I grimaced. "I'm sorry. I didn't mean to wake you."

He carefully pushed himself forward, groaning with each centimeter of movement. "No, it's all good. What time is it?"

"Almost time for me to get up and go to work." I carefully lifted his legs and sat beneath them, then rested them over my thighs. I leaned my head back and closed my eyes.

"Long night?" he asked.

"Garcia's dead. He and his guys grabbed Bishop and beat the hell out of him."

"Savannah came by with some chicken fried steak and told me. She said two of the men died."

"Garcia was our main suspect in the actual break-ins. We needed him to give up Blahut, which he did, but only to me."

"Sorry. We called Cathy. She said Bishop's got some broken bones, but he'll be okay."

"I talked to her." I rubbed my eyes. "She told me the same. She also said Bishop said Lisa to her. Nothing else. Just Lisa."

"That's odd. Who's Lisa?"

"Our suspect's wife."

"What do you think that means?"

"I don't know."

"Listen, I love you, but you look worse than I do. You're no good exhausted. Go to bed, get a few hours of sleep and get on it again."

"Can I get you anything? Do you need help getting upstairs and in bed?"

"I'm sleeping here."

"On the couch? No. Take the bed. I'll sleep in the guest room."

"Rach, that would require me to move, and I'd rather not. Besides, I breathe better sitting up. Just wake me up before you leave, okay?"

"Are you sure?"

"I'm positive."

I woke up a few hours later. I offered to help Kyle shower, but he refused, saying he had to do it himself eventually. I called Jimmy to let him know I was going to the hospital.

"Levy said you're making movement, but you're not there yet. Get there. The mayor's called me every hour on the hour for a damn update."

"Tell the mayor to go to hell."

"Just give me something today."

"Don't worry. I won't stop until I've got Blahut smiling for his mug shot."

"I don't doubt that."

～

BISHOP SAT in bed with a medical cloth wrapped around his head and jaw. I understood why Cathy said support contraption. It reminded me of the soft seat swings you'd find at a playground, only white, and Bishop's head sat where the butt would go.

"Hey." He looked awful. I wanted to touch his hand, give him some sort of comfort, but I was afraid I'd hurt him. I'd never seen my partner that vulnerable before. He seemed older. It hurt my heart. "You look like shit."

If he smiled, there was no way to tell.

"I had to google maxilla. They broke your jaw?"

He mumbled. "Part."

"And the nurse said some ribs?"

"Two."

"Are you in a lot of pain?"

"Only when I breathe."

"Cathy said you're not supposed to be talking."

He lifted his head from the swing, and his entire upper body relaxed. "This thing is bullshit."

Understanding him was still hard, but not as much as it had been with his head in the swing. "Are you supposed to do that? Take your head out of the swing?"

He tilted his head carefully. "Swing?"

My jaw stiffened. "I'm sorry, Rob. I should have been with you."

"Matt Wilson was screwing Lisa Blahut." He set his face back into the swing and closed his eyes.

"Did Blahut tell you this?"

He opened his eyes. "No, his wife did."

"When?"

"I went to her house after I dropped you off."

"That's what you were trying to tell Cathy."

"Yes."

"You were supposed to go to the Kelleys' and Morgensens'."

"I drove by the Blahuts'. Lisa was getting her mail. I pulled over, figuring I'd play dumb and pretend to be checking on the family. She offered me a coffee, so we went inside."

"What were you thinking?"

"I was thinking I wanted to know what she knew."

"And that's where Garcia grabbed you, wasn't it?"

"We walked into the kitchen, and there he and his thugs were."

I closed my eyes and breathed. "You shouldn't have gone in there. They could have killed you."

"Don't bother with the lecture. I know it by heart from giving it to you so many times."

"Bishop, I went looking for you there. She told me she hadn't seen you."

"She set me up. Go."

I laid my hand on his. "I'm so glad you're alive."

"So am I."

21

I called Levy. "Garcia grabbed Bishop from the Blahuts'. The wife was outside, he stopped by, and she invited him in for coffee. Garcia was in the kitchen with his goons."

"Didn't she tell you she hadn't seen him?"

"Yes. Oh, and she was screwing Matt Wilson."

"This wasn't about the money after all?"

"Maybe."

"You going there?"

"Yes."

"We're on our way."

I called Bubba. "Alan Blahut is supposed to be in New York city. Left yesterday morning. Can you get in touch with the DA's office and check flights?"

"On it."

"Do me a favor, check John Hagar, too."

"Will do, and those videos should be here in the next hour or two."

"Great. Thanks, but Bubba, I need the flight information ASAP."

"Will do."

I gripped the steering wheel as I sped down Hopewell Road. Lisa Blahut had lied to me. How had I missed that?

The security guards waved me through Mayfield's front gate. I ignored the speed limit signs and the two golf cart drivers yelling at me to slow down as I rushed to the Blahut home. I slammed my Jeep into park in the driveway and tucked my BUG into the back of my jeans. Easy access if needed.

I rang the bell and pounded on the door, then I looked up and stared right into the video camera and knocked again.

Lisa Blahut opened the door. Her face was swollen, her eyes were bloodshot, and her hair was in a bun on the top of her head. The media would have a field day with her mug shot.

"Why'd you lie to me?"

She blinked. "I don't know what you're talking about." She stepped into the doorframe again.

"Cut the bullshit, Lisa. You were here when Garcia took Bishop. Turn around and put your hands behind your back. You're under arrest."

Her eyes widened. "No, please. You can't do this." She cried. "Please."

I unclipped my cuffs from my belt. "Turn around!"

She twisted to the side. I grabbed her right hand, locked a cuff around it, then grabbed the other and clicked it shut. "Let's go."

"You don't understand."

Levy and Michels arrived along with two backup squads. Levy threw Blahut a look so intense it made her wince.

Michels held her arm at the bottom of the porch.

"I had to," she said. "Please. I didn't have a choice."

"You didn't have a choice in what? Screwing your neighbor or watching a cop get abducted?" I stood with my face less than an inch from hers. "They beat the shit out of my partner. They broke his face, Lisa, and you're an accessory. You're going down, and your scumbag husband is going with you."

She dropped her head and cried.

I tossed Levy my keys. "Take my Jeep. I'm riding with her."

❧

LISA BLAHUT CRIED the entire way to the station. I asked her several questions, but her one- or two-word answers made no sense. We stuck her in an interrogation room and left her there to calm down, while I checked in with Jimmy.

"We'll get the other victims to verify how they learned about Merit," I said.

Someone knocked on the door. Jimmy said, "It's open."

Bubba walked in. "Good, you're here," he said to me. He handed me several eight-by-ten photographs and a copy of Alan Blahut's driver's license. "Alan Blahut did go to New York and is probably driving back from the airport as we speak. Also, John Hagar has a trip to the Bahama's scheduled tomorrow." He gave me another photo. "Here's his passport, and he's got a checking account at Bank of America. Emptied it two days ago. Six million and some change."

John Hagar was Alan Blahut. Jimmy dropped his forehead into his palm and hissed out three f-bombs.

Bubba handed me a copy of the Hagar bank account and his driver's license. "New York?"

"I checked. It's a condo owned by John Hagar."

"Where's Michels?" Jimmy asked.

"Waiting to talk to Lisa, so probably the kitchen or his cubby."

He picked up his phone and had the receptionist page him. A minute later he was at the door.

"I want a BOLO out on Blahut and a team in Mayfield. You and Levy handle it."

"You," he said pointing to me. "Get whatever you can from the wife. Find out what she knows and how she's involved. If she won't talk, call Christopher, and see if he'll swing a deal."

"But I—"

He stopped me with a palm toward the face again. "No way. You're not going near Blahut. Don't even ask." He pointed to the door. "The wife. Now."

I rotated on my heels and left.

I set a box of tissues and a bottled water in front of Lisa Blahut. She'd stopped crying and had been staring at the wall when I looked through the window. She hadn't moved when I set the items in front of her, nor had she looked me in the eye.

I sat across from her and pretended to care what happened to her. "Lisa, I'd like to help you, but I need you to help me, too." I kept my voice even and calm even though it was raspy from exhaustion. "Do you understand?"

She finally made eye contact. "I think he's watching me."

"Who's watching you?"

"Alan. That's how he found out about me and Matt. He's watching me."

"Why do you say that?"

She sipped the water. "Because he knew details. Things he wouldn't have known unless he was . . . he saw."

"I want to talk to you about what happened to my partner first."

"You don't understand. He's watching me. He must have sent those men. He must have seen your partner talking to me."

"You're saying your husband has cameras inside your home?"

"That has to be it."

I picked up the landline and asked Nikki if any cameras were found during the search.

"None that I'm aware of," she said.

"There were no cameras in your home when we searched."

"He must have installed it after Matt . . ." Tears pooled in her eyes. "It's all my fault. Matt's dead because of me."

"Did you sleep with Matt at your house?"

"He would come when Alan was at work."

"How long has this been going on?"

"Since February of last year." She stared at the wall again. "That's what he was doing. He was putting in a camera."

"I'm sorry?"

"Alan came home early from work a few weeks ago. Matt was there, but we weren't, you know. He'd come over to drop something off for Alan. They talked outside. I couldn't hear what they said, but I knew they were arguing. Alan always jabs his finger at me when he's mad, and that's what he was doing to Matt. I asked him about it, and he said it was nothing, and to mind my own business. The next day he went to the store and bought new speakers for our home entertainment system. We have them in the walls, but they crackle, and he hates it, so he bought speakers and has them everywhere. He traded some out the other day. In the main area, the den, and our bedroom. He must have put the cameras in the speakers."

"How big are the speakers?" I asked.

"Small. Maybe the size of my hand?"

We wouldn't have looked for anything inside the speakers. "You think he watched you with Matt and saw you with Bishop?"

"That's why I didn't say anything to you. Because I knew he was listening, and I didn't want him to do anything else."

"Let me make sure I've got this right. You were sleeping with Matt, and you believe your husband put cameras in the house and saw you. Then when Bishop came over, he saw that and sent his men. So, instead of going to your car, or taking a walk to call the police, you did what? Nothing? Then lied to me about seeing my partner."

"I'm sorry."

"Why? Why didn't you call the police?"

She twisted the tissue into a tight wad. "Because the man told me if I did, he'd come back and kill me."

"Did your husband accuse you of sleeping with Matt Wilson?"

"He didn't have to. He knew I already had. We were part of that stupid group. Matt and I slept together at the parties. That's how things started with us."

"Miranda said they didn't participate."

"She didn't. Matt would take her home, find some excuse to leave, and come back."

"That was allowed?"

"I'd convinced the other women it would be fun."

"Did they sleep with him too?"

"No. It infuriated Alan." Tears fell down her face. She pulled another tissue from the box and nodded. "He was all for it at first. It was his idea for Matt and me to hook up, but when it happened, he was so upset with me."

"Did he confront Matt?"

Her eyes widened. "Oh, God no. He couldn't. He wanted Matt's business. He made good money. Alan thought my sleeping with him would help get him on board."

"Did you encourage Matt to work with your husband?"

"Yes."

"With Spectrum?"

"I assumed so, but you asked about him leaving his job. Maybe he was?"

"He was," I said. "He scammed your friends with a fake investment company called Merit Investments."

Her eyes widened. "I didn't know that, I swear."

I gave her a moment then said, "Did you have feelings for Matt?"

She looked up from the tissue. "We were in love."

"And you think your husband knew that?"

"Yes."

"What papers did Matt bring for your husband that day he came home and found him there?"

"I don't know. He put them in his bag."

"Who's John Hagar?"

"John Hagar? He's one of Alan's clients. He lives in New York. I think that's who he was going to see."

I'd brought the photos with me into the interrogation room and removed the photo of John Hagar's passport. I set it in front of her. "This is John Hagar, Lisa. Your husband has two identities." I showed her John Hagar's flight itinerary for the next day.

Her eyes widened. "I don't understand. Why would he, why would he pretend to be this man?"

"Does Alan normally go to the office when he returns from a trip early in the day?"

"Sometimes, but he didn't drive to the airport this time. He said the parking garages are always full because of all the construction, so he took an Uber."

Great. Just great.

"Am I under arrest? Do I need an attorney?"

"We haven't filed any charges, but if you want an attorney, I can't stop you."

She bit her bottom lip. "No. Not yet. I want to help."

"Can we have access to your home to find the video cameras?"

"Yes, and the remote for the room is in a tool box in the garage. Top shelf on the right side, toward the front."

JIMMY, Bubba, Nikki, and Zach Christopher sat in the conference room.

I closed the door as I spoke. "Blahut isn't going home, and he doesn't have his vehicle."

"She tell you that?" Jimmy asked.

"Yes. Said he took an Uber. There are cameras in the house. She thinks they're in the speakers for the entertainment system built into the house. Blahut saw Bishop there and sent his goons to take care of him." I made eye contact with Christopher. "She gave us verbal permission to look for them and told me where to find the key to the room."

"Room?" Christopher said. "What room?"

"A sex room."

"Oh."

"Blahut saw Lisa talking to Bishop. He must have known he was going there. He also saw us arrest his wife. He knows we're onto him. He could be anywhere."

Jimmy rubbed the back of his neck.

"Who owns the warehouse?" I asked.

He gave me the name of a well-known resident.

"And he what, rented it to these guys? Just like that?"

"They paid cash. Told them they were starting a business fixing up race cars."

That wouldn't get us anywhere.

Police work was one quarter evidence, one quarter due diligence, and half gut instinct. Christopher would easily swing a deal for Lisa Blahut's testimony against her husband. If Blahut hadn't erased the cameras, we'd have the evidence to back it, but we still needed more for a slam dunk. "What about the guy shot last night? Where are we with him?"

"He's cuffed to his hospital bed. Their security is keeping an eye on him," Jimmy said. "But he's not talking."

"I'll get Levy and Michels back to the house. See what else you can get from the wife."

"I'd like to go to the home as well," Christopher said.

I bought a Diet Coke from the machine and headed back to Lisa Blahut.

"Lisa, do you have any local rental properties or places that your husband might go?"

"We sold our lake house last year, so no."

"Any friends or family have a place where he could go?"

"His brother Brad lives on Lake Lanier. He's out of the country, so he gave Alan a key to check on the place. He's probably there."

"Do you have the address?"

"It's two down on the left from our old place." She gave me her former address.

I stood to leave.

"May I go home?"

I believed her story, and didn't expect any charges to be filed against her, but it wasn't safe for her to leave. "We're not going to charge you, but until we find your husband, I think you're safer here."

"Okay." Tears pooled in her eyes. "I'm sorry about your partner."

"So am I."

I opened Jimmy's door without knocking. "Alan Blahut's brother owns a place on Lake Lanier."

"I'll get patrol on the Blahut home, send Michels and Levy with you, and then contact Forsyth County for an assist and a sign of life drive-by. Color inside the lines, Ryder. I want him alive."

"So do I."

22

FoCo deputies met us a short distance from the house.

"Blinds are closed," one deputy said, "But there's a two-story window for the lake view with blinds just on the bottom. Our guy across the lake got a visual of a woman on the upstairs balcony. No sign of your man, though."

"A woman? Shit. Any vehicles in the drive?"

"No."

I put my hands on my hips. "If we give him a chance to see us, he'll run."

"Not sure we have any other option, detective."

"How many exits?"

"Six, plus two garages. One in front, one in back. Upstairs decks have two doors but no stairs. The main level is a walk-out with a large entertaining porch. It's got stairs leading down to the lake."

"Windows?"

"Thirty-seven, twenty-two on the main floor," he said.

"How many deputies you got nearby?"

"Five. If you want more, I can have them out in ten."

I pressed my lips together and exhaled through my nose. "No. They'll work. Keep them near the exits in case he runs. My guys and I will approach through the front entrance." I nodded to Levy and Michels. "We'll knock first. Give the woman a chance to answer."

They both agreed.

"We assume he's armed," I said. "But we want him alive, so let's try to keep him that way, okay?"

"Yes, detective," the deputy said. "I'll maintain contact with my people from the front."

"Appreciate it."

The three of us hit the ground running, leaving our vehicles on the side of the road down the street. A black BMW headed our way. I glanced at the driver. He wore a baseball cap and dark glasses. He shifted his head toward us as he passed.

"Son of a bitch! That was him!" I flipped around and chased the vehicle, but I only made it another block before the car sped away. Levy and Michels followed. I bent over and caught my breath. "RJL. RJL. I couldn't see the rest of the plate."

The FoCo deputy caught up. "I got cars watching for him."

"He saw us arrest his wife," Levy said. "He was waiting for us."

"Why come here then?" Michels asked. "He should have known his wife would tell us about this place."

"Because he's an arrogant asshole," Levy said.

I motioned to Michels and Levy to follow me. "We need the woman inside."

We stepped onto the front porch. Michels and Levy stood on each side of the door with their weapons drawn while I pounded on it. "This is Detective Rachel Ryder with the Hamby PD. We know you're in there. Open the door."

The lock clicked. I slammed my shoulder into the door and knocked the woman on her butt before she had a chance to take another breath. I aimed my gun at her, and said, "Turn onto your stomach and put your hands behind you!"

"What's going on?" she asked.

Michels pushed past me. Levy followed behind him. They stood beside the woman, their guns aimed at the middle of her forehead. She lay back down and cried. "I don't understand what's happening."

Levy said, "Do what your told, ma'am," then flipped her over and cuffed her. Michels lifted her off the ground to stand. "Forehead against the wall," he said.

"Was that your black BMW that just drove down the street?" I asked.

"Yes."

"What's the plate number?"

Her body shook. Through sobs she said, "I don't know."

Levy checked her pockets, but they were empty.

"Where's your wallet?" I asked.

"In my purse on the kitchen counter."

I flicked my head and Michels moved toward the kitchen.

"I haven't done anything. Please! My husband rented the place for the night. I have the paperwork. I can show you."

Husband? "What's your name?" I asked.

"Kristin. Kristin Hagar."

Levy and I made eye contact. She mouthed, "Hagar?"

"Who took the car just now?" I asked.

"John, my husband. He's going to the liquor store. He wanted a bottle of champagne to celebrate."

"Celebrate what?"

"It's our one-year anniversary. We're going to the Bahamas tomorrow."

"Have someone take her to Hamby," I said right before bolting out the door.

The FoCo deputy gave me quick directions to the nearest liquor store and put a call out for the other deputies to get there quickly.

I jumped into my Jeep and hit the gas so hard my tires spun on the rocky road. I reached the end of the street and waited for cars to pass before turning right. I hammered my fists onto the steering wheel. "Move it, people!"

Only one lane went each direction, and with the busy traffic, there was no way I could pass anyone. At least it would slow Blahut down. It took ten minutes to get through three lights. Cussing out the traffic wouldn't make it move any faster, but that didn't stop me.

The growing sound of sirens assured me I was close. As I waited to make the final turn onto the street where the store was located, several FoCo squads raced past.

I yanked my steering wheel to the left and landed behind the last squad. The parking lot was only a few hundred feet ahead.

And the BMW wasn't there.

MICHELS SENT AN UPDATED BOLO on Blahut posing as Hagar out for the tri-state area. Kristin Hagar whimpered in the investigation room. Jimmy and I were watching her on video when Bubba entered the room.

"I've got everything. Blahut did it all from his home computer."

"What's everything?"

"The statements, the fake contracts. He's got twelve clients under Merit Investments. Total investment amount from them all: 6,748,000 bucks. Take out the five hundred K he returned to Wilson, and it's the exact amount John Hagar withdrew from his bank account." He handed me a file. "There's more. Photos, driver's licenses, marriage licenses, and a few other documents you'll need to bust him, but get this. I found emails between him and Wilson. About Lisa Blahut."

"Holy shit, Bubba. You're a freaking genius."

"I can't connect him to the home invasions."

"I was just going to tell you," Jimmy said. "The third guy is ready to talk." Everything was falling into place. We just needed to find Blahut.

"Great work, Bubba," I said.

He blushed. "Just doing my job."

"Like a boss," I said.

He peeked at the video. "That's the other wife?"

"Yep."

"I feel bad for her," he said.

"Thanks again," I said as he closed the door behind him.

"I need to interview the wife before I go in there."

"The guy in the hospital has a public defender already, so he probably wants a deal. Christopher said to call him when you're on your way."

"Okay."

He pointed to the video. "She seems genuinely upset," he said.

"I feel bad knowing it's going to get worse."

"Same place as John Hagar. Bubba looked it up on Google Earth. It's a condo overlooking Central Park."

"Blahut's been living the life."

"Go break it to the girl."

I WALKED into Kristin Hagar's interrogation room carrying a box of tissues, a bottled water, and Bubba's file.

"I don't understand what's happening. Why am I here? Why are you looking for John?"

I exhaled. Blahut was forty-three, and his second wife only twenty-eight. She dressed conservatively, a pair of jeans, black light-weight sweater, and ankle boots. Her long, blond hair landed just past her bra strap. If there'd been a sparkle in her eyes, we'd dumped water on it. "Mrs. Hagar, where and when did you meet your husband?"

"A year and a half ago. In Manhattan, at a Starbucks. Please, what's happening?"

I placed the photos of Blahut and his aliases in a row in front of her. "Your husband's real name is Alan Blahut." I set the copy of their marriage certificate on top of the Blahut photo. "He married Lisa Blahut on December 14, 1996, in Alpharetta, Georgia. They have one son." I placed a photo of their Hamby home on top of the marriage license. "They purchased this home in Hamby, Georgia, four years ago, and are still married."

"No," she said shaking her head. "That's impossible. He wasn't married when I met him, and he lived in Manhattan. He only comes to Atlanta for work."

"What work is that?"

"He's a project manager for an outdoor mall company. He travels all over the country."

"Alan Blahut is a financial advisor for the Spectrum Group in Atlanta. He's been there for ten years."

She just stared at me wide eyed.

I set a copy of her marriage license on top of the John Hagar photo. "You two married twenty-five years after he married his first wife."

"Wait, are you saying my marriage—that John isn't really my husband?"

That was the least of her worries. "We also believe he has been scamming people by taking their money for investments, falsifying their statements, and keeping the money for himself. We also believe he is responsible for four home invasions, one being the home he shares with his legal wife, various assaults, and murder."

"This can't be true. John's a sweet man. He couldn't hurt anyone."

"The rental home where you're staying belongs to his brother. His brother is out of the country and asked him to check on the property. Just down the street is a home he and his wife recently sold."

"But I saw the receipt. He printed it out and brought it with him."

I showed her photos from the bank videos. "This is Alan Blahut posing as John Hagar. He opened bank accounts under his alias at three different banks. He stole over six million dollars from his friends."

Tears slid down her cheeks.

I placed the first of several emails between him and Matt Wilson on the table. "Alan and Lisa Blahut participated in a sex group in their community. He urged his wife to engage in sexual activities with Matt Wilson, one of his clients, and then got angry when she did."

"Please, stop. I don't want to hear this."

I gathered the documents and put them back into the file folder. "Lisa Blahut and Matt Wilson began an affair, and they fell in love. Alan found out and now Matt Wilson is dead."

"Please," she said. Then she cried.

I felt terrible for her. She was just as much a victim as the rest of them. "I know this is hard to hear, but it's all here."

"What am I supposed to say?" She plucked a tissue from the box. "I didn't know any of this. He told me he was a bachelor. That he'd been waiting for someone just like me." She blew her nose. "Why would he lie? Why would he do this?"

"I don't know, and you need to be prepared to never know. Alan wasn't at the liquor store. We believe he'll try to get on that plane to the Bahamas tomorrow. We've already alerted the necessary authorities, but I need to know where he might have gone to hide."

"I don't know. I've never been here before."

"What about his project management job? Did he ever provide any details?"

"Not really. It was all general stuff." She rolled her eyes. "And now I know why. The bastard."

Good. She'd gone from disbelief to anger. I could work with anger. "Do you have photos of you two on your cell phone?"

"Yes. Why?"

"I'd like to get copies of them. Would that be okay?"

She gave me her passcode.

"Thank you. I'm going to give you some time. Please think about the past year and a half. I need anything you can recall that might lead us to Blahut."

"May I use the bathroom?"

"Sure. Let's get you into a nicer room." I stood and opened the door. "Would you like something to eat? We have a snack machine with a bunch of sugar-laden garbage in it. I hear the powdered donuts are to die for."

We stopped and got her something to eat, then I made sure she was comfortable in the other room.

I knocked on Bubba's office door.

"It's open."

I rushed over and wrapped him into a tight hug. "You just nailed Blahut for everything!" I squeezed him so tight he yelped. I loosened the hug and stepped away. "Oh, sorry."

"I can't take the credit. Blahut was stupid enough to document everything. I'll never understand that."

"It's his arrogance," I said. "But without you, we wouldn't have what we need, so thank you." I handed him Kristin's phone and gave him the code. "Can you print out a few photos of her with Blahut?"

He cringed. "Are you going to show them to the other wife?"

"I am."

"You're a brave woman."

A few minutes later I had a photo from their wedding—that would hurt —and three photos of them in New York City.

"Thanks."

"Good luck."

Lisa Blahut plowed into me as I walked into the hallway. "Is he there? I need to see him."

"No. He knew we were coming, and he left his brother's home before we could detain him. Lisa," I leaned toward her. "Let's go back to where you were. I need to tell you something."

"There's only one way to do this," I said. I set the three photos of Blahut with Kristin on the table.

She studied them. "He's having an affair?" Her temper quickly rose. "The bastard killed Matt and he's screwing another woman?"

"He's not just screwing her," I said. I set their wedding photo in front of her.

She looked at it and leaned back in the chair. "That's impossible."

"It's not." I handed her the marriage license Bubba had provided earlier. "They're here on their anniversary. She was supposed to go with him to the Bahamas tomorrow."

"Where is she now?"

"Detained."

Her eyes widened. "Here? I need to see her."

"That's not a good idea," I said. "I know you're upset, but right now, we need to focus on Alan. Where else would he go?"

"I don't know. I don't even know this man."

"Lisa, I need you to think, please. Does he have any college friends nearby? Maybe a high school friend or a family member?"

"His best friend from elementary school lives in that townhome community across from the downtown area in Hamby, but they had a falling out, and he hasn't talked to him in a year. Probably because he married that woman." A moment later, she added, "Honestly, I don't know if he's even still there."

The friend lived in my community. "What's his name?"

"Jack Stillman." She stared straight into my eyes. "You said I don't have to stay here."

"You're not safe until we find your husband."

"I'd like to leave, please. Now."

I couldn't make her stay, but I could make sure we kept an eye on her. The last thing we needed was her confronting Blahut.

23

Michels, Levy, and I, along with a flood of patrol officers, parked behind the Methodist church a block away from my community.

We huddled together while I barked out orders. "I need a squad at each side of the road, and right outside the building behind Stillman's." I pointed to a woman and three men, the four fittest-looking of the bunch. "You four stand guard at each side of the building. We don't know if he's armed, so expect him to be." I scanned the group. "Any questions?" When no one spoke, I said, "Let's do this then. Levy and Michels, you're with me."

The group scattered.

"Standard procedure. A lot of people want justice, so let's do our best to keep him alive."

Jack Stillman lived in the middle unit of a building three streets behind mine. A black BMW was parked with the back end backed to the garage. I crept over, ducking past the neighbor's front door, then crawled between the bimmer and garage door. RJL. I motioned to Levy and Michels. Levy notified the others through a series of taps onto her radio mic.

I knocked on the door. "Hamby Police. Alan Blahut, we know you're in there. Open the door."

Tick. Tock.

"Last chance, Blahut. Open the door!" I waited a few seconds and then gave Michels the go-ahead.

He removed the blasting tool and attached it to the door. Once finished, he moved to the left, and Levy and I moved to the right. He hit the button on the remote and the door opened.

A man tied up with ropes crashed into us, his body heavy and dense.

Michel took the brunt of the crash. "What the—"

Alan Blahut slammed into Levy, knocking her into the body as Michels pushed it aside. Levy lost her balance and hit the ground. Blahut took off running.

I jumped over Levy and the body, screamed, "He's unarmed," and bolted after him.

Michels passed me less than a second later. The patrol officer standing near the front of the home fired a shot at Blahut but missed. Someone said something on the mic, but my loud breathing made it hard to hear. "Check the man," I screamed at the officer.

Blahut darted right and ran between the two buildings. We couldn't shoot without endangering others. "Don't shoot him," I screamed.

Levy ran next to me.

"Go left and cut through. I'll take the right." I sucked in air as sweat poured down my face. My leg throbbed, sending a cramp from the puncture wound down to my ankle. "Shit!" I slowed for a moment, then said, "Fuck it," and pounded my feet into the ground. Porch and garage lights flicked on, lighting up the area. Sirens blared as the squad cars sped past. A woman stood on her front porch as I ran by. "Get inside!"

Levy and I rounded the corners as Michels flung himself on top of Blahut. Michels wrapped his arms around him and rolled onto his back. He grabbed onto his wrists as he drew his knees up and thrust them into Blahut's waist. Blahut's back arched as Michels slammed his knees into the arch, flipping him onto his back once more while pulling his wrists behind him.

Levy tugged her cuffs off her belt and cuffed him while Michels held him down. Once she finished, Michels rolled him over and said, "What the hell is with all these damn runners lately?"

I returned my weapon to its holster. "Read him his rights and bring him in."

I CALLED Jimmy on my way to the hospital. "We got him. Levy and Michels will process him. I'm going to talk to the suspect. I'll call Christopher now."

"Don't say a word until he gets there."

"Not my first rodeo, chief." I ended the call and asked Siri to call Zach Christopher.

He didn't bother with a hello. "Did you get him?"

"He's on his way to be processed as we speak. I'm heading to the hospital. We need that guy to confirm what we already know."

"I'll be there in twenty. Do not speak with him or his lawyer before I'm there."

"You'd better make it fifteen then."

I checked on Bishop first. His head rested in the swing contraption, but his eyes were open. As open as the swelling would allow. "You still look like shit," I said.

He mumbled, "Can't talk. Got in trouble."

I smiled for the first time in a while. "I think I could get used to this."

I was pretty sure he was cussing me out in his head.

"We got Blahut. I'll fill you in later. Right now, I'm meeting with the guy who did this to you. We'll get what we need." I set my hand on his. "I won't let Christopher let him off easy."

I waited for Christopher outside the man's room.

A nurse walked over. "Are you with the police?"

"Yes."

"You can go in. The officer who was here just took a break. He's getting a coffee downstairs."

"It's okay. I'm waiting for the assistant district attorney. How is he doing?"

"He'll be able to go home in a day or two."

"He's not going home."

"I should have assumed."

Christopher walked up. He smiled at the nurse and then turned toward me. "Ready?"

"More than."

Morgan Clayton sat in a chair beside the hospital bed. She stood when she saw us. "Good evening. Mr. Lopez would like to discuss the night your officer was injured. He is willing to provide information that will lead to the arrest of Santos Garcia and—"

"They're dead," I said.

She showed no emotion.

I stared at Lopez and asked, "Are you related to Rosy?"

He glanced at Clayton, who nodded. He said, "She's my sister."

I clenched my fists and pressed my heels down inside my boots. It took every ounce of strength I had to not go at him. "Who shot her? Was it you?"

"Detective Ryder," Christopher said. "Let's put our cards on the table and then we'll ask the questions."

I took a step back so I could breathe, and Lopez wouldn't get hurt.

"Ms. Clayton," Christopher said. "We're prepared to listen to your client's requests, however, given the extent of his charges, including, but not limited to the attempted murder of a police officer while performing his duties, I can't make any promises without an honest discussion of the events and what he knows first."

She glanced at her client, then back to Christopher. "May I have a minute with my client, please?"

We turned and walked out.

"We need him to name Blahut. It's the only way we'll get him for any of the invasions or the rest of this."

"We will," Christopher said.

~

LISA BLAHUT CALLED me on my way back to the department.

"I want to see him."

She must have been nearby, watching. "We need to talk to him first."

"I don't care. I'll wait. I'm coming there now." She ended the call.

I arrived at the station. The team sat in the investigation room waiting for an update from me and Christopher. I grabbed a bottle of water and sat next to Levy.

"It's solid," Christopher said. "Blahut paid him, Perez, and Garcia each ten thousand bucks to break into the first three homes. He arranged it so they couldn't take anything from his place. They could keep the jewelry, but Blahut wanted the cash."

"Not surprising," Michels said.

"Right," I said. "He said Blahut explained he wanted them to mimic the crimes at the Wilson house, and he'd pay an additional five thousand to whoever killed him."

"Did he say why he wanted him killed?"

"For screwing his wife," Christopher said.

"Damn," Michels said. "The dude's a selfish hypocrite."

"That's putting it mildly," Levy said. "Who did it?"

"This is where it gets interesting. Perez and Garcia fought about it, then Perez winds up dead. Garcia brings in Lopez, tells him the deal—"

"Lopez?" Michels said. "Is he related to Rosy?"

"Sister. He shot her."

"What a POS."

"While they're there emptying the safe, Anthony says he wants the money, so, he's going to kill Wilson. They argue. Garcia drags Wilson out of the room with his gun pointed at Anthony. Anthony follows. Garcia shoots Wilson, and they both bolt."

"Anthony didn't have a gun?"

"Garcia snatched it out of his hand in the office," Christopher said.

"Lopez hears the shot and freaks, tosses a few pieces of jewelry into the bag, and takes off."

"No one even thought about the cash," Michels said.

"Nope."

"It's Lopez's word against Blahut's," Levy said. "The jury could go either way."

"Lopez can pick Blahut out of a lineup, and he admits to being at Lisa Blahut's home," Christopher said.

"And we've got the camera footage," Jimmy said. "It'll be on there."

"Where's Maria Perez in all this?" Levy asked.

"MIA. Lopez swears they didn't grab her."

"Did you tell Forsyth?"

"I'll call before we interrogate Blahut."

"So, is Lopez trying to plea?" Michels asked.

Christopher smiled. "He'll go in for twenty to thirty. I said we'd give him five off."

"Please tell me we're all going in to question Blahut," Levy said.

"Just me and Christopher," I said.

"He's already lawyered up anyway. He won't talk."

"Maybe not to us, but he might to his wives," I said. "Lisa Blahut is waiting in the lobby, and we've got Kristin Hagar in a conference room."

Michels laughed. "Now this, I have to watch."

It took some convincing, but Jimmy allowed Kristin Hagar to watch the conversation between Blahut and his wife. She didn't say a word while Lisa laid him out.

"Damn," Michels said. "That's a dull knife she's using to cut off his balls."

Christopher and Jimmy both grimaced. I laughed.

"A pair of dull scissors would be better," Levy said.

The men stared at her and then backed away.

"How old is she?" Lisa asked Blahut.

He stared down at the metal table. "Old enough."

"Do you love her?"

"No."

Kristin gasped, then turned around, pushed Michels out of her way, and ran out of the room.

I exhaled. "I've got her."

She leaned her back against the hallway wall and sobbed. "He's going to prison, isn't he?"

"For a very long time."

"Good."

"I want my stuff from that house. I'm going home."

"I'll get an officer to take you."

~

CHRISTOPHER LISTED the fifteen charges filed against Blahut to his attorney. "We've added the additional charges since you arrived, and there may be more."

"My client has offered to give you whatever information you request if you'll consider dropping the charges."

I busted out laughing. "You've got to be kidding."

"I'm not."

"Not going to happen," Christopher said. "And you should be embarrassed for asking."

Blahut's lawyer turned toward him. "Now do you understand?"

Blahut exhaled. "Fine."

The guy lived in an alternate version of reality.

The lawyer looked at Christopher, "What's your offer?"

"He tells us everything, and I mean everything, we give him life in a minimum security prison instead of a maximum."

Blahut's eyes widened. "This is ridiculous! I have a child!"

"Should have thought about him before you decided to be a piece of trash," I said.

ALAN BLAHUT PLEADED GUILTY, waiving his right to a trial, and accepted the assistant district attorney's initial offer.

Jimmy convinced Bishop's nurse to let us all visit and give him the good news. Savannah smiled as he worked his Southern charm on the woman.

Michels popped open a bottle of champagne and poured it into plastic cups. I handed Bishop a hospital cup with the plastic straw, while Levy gave everyone their champagne.

"Some cases hit close to home, and we've had several of them over the past few years." He tilted his head and pointed to me. "They started about the time you came on board."

Everyone laughed.

"All kidding aside, you all worked hard on this, and through every frustration, every setback, you came back and kept swinging until finally hitting it out of the park. I am so grateful we're all on the same team." He held up his glass. "Cheers."

"Cheers," we all said.

Savannah snuck to the side and dumped her drink in the garbage. Nikki caught her. "Why'd you just—oh, my gosh! Are you pregnant?"

Savannah blushed, and for the first time in forever, she couldn't speak. Jimmy wrapped his arm around her. "Busted."

The nurse kicked us out a few minutes later. Since Rosy was out of intensive care, I stopped by to see her. She was sitting up in the bed watching a Spanish station on TV.

"How are you feeling?"

"I'm better. You arrested my brother, yes?"

"Yes. Rosy, I'm sorry this happened to you. I shouldn't have brought you to my house. I didn't think they'd find you."

"They didn't," she said. "I called my brother. I was afraid. I did not know he was working with Santos."

Her brother refused to talk about her. "And you told him where you were?"

"Yes. It is not your fault."

I wasn't sure what to say. "Is there anything I can do? Pick you up some decent food maybe?"

"It is too late to eat. I don't want to upset you, but I just want to be left alone."

"Okay." I walked out.

KYLE WAS STANDING in the garage when I pulled in.

"What are you doing out here? You should be resting."

He shuffled toward me, his movements still and slow, but successful. "The doctor said I should walk some when I'm feeling better."

"And do you feel better?"

"I figured walking would help with that."

I helped him inside and closed the door. "Go sit. Do you want something to drink?" I spied a pile of plastic bags on the kitchen counter. "How did you get to the store?"

"I didn't. I ordered through Instacart on my phone."

I guided him down onto the couch. "Wow. Very impressive."

"You have no food in this place. I had to have crackers with all-natural peanut butter."

"Oh, I forgot I had that. Did you eat all the carrots?"

He rolled his eyes. "Do you really eat that peanut butter? It tastes like cardboard drenched in oil."

"It really does, and no. I think that's like a year old, maybe?"

"Great. I survive a shooting, but I die from spoiled peanut poisoning."

I laughed. "Not at all dramatic."

He patted the couch. "Savannah's been updating me, but all I know is you got your guy. I want specifics."

I leaned back against the couch and groaned. "Tomorrow, okay? I just want to strip out of these clothes, take a shower, make us something to eat, and sit with you."

"That sounds perfect."

I leaned my head carefully against his shoulder and yawned. "Good. I'll do it in a minute."

FINAL FIX
Rachel Ryder Book 8

Detective Rachel Ryder stumbles upon a case that will force her to confront her past like never before.

At a local fair, Rachel unexpectedly crosses paths with Sean, a familiar face from her past. The encounter, laced with awkward tension, takes a harrowing turn when Sean sends her a cryptic message, begging to meet. When Rachel arrives, she's met with a chilling scene—Sean, deceased from an apparent overdose. But the presence of his baby at the scene whispers a different tale, one Rachel is determined to uncover.

The investigation takes a sinister turn as she discovers Sean's secret dealings. Heated confrontations, clandestine exchanges with ranch owners, and a rising body count point to a puzzle far more intricate than a straightforward overdose.

As Rachel and her team navigate a treacherous web of lies, they must outwit a ruthless adversary whose reach extends far beyond their city. The stakes rise when the lives of those closest to her hang in the balance, forcing Rachel to question just how far she's willing to go to unmask the truth and deliver justice.

Final Fix by Carolyn Ridder Aspenson is a gripping crime thriller that takes readers on an intoxicating journey into the underbelly of crime, where the price of truth is higher than ever before.

Get your copy today at
severnriverbooks.com

ABOUT CAROLYN RIDDER ASPENSON

USA Today Bestselling author Carolyn Ridder Aspenson writes cozy mysteries, thrillers, and paranormal women's fiction featuring strong female leads. Her stories shine through her dialogue, which readers have praised for being realistic and compelling.

Her first novel, *Unfinished Business,* was a Reader's Favorite and reached the top 100 books sold on Amazon.

In 2021 she introduced readers to detective Rachel Ryder in *Damaging Secrets. Overkill,* the third book in the Rachel Ryder series was one of Thrillerfix's best thrillers of 2021.

Prior to publishing, she worked as a journalist in the suburbs of Atlanta where her work appeared in multiple newspapers and magazines.

Writing is only one of Carolyn's passions. She is an avid dog lover and currently babies two pit bull boxer mixes. She lives in the mountains of North Georgia as an empty nester with her husband, a cantankerous cat, and those two spoiled dogs.

You can chat with Carolyn on Facebook at Carolyn Ridder Aspenson Books.

Sign up for Carolyn's reader list at
severnriverbooks.com

Printed in the United States
by Baker & Taylor Publisher Services